Dear S
Hope

Jerry Bentz
Dec. 3, 2022

OPERATION COYOTE

A JOHN BENSON NOVEL

JERRY BENTZ

Suite 300 - 990 Fort St
Victoria, BC, V8V 3K2
Canada

www.friesenpress.com

First Edition — 2021

Cover Design Credit: Sarah Schulz Creative
www.sarahschulzcreative.com
Instagram: @sarahschulzcreative

Photo Credit: iStock Photography
(Stock photo ID:104517501)

ISBN
978-1-03-910550-8 (Hardcover)
978-1-03-910549-2 (Paperback)
978-1-03-910551-5 (eBook)

1. FICTION, TECHNOLOGICAL

Distributed to the trade by The Ingram Book Company

For my daughters Sarah, Andrea, and Lisa,
and for Syd and Nelle.

PROLOGUE

3:00 p.m. Wednesday, February 24, 2021
RCMP K Division Headquarters, Edmonton, Alberta, Canada

Dr. John Benson looked up from his office desk on the third floor of the Royal Canadian Mounted Police (RCMP) K Division Headquarters over at his two German shepherd dogs, Sydney and Nelle, sleeping in their dog beds in their corner of the office. They were beginning to show their age, just like him. They were sisters from the same litter and were former police dogs trained at the National RCMP Canine Training Centre just north of Bowden, Alberta. They had proven to be a little small for RCMP police dogs and were not quite aggressive enough for regular canine unit duty. The dog handlers decided to redeploy them and offered John's team in the RCMP Wildlife Crime Forensic Unit the opportunity to retrain them for their international wildlife enforcement work.

The two dogs went along with John's team to most of their overseas INTERPOL assignments, but when John was home in Edmonton, he liked to have them stay with him. They were getting older now at ten years old, and not quite as agile, but probably had a few more good years left for active service before they were retired, maybe at the same time as John. They had adapted very well to the wildlife trafficking enforcement work and all the international travel involved. They came along on many of the field take-downs of bad guys with the local wildlife law enforcement agencies or police, and they were often instrumental in helping to track down and capture the wildlife poachers and traffickers.

John Benson was sixty-three years old now and starting to feel his age. He was always battling with his weight, especially when he was office-bound like the last two months, and his knees were always sore. He was just over six feet tall and his nickname within INTERPOL circles was John "Indiana Jones" Benson because they thought he looked a little like the actor Harrison Ford and had a similar swagger about him and a keen sense of humour.

For periods of the last three years, John Benson had been involved in Operation Thunderball. He and his Canadian team had worked with a larger team of international customs and police officers to coordinate global enforcement activities from an Operations Coordination Centre at INTERPOL's Global Complex for Innovation in Singapore. The operation led to the identification of almost six hundred illegal wildlife poaching and trafficking suspects, triggering arrests worldwide.

John Benson had been back in Canada for more than two months now writing reports and preparing for his testimonies at the various trials of the leaders of the trafficking networks and gangs. He had tried to come back to Edmonton as often as possible for short visits over the last three years, and he had really missed his three daughters and his now seven grandkids. During the last year, he had to spend several consecutive months in Singapore in early and mid-2020 while the COVID-19 international travel bans were in place before the RCMP were able to charter a plane and bring the Canadians back home.

The office next to John's belonged to Corporal Anna Dupree. She had been a senior member of his team for the last ten years. She was technically also the operations manager of the small wildlife forensics lab in the sprawling complex of the RCMP K Division Headquarters in north Edmonton. Since she was away with John on INTERPOL overseas assignments a lot of the time, the assistant manager of the lab supervised most of the lab work while they were away.

Anna Dupree came into the doorway of John Benson's office and said, "Hey, John, RCMP Commissioner Michael Alden's executive assistant, Jeannie Hoxton, is on the phone for you from Ottawa."

"Thankyou, Anna. I wonder what they want now. Hi, Corporal Hoxton, what can I do for you?"

Jeannie Hoxton said, "Hi, Inspector Benson, I have Commissioner Alden on the line for you."

"Hi, John, I am going to have Jeannie send a document to your classified email account. When you have finished reading it, please give me a call right back."

John thought to himself, *Holy shit, this seems weird.*

John saw the email come up in his classified email inbox and opened the document.

The title on the front cover was "Operation Coyote" with the watermark "Classified Level 1 — Office of the Vice President of the United States of America."

CHAPTER 1

8:30 a.m. Thursday, January 21, 2021
Broomfield, Colorado

Dr. Jill Smylie was sitting at her kitchen table with a cup of coffee and thinking about how to spend the rare four days off from her job. She was the chief of trauma medicine at the Denver Health Medical Center, one of five Level I trauma centres in Colorado. Its emergency department was colloquially known as the "Knife and Gun Club" because almost every shift saw a stabbing or shooting victim. The main hospital housed the Rocky Mountain Regional Level 1 Trauma Center with 555 beds. She was only forty-one years old and was probably a little too young to have achieved the position of "chief," but her former boss and mentor died from the COVID-19 virus in May 2020, and then his replacement also died in late June. She was next in the line of seniority so reluctantly took over as chief amid the worst virus pandemic in the last one hundred years.

She herself had caught the virus in early June, but fortunately her symptoms were relatively mild and after self-isolating at home for the standard fourteen days, she returned to work. During the height of the pandemic from the beginning of April to the end of June, suspected COVID-19 patients were triaged in a large tent in the parking lot and sent to other Denver hospitals or to temporary hospitals set up at the Denver Convention Center and several city arenas. The health centre's ICU was filled for months until the virus cases finally slowed to more manageable levels in late summer and fall.

Her fiancé, Dr. Drew Kerber, was an epidemiologist who lived in Fort Collins and worked for the Center for Disease Control, CDC's National Center for Emerging and Zoonotic Infectious Diseases (NCEZID) located at the Colorado State University campus in Fort Collins. The Fort Collins site was the only major CDC infectious disease laboratory outside of Atlanta, Georgia.

She and Drew were supposed to have gotten married in August last year but had to postpone the wedding because of the pandemic and their crazy work schedules. Drew had been working on the control of Lyme disease until a year ago and then was transferred to the CDC team working on the COVID-19 vaccine development.

The ban on international travel had finally been lifted a couple of months ago and she had been invited to do a presentation at a medical conference in London, England from February 6th to the 8th about practising trauma medicine during a global pandemic. There were going to be about three hundred attendees from around the world and there were very strict rules about who could attend, one of the major ones being that you had to have already had the COVID-19 virus and had obviously survived. The organizers had assumed that since everyone in attendance had already survived the virus, that they were now immune from reinfection and could safely travel and attend the conference. Jill had already been working on her presentation but was hoping to spend some time during her upcoming days off to edit her talk and finalize her PowerPoint slides.

Jill's family had been lifelong Democrats and she was as well, so she was very relieved that the Democrats had won the November 2020 election and Jim Borden was now the new president and former Senator Amanda Kincaid was now the vice president. The election was closer than it should have been, but Donald Trump was now finally gone, and the Democrats had removed almost all the former Trump appointees from their government positions in the Cabinet and senior administrative jobs. It seemed that most people in the country were relieved that a human being who was capable of empathy and understanding and had some real experience at the highest levels of government was now the president.

The country was in very tough shape, but things were starting to improve, and most people were now back at work and the schools and universities were open again. People around the country were starting to do all the normal things again like going to movies and out to dinner at restaurants and attending sporting events and music concerts. Her fiancé, Drew, since he had some inside information working at the CDC, had assured her that several of the new vaccines for the COVID-19 virus were within weeks of being rolled out within the United States and worldwide, which would hopefully eradicate the pandemic once and for all.

While she was sitting at the kitchen table contemplating her upcoming day, her cat Pippin came into the kitchen and started rubbing herself against Jill's leg, her way of saying good morning.

"Well, hello, Pippin, so you thought you would finally get up and join me. Do you want to go outside and get some fresh air?"

Pippin sneezed a couple of times and it looked like her nose was running and there was a little discharge under her eyes. "Hey, Pippin, are you getting a cat cold or something?"

Jill opened the patio doors and Pippin went out onto the deck. There were still some patches of snow in the backyard, but the weather had been quite pleasant the last few days and there was no snow left on the deck. Jill went back to her coffee and started looking over the draft of her presentation in London. After about thirty minutes she heard a loud yelp from the backyard and she looked out the window and saw that two coyotes had Pippin cornered against the chain-link fence, but Pippin was putting up a brave fight spitting and hissing at them and trying to claw them if they got close. Jill could see a little blood on the patch of snow that Pippin was on. Jill grabbed a pot from the counter and a large metal serving spoon and rushed out onto the deck banging the spoon on the pot as loudly as she could. The two coyotes looked up at her startled and immediately jumped over the fence and ran down into the river valley.

Jill ran over to Pippin and could see that she had a deep gash on her back where one of the coyotes had grabbed her. She was not bleeding too badly but the gash was about three inches long and looked quite deep, and Jill picked her up and took her back into the house. She found a towel and wrapped Pippen up and put her in her travel kennel.

Her regular vet worked at the Broomfield Veterinary Hospital which was normally about a fifteen-minute drive from her house. She made it there in twelve minutes and rushed in with Pippin and told the receptionist what had happened. Her veterinarian, Dr. Pamela Towns, came out of her office and took Pippin out of her kennel and examined the gash on her back. Jill reluctantly found a seat in the waiting area. As a trauma doctor, she was usually the one in control and talking to the distraught family members and giving them either the encouraging news about their loved one, or unfortunately in many cases, the bad news no one ever wants to hear.

After about an hour and a half, Dr. Towns emerged from the back area of the clinic and came up to Jill. She said, "So you can stop fretting now, Jill, we got Pippin all stitched up and she should be fine. She is still coming out of the anesthetic right now and will probably sleep for most of the rest of the day so we will keep her overnight just to be sure there are not any complications. The wound was deep but none of her ribs were damaged, so it was mostly just damage to the muscles on her back. We did notice that her temperature was a little high and that she had some discharge from her eyes and nose. Did you notice that she hadn't been feeling well the last few days?"

Jill said, "I did notice that she had sneezed a few times this morning and had a runny nose and had slept longer than normal last night. I thought that she may have just been coming down with a cat cold or something. Thank goodness I have the next few days off from work so I can take care of her."

10:00 a.m. Friday, January 22, 2021
Broomfield, Colorado

Pippin was a forlorn-looking cat when Jill went to the kennel area to pick her up the following day. She had a large, shaved area on her side and back with about four inches of stiches along her front shoulders and back. Jill put her in the travel kennel and drove home. She had put an extra blanket in Pippin's cat bed and put the bed in her favourite place to sleep in the living room close to the big picture window so she could look outside into the backyard even though she wasn't allowed to go outside while she healed. She immediately curled up and went to sleep when Jill took her out of the kennel and put her in the bed. With Pippin now safe at home Jill got back to work on her London presentation since she would not have much time to work on it for the rest of the weekend after Drew arrived on Saturday morning.

Jill gave Pippin the antibiotics two times per day by crushing them into her cat food. She had a pet digital thermometer and took Pippin's temperature a couple of times per day, and it was still a little high but did not seem to be getting any worse

11:00 a.m. Thursday, February 4, 2021
Denver International Airport

Dr. Jill Smylie was in the waiting area at Gate 37 in the Denver International Airport with about one hour to go before the departure of her flight to London, England to attend the medical conference. She had a three-hour layover at JFK Airport in New York to change planes and then fly on to London. The last couple of weeks had been crazy busy working at the hospital, finalizing her presentation for the conference, and looking after Pippin whose recovery from the coyote attack had been very slow, and then had taken a turn for the worse yesterday. Pippin had continued to be very lethargic and had not been eating very much, and then yesterday her low-grade persistent fever had gotten a little worse. Jill had considered not going to London for the conference but could not cancel at this late date. So, she called Dr. Towns at the vet clinic and asked if she could leave Pippin at the clinic kennel while she was away so they could keep an eye on her. They had of course agreed, and Jill had dropped her off on her way to the airport.

They announced that her flight was ready for boarding, so she proceeded to the gate and found her seat in first class, a perk paid for by the conference organizers for the people doing presentations at the conference. She was grateful for her first-class seat so she could hopefully get a little sleep during the flight. She had been feeling a little run down the last couple of days and had what felt like the beginnings of a cold. She hoped that it would hold off until after she was back home next Monday evening.

4:00 p.m. Wednesday, February 10, 2021
Broomfield, Colorado

Dr. Jill Smylie had picked up Pippin from the vet clinic on her way home from the airport on Monday. Her presentation at the medical conference seemed to be a big hit and she had met lots of people from all over the world wanting to talk to her about her experiences trying to run a major urban trauma centre during the pandemic. Pippin was not doing well and was still very lethargic and not eating very much. She also still had a high fever and the antibiotics they have been giving her did not seem to be helping her much.

Jill was scheduled to go back to work the next day so she called her next-door neighbour and friend Nicole Barber again to see if she could look in on Pippin while she was at work. She was feeling very tired from her trip to London and the long flight home, and her cold seemed to be getting worse, so she took some cold medicine and went to bed early.

The next afternoon, Jill got a phone call at the hospital from her neighbour Nicole that she had just looked in on Pippin and that Pippin was just laying in her bed sort of gasping for air and looking awfully bad. Jill immediately booked off work and jumped in her car and headed for home. When she got home, she saw that Pippin was having trouble breathing and had an even higher temperature than she had that morning, so she put her in the travel kennel and drove to her to the vet clinic. Dr. Towns examined her and said they would admit her and see if they could bring down her fever and help her breathing with some oxygen.

Dr. Towns said, "Jill, I know you love Pippin, but things are not looking very good for her so you should decide how much you want us to do for her."

Jill said, "You have no idea how often I have had this same conversation with the family members or loved ones of the patients that I treat at the trauma centre in Denver, and I never really thought I would be on the receiving end, even if it's only for a cat. Let's see how she does overnight and make the decision in the morning."

7:00 a.m. Thursday, February 11, 2021
Broomfield, Colorado

While Jill was making herself a cup of tea and some toast, her cell phone rang. An instant chill went through her and she reluctantly hit the green button.

"Hello, Jill, this is Pamela Towns. I have some bad news, Pippin died last night. I am sorry for your loss, Jill. We know how attached people get to their pets and we never underestimate the grief that they feel when the pet dies." Although as a doctor, Jill was not really surprised to get the call, it still shocked her, and she felt an overwhelming sense of loss.

Dr. Towns said, "Jill, because of the COVID-19 situation, veterinarians in Colorado are required to do a comprehensive autopsy on animals that die with symptoms like Pippin had, and to send swabs and blood samples to the CDC forensic lab in Fort Collins. After we are done with the autopsy, we are also required to keep the body of the animal until the autopsy results are finalized and the CDC are finished with their tests. When all the autopsy tests are completed, and if there are no problems, we can release Pippin's body to you, or you can use our cremation services."

Jill said, "I understand, I know the routine. Please let me know when you get the autopsy results and I'm quite sure that I will be using your cremation services when the time comes."

Jill sat down on the couch and had a good cry over her sweet little Pippin. She had been a good housemate, and although a little aloof at times as most cats tend to be, it would be strange not to have her around anymore. She decided that the hospital could survive without her today, so she called in and told her assistant about Pippin and that she would not be coming in today. Besides, she could use a day in bed feeling sorry for herself and trying to shake her nagging cold and since last night, a sore throat as well.

7:00 a.m. Monday, February 15, 2021
Broomfield, Colorado

Jill went back to work on Friday and then had the weekend off. Over the weekend her cold did not improve, and her sore throat got worse and she was even having trouble swallowing by Sunday evening. She hardly got any sleep on Sunday night and got up Monday morning with an even worse sore throat and a splitting headache. She had similar symptoms during her bout with the COVID-19 virus last June, but they only lasted a few days and then had started to subside and were totally gone after the end of the second week of self-isolation. This was feeling worse, but everyone assumed that if you had contracted the COVID-19 virus and then had gotten better, that you were immune from getting it again. Since her infection last June, she had been in contact with hundreds of COVID-19 patients in the ER at the hospital and had not worried about getting it again. She decided to drive into work at the hospital and get herself looked at by one of her colleagues in the ER.

Once she got to the hospital, she was feeling even worse and was starting to panic a little. She talked to one of her closest colleagues in the ER, Dr. Robert Godwin, and he became quite alarmed when he saw what condition she was in. He immediately put her into one of the observation rooms that were reserved for COVID-19 patients and started to examine her. In addition to her cold, sore throat, cough, and splitting headache, she also had a fever, and he became even more alarmed since he had seen thousands of patients with these same symptoms over the past year. He decided that since Dr. Jill Smylie was the chief of trauma medicine and technically his boss, that he would not take any chances and he had her admitted to the ICU.

10:00 a.m. Wednesday, February 17, 2021
Denver, Colorado

Since Monday, when Dr. Jill Smylie had been admitted to the ICU, her condition had worsened, and her breathing had become so laboured that she was put on a ventilator. Her fiancé, Drew Kerber, had rushed to Denver as soon as he had gotten the call about Jill from the hospital. He was initially able to see Jill in the ICU but was no longer able to see her until the doctors had figured out what was going on and why she wasn't responding to any of the treatments that had worked on other COVID-19 patients. She was getting worse by the hour and the doctors told Drew that they were afraid that they might not be able to save her so he should prepare for the worst. There was nothing he could do at the hospital, so he went back to the hotel to wait for any news. She was still holding on in the late evening, so he went to bed hoping for a miracle during the night.

Unfortunately, there was no miracle, and at 7:00 a.m. Thursday morning he got a call from Dr. Robert Godwin informing him that Jill had died during the night.

CHAPTER 2

11:00 a.m. Thursday, February 18, 2021
Office of the Deputy Director, CDC Laboratory, Fort Collins, Colorado

The deputy director of the Center for Disease Control and Prevention facility, Dr. Fred Pryor, was sitting at the conference table in his office. Also, at the table were four of the division heads at the Fort Collins lab and on a video link, his boss in Atlanta, Georgia, the director of the CDC, Dr. Miriam Bateman.

Dr. Pryor said, "Thanks, everyone, for assembling here in my office on such short notice. As you can see, we have Dr. Bateman also joining us via video link from her office in Atlanta. Something very worrying has just come to my attention and I wanted to get everyone up to speed as soon as possible. At about 9:00 a.m. this morning I got a phone call from a Dr. Robert Godwin, the acting chief of trauma medicine at the Denver Health Medical Center. He told me that the former chief, Dr. Jill Smylie, had just died last night from what appeared to be the COVID-19 virus. What worried him was that she had already contracted the virus last June and had recovered after experiencing quite mild symptoms. What further worried him was that her cat had also just died on February 11th at a vet clinic in Broomfield and the cat's symptoms were consistent with the standard COVID-19 symptoms in humans.

"Apparently, the cat had been attacked by a coyote in the backyard of Dr. Smylie's acreage on January 21st but had survived and should have made a full recovery from its injuries. Dr. Smylie had also just travelled to London,

England to do a presentation at a medical conference attended by about three hundred trauma medicine practitioners from around the world, all of whom had previously contracted the COVID-19 virus but had survived and had continued on with their work."

The others at the table looked at each other with alarm showing on their faces since they were worried about what they could be facing.

"Dr. Smylie's body is being transferred to our autopsy facilities here at the CDC as we speak. We have also contacted the Broomfield Veterinary Hospital to have the cat's remains sent here as well. They had apparently followed all the proper protocols when they did their own autopsy and had sent blood samples and swabs to our forensic lab here at the CDC, but they have not been processed yet because of our backlog."

Looking around the table grimly with a little sweat glistening on his forehead he said, "I have a bad feeling about this situation, and we need to complete the autopsies of Dr. Smylie and her cat as soon as possible and make the testing of all the samples from the autopsies our top priority. I hope to God that this is not our worst nightmare at this point, that we are dealing with a mutated version of the COVID-19 virus when we have finally approved a vaccine and are about to distribute it around the world. Do you have anything to add, Director Bateman?"

"Thanks, Dr. Pryor, for your very succinct assessment of the situation," said Director Bateman. "I also share your concern about Dr. Smylie and her cat, and the possibility of a mutated COVID-19 virus being introduced into the Denver area population. The fact that Dr. Smylie had travelled to London and attended a medical conference while she may have been in an infectious condition is even more worrying. I agree that we must get on top of this situation immediately and I will make sure that all the resources of the CDC are available if you need them."

While the group of scientists looked at the monitor with worried expressions, Dr. Bateman continued, "We should also activate our CDC tracking protocols and try to identify all the people Dr. Smylie may have come in contact with during the last three weeks of her life, which I am sure are considerable given her job at the Denver Health Medical Center and her recent travels to London. Let's get to work and we can schedule another meeting when you get the results of the autopsies and we know what we are up against. My next phone call is going to be to President Borden to give him a heads-up about this situation. Hopefully, we will catch a break and it won't be as bad as we fear."

Dr. Pryor got the results of the autopsies of Jill Smylie and her cat Pippin at 5:00 p.m. that afternoon. After reading through the reports and trying to decipher all the scientific and medical jargon, the bottom line was not good. He called his assistant into his office and told her to schedule another meeting with the whole senior team again for the next morning at 9:00 a.m., as well as Director Bateman in Atlanta.

His assistant looked at him and asked, "Are you alright, Dr. Pryor? You don't look very good."

"I'm sorry, Michelle, I didn't mean to alarm you. It is just looking like we are probably in for some serious problems again. I was hoping that after what we have all just gone through over the last year, that we were finally over the worst of it."

9:00 a.m. Monday, February 22, 2021
Office of the Deputy Director, CDC Laboratory, Fort Collins, Colorado

Deputy Director Dr. Fred Pryor was at the conference table in his office again. Also, at the table again were his four division heads at the Fort Collins facility, and in addition, the Head of the Forensic Virology Lab Dr. Dana Schroeder, and the Head of the Virology Genetics Lab Dr. Richard Norris. On a video link again, was the Director of the CDC Dr. Miriam Bateman from Atlanta, as well as Vice President Amanda Kincaid and Dr. Stephen Favaro, director of the National Institute of Infectious Diseases, from Washington.

Deputy Director Dr. Fred Pryor began the meeting. "Good morning, everyone. Once again, a lot has happened since our last meeting Friday morning. I would like to welcome Vice President Amanda Kincaid and Dr. Stephen Favaro via video link from Washington to the meeting. I have been in constant contact with Director Bateman over the weekend and have met with most of you either individually or in smaller groups with your staff over the weekend as well.

"We have all been busy over the weekend, so I will give you a quick rundown before we start discussing what actions we need to take to move forward today. First of all, the autopsies of Dr. Smylie and her cat Pippin were completed Thursday afternoon and we have copies for everyone if you are interested in all the details, but the bottom line is that they both died from what appear to be the standard, very severe symptoms of the COVID-19 virus. As usual, the final cause of death was catastrophic respiratory failure. We completed all the tests we usually do including detailed genetic testing of the virus present in the tissue and blood samples. Since this is not really my specialty, I will let Dr. Dana Schroeder, the head of the Forensic Virology Lab explain briefly what they found from the autopsy results."

"Thanks, Dr. Pryor. As you know, during the development of the current COVID-19 vaccines, we were able to map out the genetic makeup and sequencing of the COVID-19 virus and that allowed scientists to formulate several specific vaccines to neutralize the virus. This may sound simple, but as you know it involved the work of not only our own scientists at the CDC, but hundreds of other scientists from labs around the world. The only reason we have several mRNA-based vaccines right now for COVID-19 that are ready to be distributed around the world after only one year is testament to the work of hundreds of scientists working cooperatively in dozens of countries. The pharmaceutical companies also stepped up. big time, to produce the vaccines in the volumes required to eventually vaccinate most of the world population."

Continuing, Dr. Dana Schroeder said, "So, as I explained on Friday to our team here in Fort Collins, this is what we discovered. The virus isolated from the tissue and blood samples from Dr. Smylie and her cat Pippin is genetically slightly different from the COVID-19 virus we have been dealing with. Since the most obvious element introduced into the equation was the attack by the coyote on the cat Pippin on January 21st, we concentrated our efforts on assessing whether the genetic differences in the virus had some connection to what we know about the genetic makeup of the Plains coyote present here in Colorado. Our initial testing confirmed that the new genetic makeup of the virus from both the cat and Dr. Smylie was consistent with a small segment of the Plains coyote genetic sequencing.

"The coyote DNA basically attached itself to the COVID-19 virus molecules in some way. For this to have happened, it was also necessary for the cat to have already been infected with the COVID-19 virus, which in itself is an extremely rare possibility since this has only been reported in a couple of incidents around the world. Although, it may be more common than we think since we were not too worried about testing common house cats for the COVID-19 virus if they got sick. So, we contacted the Broomfield Veterinary Hospital and they had fortunately collected a blood sample from the cat when she was first brought to the vet hospital after the coyote attack. We had them send us the blood sample and sure enough it tested positive for the COVID-19 virus. So, we concluded that as far as we knew at that point with our current testing and analysis, we are likely dealing with a stable mutated version of the COVID-19 virus that more than likely would not be neutralized by the vaccines that we have spent the last year developing and producing. I'm sorry that I don't have better news."

Dr. Pryor said, "Thanks, Dana, your people have done some very impressive work in a truly short time. So, as we all realize now, we did not catch a break and we have a huge problem to contend with again. We don't know at this point if this new coronavirus — let's call it COVID-21 for now — is as infectious as the COVID-19 virus or how many people Dr. Smylie may have infected before she died. Over the weekend, our CDC scientists here in Fort Collins, assisted by their counterparts in Atlanta, made this our top priority to confirm exactly what we are dealing with and try to come up with a strategy to combat the spread of this new COVID-21 virus. Director Bateman, I assume you would like to say something as well."

"Yes, thanks, Fred," said Dr. Bateman. "I would once again like thank you and your team there in Fort Collins for your excellent work. Every hour now that we have left to solve this problem before it develops into another pandemic is critical. The fact that we already have several existing vaccines will hopefully assist in the development of a new version for the COVID-21 virus.

"One of the most important developments over the weekend has been the confirmation by our CDC contact tracking team that the new COVID-21 virus is indeed highly infectious and that at least thirty people who attended the London medical conference with Dr. Smylie have been infected, and five of them have died. They have managed to contact almost all the three hundred attendees and have instructed them to isolate themselves for at least fourteen days and have been provided with all the appropriate information about safeguarding the people around them. We have also done the same for all the people in the Denver area who may be at risk from contact with Dr. Smylie. This will certainly help but will not guarantee that the eventual spread of the COVID-21 virus will not occur. It only buys us a little more time until we find a more permanent solution. From the very preliminary data we have so far, it appears the COVID-21 virus likely has a somewhat higher mortality rate, perhaps as high as 3 percent.

"They have also found that one of the veterinary technicians at the Broomfield Veterinary Hospital who was looking after Pippin the cat has also been reinfected and is in the hospital in Boulder. Also, Dr. Smylie's fiancé, Dr. Drew Kerber, who I understand works at the CDC there in Fort Collins, was contacted at his home and he said that he had come down with what he thinks is a cold, a slight cough and mild fever. He was advised to immediately go to the hospital in Fort Collins and go into a quarantine unit."

Dr. Pryor then continued, "Our CDC geneticists, virologists, and epidemiologists worked extremely hard over the weekend and came up with a couple of scenarios for tackling the situation. I will defer to Dr. Richard Norris, head of the Virology Genetics Lab, to give you a briefing of what the scientists have collectively agreed are the two most viable options at this point, given our current state of knowledge about the COVID-21 virus."

"Thank you, Dr. Pryor," said Dr. Norris. "As you all can appreciate this is a very unprecedented situation in the world of virology. However, we do have a unique and opportune situation in that we have already developed several messenger RNA or mRNA-based vaccines for the extremely closely genetically related COVID-19 virus. I have a series of animation slides that my staff put together that hopefully will illustrate the science involved."

As he was talking, he got up and gestured to different areas of the animation slides. "So, very simply, in assessing the new mutated coronavirus we looked at the genetic component of the mutation that affected the virus's 'spike' — the protein on its surface that it uses to recognize and enter human host cells. COVID-19 mRNA vaccines give instructions to human cells to make a harmless piece of what is called the "spike protein." The spike protein is found on the surface of the virus that causes COVID-19. Once the vaccine is injected, enclosed in lipid nanoparticles, our immune systems recognize that the protein does not belong there and begin building an immune response and making antibodies. The vaccine then creates a memory response to the virus which creates immunity. The COVID-19 vaccines that have currently completed their Phase 3 clinical trials and have been approved in the United States need two shots to be fully effective, given about three weeks apart.

"The coyote genetic material seems to have changed a few of the protein molecules that make up the spike, subtly altering the spike's genetic structure. In simple terms, we have found that the only significant difference between the two viruses is the attachment of a very small amount of DNA protein material from the Plains coyote to the genetic structure of the COVID-19 virus, unfortunately resulting in a stable mutated version of the virus which we have named the COVID-21 virus.

"This new virus can infect people and replicate in much the same way as the existing COVID-19 virus. Unfortunately, based on the testing we have done over the weekend, the two viruses are genetically different enough that the new vaccines will not consistently work on the COVID-21 virus. We will need to introduce the coyote protein material into the existing structure of the mRNA-based vaccines for them to work on both viruses. Obviously, this is an overly simplistic scientific explanation of the situation, but I will not bore you with all the scientific jargon.

"So very simply, there are two basic solutions we have decided would work from a genetic standpoint, a longer, more conservative and standard solution based on synthesizing the required coyote genetic protein material which we estimate would take about three to four months on a best-case scenario. The second solution is the 'out-of-the-box' solution that Director Bateman suggested we consider. Forgive me if it sounds a little crazy initially, but we have done some initial testing and we are quite certain that it will work at the genetic level. It involves using actual genetic protein material from wild coyotes, more specifically the brain tissue from coyotes which we would then use to extract the required genetic protein material to start producing a new and improved vaccine.

"The main benefit of this approach is time. We estimate we could start production of a new vaccine for the initial testing within about two weeks of getting the first coyote brain tissue. We estimate that each brain from an adult coyote would produce enough genetic material to manufacture about half a million doses of vaccine during the production phase. We think we would need about one thousand coyote brains to give us the three to four months of additional time to synthesize the required coyote genetic protein material through normal processes and then produce enough new vaccine for targeted worldwide distribution, concentrating on countries with the most COVID-21 infection problems. And obviously, there are only a finite number of adult Plains coyotes and we cannot kill all of them to make this new vaccine.

"I do not know how we would go about acquiring one thousand coyote brains in the next few weeks because obviously I'm a lab guy, but I'm sure that there are people out there that can figure that part out. We lab scientists will handle our part of the operation if some other people figure out how to get the coyote brains to the lab. There will obviously have to be strict protocols for the collection and preservation of the coyote brain tissue to make sure it is viable for our purposes; however, we can discuss that when the time comes. Questions?"

Vice President Kincaid said, "Thank you, Dr. Norris. I must commend you in that you have certainly taken Director Bateman's advice and thought of a very 'out-of-the-box' solution. I can see the logic from a very non-scientific perspective; however, if I am going to take this solution back to the president, I will need to know as precisely as possible the probability of success. As you all can appreciate, President Borden is approaching the completion of just the second official month of his presidency, and he has a lot of work to do to get this country back on track. On behalf of the United States and the other countries around the world, we cannot afford to be wrong about this. So, do whatever you need to do over the next twenty-four hours, and I will get back to Director Bateman and Deputy Director Pryor about the CDC's final recommendation for the best plan of action. Do you have anything to add, Dr. Favaro?"

"As the director of the National Institute of Infectious Diseases, and an advisor to the president, I will be doing my own due diligence on what we have discussed here today," said Dr. Stephen Favaro. "I agree that we don't have a lot of good options available right now, however we need to be sure that the option we decide to move forward with has to be the right one, since being wrong is not an option."

Director Bateman said, "Our CDC contact tracking team will continue their work and we will attempt to contact everyone that is at risk in the

Denver area and overseas. We will have to start contacting other world leaders and health authorities and alerting them to the danger of a possible new mutated version of the COVID-19 virus; however, we will try to avoid a panic situation at this point until we are able to come up with some possible solutions. In the meantime, the general US rollout of the approved COVID-19 vaccines will go ahead as planned to start on March 15th, with more targeted vaccinations of health care workers and first responders in the upcoming first two weeks of March.

"I want the Fort Collins CDC facility to continue to take the lead in the COVID-21 virus situation and we will provide backup as required here in Atlanta. This whole situation must be on an extremely strict need-to-know level at this point and your staff in Fort Collins should be made clear about that. We do not need any leaks to the media about what is going on right now until we have more information and hopefully some good news."

9:00 a.m. Tuesday, February 23, 2021
Office of the Director, CDC Facility, Atlanta, Georgia

Dr. Miriam Bateman, director of the CDC, was in her office in Atlanta and was on a video link with Vice President Amanda Kincaid and Dr. Stephen Favaro in Washington, and Dr. Fred Pryor in Fort Collins.

Dr. Miriam Bateman said, "Good morning, Vice President Kincaid, Dr. Favaro, and Dr. Pryor. I will get right to the point. Over the past twenty-four hours since we last met, the CDC scientists in Fort Collins have been doing more testing and analysis. They were also able to get some actual coyote brain tissue to use in the testing from the local Fish and Wildlife people in Fort Collins. The results of the testing and analyses they have done show that the process of using the coyote brain tissue for modifying the existing COVID-19 vaccine is genetically and operationally viable and they recommend proceeding with that option. They would also immediately initiate a parallel, more traditional process of synthesizing the coyote DNA material to replace the need for actual coyote brain tissue but confirmed that it could take three to four months to do that as a best-case scenario. Dr. Favaro, I know that you have been doing your own scientific due diligence and have had discussions with Dr. Pryor and his team in Fort Collins. What is your opinion on this?"

Dr. Stephen Favaro said, "Since yesterday morning, I have had discussions with my coronavirus scientists at the Institute of Infectious Diseases, as well as several discussions with Dr. Pryor and his team in Fort Collins. I concur with the CDC recommendations that the genetics involved in using the coyote brain tissue is a viable process. Obviously, the operational details of acquiring the required amount of coyote brain tissue under very tight national security protocols is out of my area of expertise; however, I trust that there are others who will figure that part out."

"Thank you all for your efforts in this situation over the past number of days," said Vice President Kincaid. "I now feel confident in taking this solution to the president. Assuming we would be moving forward with this plan of action, I have also been doing my due diligence. I have contacted the heads of the agencies in the US government that would likely be involved in the field operations of what we are calling 'Operation Coyote'. The lead agency would most likely be the US Fish and Wildlife Service Office of Law Enforcement. They would be assisted by state Fish and Wildlife personnel and US Army Special Forces personnel as required. We have also touched base with the Canadian prime minister to fill him in on the situation, and he has alerted his top people in the RCMP and CSIS, and the Canadian Health Ministry.

"I will be having a briefing session tomorrow morning with the president and the key people in Washington who will likely need to be involved in Operation Coyote. In the meantime, we will now move forward with contacting the lead agencies involved in Operation Coyote in both the US and Canada and instructing them to start their operational planning processes. I have also scheduled a tentative Operation Coyote strategic kickoff meeting at the FBI Field Office in Denver for Monday morning on March 1st. So, that leaves us about five days to get everything in motion.

"We will be needing someone to assume overall operational and logistical control of Operation Coyote, so I have spoken with various people who work in the world of international wildlife law enforcement, and they recommend a Canadian forensic wildlife biologist who technically is an employee of the Royal Canadian Mounted Police and a special agent with the Canadian Security Intelligence Service, but has been working mostly with INTERPOL for the last ten years or so breaking up international wildlife trafficking networks. His name is Dr. John Benson, and he is currently at his home base in Edmonton, Alberta, writing reports and preparing for upcoming court testimonies. He does not sound like an office guy, so I am sure he would appreciate some field action.

"His counterpart in the US is a federal Fish and Wildlife special agent, Dr. Kate Beckett, who has worked with John Benson on quite a few INTERPOL assignments over the past ten years. She is working out of her US home base right now which is the National Fish and Wildlife Forensic Laboratory in Ashland, Oregon, also writing reports and preparing for upcoming court testimonies. Apparently, they have just spent a lot of the last three years working together on Operation Thunderball, the largest INTERPOL international wildlife trafficking takedown in agency history.

"Thanks again, everyone, and I will be providing more information about Operation Coyote as soon as I have some."

As their computer monitors faded to black, three of the most senior health care administrators in the United States were thinking the same thing — I hope to hell this works because if it didn't they were in for another very tough year.

CHAPTER 3

10:00 a.m. Wednesday, February 24, 2021
White House Situation Room, Washington, DC

In the White House Situation Room were President Jim Borden, Vice President Amanda Kincaid, White House Chief of Staff Peter Higgins, FBI Director Arthur Hammond, CDC Director Dr. Miriam Bateman, Director of the National Institute of Infectious Diseases Dr. Stephen Favaro, Secretary of Homeland Security Harold Jackson, and Joint Chiefs of Staff member and commander of the US Army Special Forces General Frank Shields.

President Jim Borden said, "Good morning, everyone. As you know we are here to discuss this new COVID-21 pandemic threat and to set in motion our response to solving it as soon as possible. You have all been provided with the briefing report drafted by the vice president's office, so we will not spend a lot of time backtracking on how we got to this point. Suffice to say that the plan we are proposing has been vetted by the scientists at the CDC and National Institute for Infectious Diseases, and although it may seem to be a departure from how we usually do things, these are extraordinary times, and we need to get the job done by whatever means we have available. I have once again assigned Vice President Kincaid to chair the new COVID-21 Task Force and one of the first phases will be to get Operation Coyote up and running. I'll now turn over the meeting to the vice president."

"Thank you, Mr. President. As the president has said, the first critical part of the plan is to get going on Operation Coyote. We have been talking with the heads of the various government agencies who will be directly involved in the operation and they are waiting for specific instructions from us as to how they are to proceed, Operation Coyote will be on a very tight need-to-know basis. We hope to carry out most of the operation under the guise of a rabies control and testing program and most field personnel won't be aware of the true nature of the operation and what the end use of the coyote brain tissue will be. We hope to keep the whole operation very compartmentalized on a state by state or province basis so we can minimize conservation group or media interest. We will prepare a PR package explaining the rabies control and testing program which we can use if necessary.

"With respect to who will head up the field component of Operation Coyote, we have been advised that the best person for the job is a Canadian, Dr. John Benson. He has a Ph.D. in forensic wildlife biology but has been an employee of the RCMP and a special agent with CSIS for most of his career. His partner for the past fifteen years is Dennis Bear, a Cree Indian from northern Alberta and a former Canadian Military Special Forces sniper with quite the reputation. According to his file he was apparently known as "The Ghost" in the special forces circles back in the day.

"Benson's counterpart in the US is a federal Fish and Wildlife special agent, Dr. Kate Beckett, who has worked with John Benson on quite a few INTERPOL assignments over the past ten years. When in the US, she works out of the National Fish and Wildlife Forensic Laboratory in Ashland, Oregon. Apparently, she and John Benson have just spent a lot of time over the last few years working together on INTERPOL's Operation Thunderball as well.

"General Shields, do you have anything to add about our choice of John Benson to head up Operation Coyote?"

"Thank you, Vice President Kincaid," said General Frank Shields. "I have never met Dr. Benson personally, but I do know him by reputation, and I think he is an excellent choice to run the field component of Operation Coyote. He obviously has the scientific background, but he also has high-level law enforcement experience and he even spent some time training with the Canadian Special Forces in his younger days. I believe that is where he first hooked up with Dennis Bear.

"I did meet Dennis Bear a few times while we were both serving in Afghanistan in 2004. He was one of the most respected snipers not only in the Canadian military, but in the US military as well. He was known as "The Ghost" and his exploits were legendary. Many of the kills of top al Qaeda and Taliban fighters that the US military took credit for, were actually his kills because he did not want to bring any notice to himself. The Taliban apparently had a $10,000 US dollar bounty on him in those days, so he liked to keep a very low profile.

"One story about his exploits stands out for me. We had located the hideout in the mountains of one the top al Qaeda fighters, a former lieutenant of Osama bin Laden's. With the consent of the Canadians, we sent Denny Bear and his spotter, also a Cree Indian, to see if they could take hm out. They dropped them off with a helicopter about twenty miles away and they hiked through the mountains to the hideout location. They dug themselves a couple of holes on the top of a hill overlooking the hideout and covered up with some shrubs and camouflage material. The hideout was just a cave with some camouflage awning in the front. The bad guy was very wary about showing himself during the day and Denny and his spotter stayed in their holes for seven days waiting to get the shot. Finally, in the early evening of the seventh day, with barely enough light left, the bad guy ventured a little too far out from under the canopy and Denny blew his head off at a range of fifteen hundred yards. He and his spotter then hiked back the twenty miles to the helicopter pick-up site and went back to the base.

"I just happened to be at the same base for a couple of days which we were sharing with the Canadians and I got a message from our intelligence people that the al Qaeda fighter had been killed by a sniper. The next day I saw Denny in the mess tent, looking a little tired, and I walked over and introduced myself. I said I had heard he had been gone for the last couple of weeks and he looked at me and winked and said, 'You know how it is, Colonel, sometimes you just need a little alone time.' The only reason I know the story is that his spotter was playing cards with one of my guys and he told him about it.

I guess he hooked up with John Benson when Benson was doing his special forces training in Afghanistan and he persuaded Denny that it might be more fun catching wildlife traffickers than killing al Qaeda fighters. Denny left the military after his term was up and has been together with John Benson for the last fifteen years. They are getting older now, so I assume they are stuck mostly in the command centres and do not get out in the field as much taking down the bad guys. These are two badass guys though and I look forward to working with them. I am quite sure that they will think hunting coyotes is tame stuff unless we give the coyotes guns as well.

"I have also met Dr. Kate Beckett a few times as well over the years. She travels in the same circles as Benson and Bear and is badass in her own right. They should make a good team on Operation Coyote."

Vice President Kincaid said, "Thanks, General Shields. Although most of you are aware, I would just like to confirm that we are still on track to roll out several of the US-manufactured COVID-19 vaccines within the United States and then worldwide starting on March 15th. There will be standard needle vaccinations available on a pre-determined priority basis and the final distribution infrastructure is now almost finalized around the country.

"We have also contacted all of the leaders of the countries with people that may be at risk so far and have told them that we suspect that a new mutated version of the COVID-19 virus has emerged and have traced it to a US citizen and have told them about the London medical conference connection. So far, we have not disclosed the exact nature of the mutation or the coyote connection. With our current plan we hope to buy ourselves a few weeks before we must disclose the whole story and our efforts to develop a new version of the vaccine. By this time, we assume Operation Coyote will be mostly completed and we will be well on our way to manufacturing enough new vaccine that we can start distributing it to the countries most affected by the COVID-21 virus at that point. As we produce the new COVID-21 vaccine, we can then start swapping it out for the existing COVID-19 vaccine.

"What we want to ensure is that Operation Coyote is completed before countries like China and Russia find out what is happening. We are already in a desperate fight for the recovery of our economy here in the US and we do not need these countries sabotaging our plans for containing the COVID-21 virus and avoiding another pandemic. Both China and Russia have been able to get their economies back up and running much sooner that we have, and they would like nothing better than a new pandemic starting, with its epicentre being here in the United States.

"Alright, I think that is all for now unless anyone had any questions. As I have mentioned, we have scheduled a kickoff meeting for Operation Coyote on Monday March 1st at the FBI Field Office in Denver. We will be contacting the select people in the US government who need to be there, and the heads of the Canadian agencies that will need to be involved. I will contact Dr. Kate Beckett and the US Fish and Wildlife Service director myself and leave Dr. Benson's superiors to contact him and fill him in on Operation Coyote. Mr. President, do you have any comments before we end the meeting?"

"Thank you, Vice President Kincaid. We have a huge challenge ahead of us again, but we have learned a lot about the control of coronavirus pandemics over the past year which should be extremely helpful. We have also been able to get ahead of this new COVID-21 virus so I am hopeful we will be successful. I'll let you all get back to work now as seems we have a lot to do."

CHAPTER 4

3:00 p.m. Wednesday, February 24, 2021
RCMP K Division Headquarters, Edmonton, Alberta, Canada

Anna Dupree came into the doorway of John Benson's office and said, "Hey, John, Commissioner Alden's executive assistant, Jeannie Hoxton is on the phone for you from Ottawa."

" Thank you, Anna, I wonder what they want now. Hi, Corporal Hoxton, what can I do for you?"

"Hi, Inspector Benson, I have Commissioner Alden on the line for you."

"Hi, John, I am going to have Jeannie send a document to your classified email account. When you have finished reading it, please give me a call right back."

John thought to himself, *Holy shit, this seems weird.*

John saw the email come up in his classified email inbox and opened the document. The title on the front cover was "Operation Coyote" with the watermark "Classified Level 1 — Office of the Vice President of the United States of America."

Suddenly extremely focused, John spent the next twenty minutes reading the document and then called the RCMP commissioner, Michael Alden, in Ottawa.

"Hi, Mike. What the hell is going on?"

"Hi, John. I take it that you have read the Operation Coyote file."

"Yes, I just finished it, is this for real?"

"Yes, I just left a meeting about an hour ago at the prime minister's office with Mathew Venable, the CSIS commissioner. We were on a video link call with US Vice President Amanda Kincaid and the president's chief of staff and she ran through basically what is in the file I sent you on Operation Coyote. At the request of the vice president and prime minister, my instructions were to send you the file and then give you a call and let you know that you will be expected to attend a meeting in Denver, Colorado, on Monday morning with a tentative plan on what you will need to head up Operation Coyote. Sounds pretty simple for a guy like you, right?"

"Why me, I would think that Kate Beckett and her people could run this operation without our help."

Michael Alden said, "It seems your reputation has preceded you and they thought that they needed the heavy hitters on this operation, so they want both you and Kate to run the show together, with you being the lead agent. They are being extremely cautious about leaks getting out to the Russians and Chinese who would like nothing better than have another pandemic ravage the US economy. So, John, did you ever think that this would be where we would end up when we were both at the RCMP Training Academy in Regina together, me the RCMP commissioner and you the famous INTERPOL wildlife trafficking hero?"

John Benson said laughing, "Yes, I was fairly sure where I would end up, but you being the RCMP commissioner seems pretty weird to me since I had to help you with almost every exercise at the RCMP academy. It's a good thing you were good at paperwork and kissing the asses of all the bureaucrats and politicians."

Laughing, Michael Alden said, "Be careful, John, I am technically your boss you know. I could have you demoted back down to constable. How is Denny Bear doing these days?"

"Denny is good. He has mostly been at his cabin at Slave Lake with his family for the last two months ever since we got back from Singapore. He doesn't do paperwork and reports, so I have been stuck here at my office with Anna Dupree for the last two months writing reports and preparing for my testimonies for whenever they schedule the trials for all the bad guys we took down in Operation Thunderball. I will call him later and let him know that our services have been requested again. I am sure he is getting itchy to get out there in the action again. Although hunting coyotes might seem tame stuff to him considering the adventures' we have gone through in the last fifteen years. So how is this going to go down on our end?"

"Since all the Canadian action on Operation Coyote will be happening in Alberta and Saskatchewan, we will let K Division in Edmonton handle all the logistics," Michael Alden said. "We have already reserved the RCMP corporate plane to fly you down to Denver. You can check with Kate Beckett, but I assume you can pick her and the US Fish and Wildlife director up in Oregon on the way there. Bill Shaw, the RCMP K Division superintendent, and John Clark, the CSIS station chief in Edmonton there at K Division, will fly down to Denver with you. I would suggest that you also take Corporal Anna Dupree with you so she can keep you organized like she always does when you are on a field assignment."

After a pause, Michael Alden continued, "All kidding aside, John, I am sure I do not have to tell you how big a deal this is. Failure of Operation Coyote is not an option. It may turn out to be one of the most important assignments of your career, not to put too much pressure on you. Kate Beckett has been briefed about Operation Coyote this afternoon as well, so I am sure she is expecting a call from you. Please let me know if there is anything you need from the RCMP or CSIS, and I mean anything, John. I will be getting the daily briefings from the task force so I will be up to speed all the time. Good luck, John, and I will talk to you again soon."

John Benson sat back in his office chair and thought about his relationship with Michael Alden. They had ended up in the same class at the RCMP Training Centre in Saskatoon in 1990. John was a few years older and a little more "world wise," but Michael was one of the smartest people he had ever encountered. He breezed through all the academic stuff at the academy but struggled with his firearms certification and the more physical parts of the training. Those were the parts that John had excelled at, so he had worked with Michael after hours and he eventually got through the training program. After graduating, they went their separate ways, John to the wildlife forensics unit, and Michael to begin his path upwards through the RCMP ranks. He eventually was promoted to the position of superintendent of K Division in Edmonton where he and John were able to renew their friendship. And then six years ago, he was promoted to RCMP commissioner and had to move to Ottawa. John and Michael always kidded each other about their days at the RCMP academy, but John knew that Michael Alden had earned every accolade and promotion in his distinguished career. Also, it had proven to be very opportune to have a friend in the RCMP commissioner's office on more than one occasion in the last six years.

He thought he had better call Dennis Bear right away to let him know what was going on. It was getting close to dinnertime so he thought Denny would probably be home.

"Hi, Denny, John here. Have you been enjoying your time off?"

Denny Bear answered, "Hi, John. I have, but my freezer is full of moose meat and the winter ice fishing season is almost over on the lake, so I was happy to see your name on my phone with maybe some news about getting out there chasing bad guys again."

"Well, I guess I have good news for you then." After John briefly told Denny about his conversation with Michael Alden he asked, "Can you come to Edmonton tomorrow morning? And Denny, pack enough clothes for at least a month and bring your assortment of weapons with you. You can stay with me at my house until we leave for Denver on Sunday on the RCMP corporate plane. Syd and Nelle miss you so you can spend some quality time with them. They will be coming to Denver with us as well as usual. And of course, Anna Dupree will also be coming with us so she can keep us organized so we don't get ourselves in trouble with all the paper-pushers."

"No problem, boss, I should be there by lunchtime. It must be important if they busted out the RCMP corporate plane for us."

John Benson grew up on a farm about one hundred kilometres northwest of Edmonton and had a twin sister, Julie, who now lived in a small town east of Edmonton, and a younger sister, Nina, who lived in the Okanagan Valley in British Columbia. He moved into Edmonton after high school at the age of seventeen in 1976 to go to the University of Alberta where he got a B.Sc. in Wildlife Biology and then, after a few years of working for the Alberta provincial government, went back to the U of A and got his M.Sc. in Forest Science. He did his M.Sc. thesis research on Rocky Mountain bighorn sheep and the effects of wildfires on their habitat. After graduating he worked in the environmental consulting industry for about three years.

He had met a professor at the U of A who was doing some interesting research in forensic wildlife biology. He was trying to develop genetic bioassay techniques to be able to trace the geographic origin of ungulate trophy animals confiscated from poachers by the Fish and Wildlife Service. It was assumed that most of these animals came from National Parks, but it was difficult to prove using the current scientific tools. Since bighorn sheep were one of the most popular animals confiscated from poachers, it sparked John Benson's interest and he ended up spending two years in a Ph.D. program working on developing the genetic bioassay techniques specific to bighorn sheep. After completing his Ph.D. in 1989, he was recruited by the RCMP to work in the Environment and Wildlife Enforcement Branch, but first he had to go to the RCMP Training Academy in Regina, Saskatchewan, just like any new RCMP recruit. The National Wildlife Enforcement Headquarters was in Gatineau, Quebec, but he could set up a small forensic lab and hire a team of forensic biologists to work out of K Division Headquarters in Edmonton, since he was married and had three young daughters at that point.

His small team of RCMP wildlife forensic biologists in Edmonton concentrated their efforts mostly in western Canada but soon developed a national reputation for solving some very complex cases of international wildlife trafficking originating in Canada and involving the illegal harvesting of animal parts, mostly for the Asian market. They often worked in partnership with the Alberta Fish and Wildlife Enforcement Branch's forensic lab in Edmonton, and the Wildlife Enforcement Directorate of the Environment Canada Enforcement Branch headquartered in Gatineau, Quebec.

John Benson's work in Canada eventually caught the interest of INTERPOL's Wildlife Crime Working Group. The wildlife experts who make up the Wildlife Crime Working Group devise strategies and initiatives for law enforcement to combat wildlife crimes on an international scale. The group initiates operations aimed at capturing wildlife criminals, seizing poached items, and dismantling the organized networks responsible for wildlife crime. It also engages with key players in wildlife conservation and law enforcement to maximize the global impact of its projects and operations.

Beginning around 2007, John Benson and his team were requested by Environment Canada's Wildlife Enforcement Directorate and INTERPOL's Wildlife Crime Unit to begin training local and state wildlife enforcement agencies in various countries around the world in the scientific principles of forensic wildlife biology and wildlife crime scene processing. This often involved not only classroom instruction but participating in field raids and takedowns of the wildlife poachers and traffickers. These people were often involved in criminal networks or gangs and were generally heavily armed, so firefights were not uncommon. Wildlife trafficking was often only one of the criminal enterprises the gangs were involved in, they were often diversified into things like drug trafficking and human trafficking. The Chinese Triads were particularly nasty bad guys and operated in many countries to satisfy the insatiable demand for various exotic animal parts in China and other Asian countries. Over the years, John Benson and his team's reputation grew and his services were in great demand.

The most recent INTERPOL operation John Benson had been involved in for periods of the last three years, together with the World Customs Organization (WCO), was Operation Thunderball, with police and customs administrations leading joint enforcement operations against wildlife and timber crime across 109 countries. The intelligence-led operation identified trafficking routes and crime hotspots ahead of time, enabling border, police, and environmental officers to seize protected wildlife products ranging from live big cats and primates to timber, marine wildlife, and derived merchandise such as clothing, beauty products, food items, traditional medicines, and handicrafts. Benson worked with a team of customs and police officers to coordinate global enforcement activities from an Operations Coordination Centre at INTERPOL's Global Complex for Innovation in Singapore. The operation led to the identification of almost six hundred suspects, triggering arrests worldwide. Further arrests and prosecutions were anticipated as ongoing global investigations progressed.

Although he was not a big fan of report writing and RCMP paperwork, his time back in Edmonton had given him the chance to spend a lot more quality time with his family for a change. He could see retirement looming in the not-too-distant future and maybe he would take Denny up on buying the lot next door to Denny's cabin on the south shore of Lesser Slave Lake and building his own get away where he could fish in the lake and whittle on the front porch in his rocking chair.

He had been divorced for the last twenty years. He had met his now ex-wife June while he was an undergraduate science student at the University of Alberta, and she was a pre-med student. They got married in 1979 in the summer after they had both graduated. The first of their three daughters, Sally, was born in 1983, and then Angela in 1985 and Laura in 1988. They were now thirty-eight, thirty-six, and thirty-three years old, respectively, and were all married to great guys. Sally was a senior graphic designer and art director for an advertising company and had two daughters, Angela was a physiotherapist and had two daughters and a son, and Laura was also a senior graphic designer and the operations manager working for a different advertising company and had a son, and just recently, the youngest of his grandkids, a daughter. They had all settled in Edmonton, so the decision about where his home base had to be was not ever really an option during his career.

Unfortunately, because of the demands of both his and his ex-wife June's careers, and his frequent absences travelling around the world, their marriage did not survive, and they were divorced in 2001. Ironically maybe a little, June had recently gotten remarried to a retired Edmonton Police Service detective with whom John got along with very well. John tried to be home for family celebrations like birthdays and holidays as much as possible but could not always be there if he were away on some INTERPOL assignment in Africa, South America, or Asia.

John lived in an historic bungalow on Ada Boulevard in north Edmonton overlooking the North Saskatchewan River valley. It was in the Highlands neighbourhood of Edmonton, one of the older suburban areas of the city with many houses dating back one hundred years. Ada Boulevard was a very trendy street running for about twenty-five blocks along the top of the river valley and had a mixture of older historic houses and new large infill houses. John lived alone in the house, except for Syd and Nelle, the German shepherds.

When the dogs could not come along with John's team on an assignment, they usually stayed with Denny's cousin at Slave Lake who lived just down the road from Denny. His cousin Mike Giroux was Denny's former spotter when they were both in the Canadian Military Special Forces. He had left the military at the same time as Denny and had also joined the RCMP and was now a special constable working out of the Town of Slave Lake RCMP detachment. There were several First Nations and Metis reserves in the Slave Lake area, and Mike Giroux was busy working primarily in the reserves and local settlements. Syd and Nelle liked their time with Mike at Slave Lake, and he would often take them along in his RCMP SUV while he was on duty.

John forwarded the Operation Coyote file to Anna Dupree and asked her to come into his office once she had read it.

Anna Dupree was now thirty-eight years old and was originally from Montreal. She had completed her B.Sc. in Genetics and M.Sc. in Wildlife Forensic Biology at McGill University. After completing her M.Sc. degree, she had been recruited by the RCMP to work in the National Forensic Laboratory Services out of the Environment Canada National Enforcement Headquarters in Gatineau, Quebec. John Benson had first met her in Gatineau about eleven years ago while she was working on some tissue samples' he had submitted for DNA testing from the Edmonton forensics lab. After numerous discussions both in person and over the phone, he realized she would be the perfect person to take over the management of the Edmonton lab. He wooed her for a year with stories of the chance to not only manage the forensics lab in Edmonton, but to travel to all the exotic locations around the world working with INTERPOL She finally took him up on his offer and had been in Edmonton for the last ten years.

Anna was an attractive brunette and all muscle. She was an over-achiever in almost every facet of her life. While he was reading her RCMP background security checks, he discovered that she had an IQ of 150+. She also ran marathons for fun and had a black belt in a couple of different martial arts. She had also taken the RCMP advanced firearms and sniper training while at the RCMP Training Academy. She was not only fluent in both English and French, but she also spoke Spanish like a native Spaniard, and for something to do in the evenings in hotel rooms while on assignment, she had taught herself Swahili, because she thought it might come in handy on the job sometimes.

Often, while they were on overseas assignments, she and Denny would go to a local law enforcement shooting range and have friendly shooting competitions. Whenever she would mange to beat Denny, which was not easy since he was one of the best shooters in the RCMP service and a former special forces sniper, he would come sulking into John's hotel room complaining about, "Why that damn woman had to be the best at everything she did." They were best friends though, so it was all in good fun.

Although John would never dare to mention it to Anna, she also had a mild case of obsessive-compulsive disorder which turned out to be very opportune for him. She was a stickler for neatness and organization. She always seemed to know where everything was and what administrative or operational paperwork needed to be completed, which were not strong points for either him or Denny. John relied on her for many things, not the least of which was keeping him out of trouble with the many administrators and paper-pushers in the RCMP.

After about thirty minutes Anna came into his office and sat down and said, "So, John, it seems that your reputation has gotten us involved in something pretty big here."

"Not just my reputation, yours as well. Commissioner Alden specifically told me to bring you and Denny with me to Denver to help set up the forensic protocols and training of the field teams. I guess we should probably give Kate Beckett a call since she will be running this operation with us."

Dr. Kate Beckett picked up the phone in her office at the Clark R. Bavin National Fish and Wildlife Forensic Laboratory in Ashland, Oregon, when she saw the call was from John Benson. She said, "Hi, John. I've been expecting to hear from you. I just got a phone call from the vice president, which has not happened before. I assume you got the Operation Coyote file too?"

"Yes, I got the file. I had a chat with Michael Alden, the RCMP commissioner, about two hours ago. Seems we are in for some fun for the next month or so! I will brief Denny when he gets to Edmonton tomorrow morning. Anna's here in my office, by the way — we have you on speakerphone. How is the Thunderball testimony prep going?"

"Hi, Anna. I hope John hasn't been driving you too crazy stuck in the office with him for the last two months. I have been busy slogging through all my notes and field reports trying to put coherent final reports together. You wouldn't want to lend me Anna for a few months, would you, John?"

John said laughing, "Kate, I think you know the answer to that question. I am not the best note taker and my memory's slipping with my advancing age. Without Anna, I'd be in big trouble. And besides, it looks like we are all going to be able to put the report writing aside for at least the next month while we save the world. Any thoughts, Kate, on how we might go about doing that?"

Getting down to business, Kate said, "As you read in the Operation Coyote file, the COVID-21 Task Force have already done quite a bit of planning and have some good ideas. The plan to run the whole field operation under the guise of a rabies testing and research program is brilliant since the field collection and preservation of the coyote brains for the COVID-21 vaccine production is almost identical to the forensic protocols for rabies specimen collection and submission. As you both know, the only definitive way to determine if an animal has rabies is to examine the brain. Since this is impossible to do while the animal is alive, it means that cutting the head off and submitting it to a state lab for rabies testing is generally the only way to reliably do the testing. So, we can easily run the operation under the guise of a routine rabies testing program.

"The field teams in the individual states or provinces, will not for the most part, even need to know why they are actually collecting all the coyote brains. We will just have to assemble and train enough field teams to get the minimum one thousand coyote brains in a couple of weeks, and make sure all the brain tissue is delivered to the CDC in Fort Collins within no longer than twelve hours after collection to make sure it is still viable for the vaccine production. And we also must do it under extremely tight national security protocols before the Russians and Chinese find out what is going on. Seems pretty simple, right?"

Laughing, John said, "It seems you have everything already figured out, what do you need us for?"

"That's what I asked the vice president. Why do we need these Canadians coming down here and helping us run this operation? However, she seems to think it might not be that simple, so I agreed to let your team tag along as long as you didn't slow things down."

"Thanks for the solid endorsement, we'll try not to get in your way," John said laughing." So, Kate, all kidding aside, it looks like we have some serious operational planning to do before Monday morning. It is getting late, why don't we discuss this more tomorrow morning? I'll send you a secure video link once Anna and I brief Denny on the operation tomorrow morning. Just to let you know, we have the RCMP corporate plane reserved for Sunday and we can pick you up on our way to Denver. That will give us some time to finalize our presentation to the task force on Monday morning."

"That sounds good to me, John," Kate said. "I will let my director know since he will be coming to the meeting as well. Just give me a call later tomorrow morning after you are ready on your end and we can start working out the details of Operation Coyote."

Dr. Kate Beckett was fifty-three years old, divorced with one adult daughter, Dianna, who lived in Portland, Oregon. In many ways she was a somewhat older version of Anna Dupree, an attractive brunette, and almost always smarter than everyone else in the room. John Benson had known her for about fifteen years and had been working with her on INTERPOL assignments for about the last ten years. She and John had been a romantic couple off and on for the last ten years as well.

Kate grew up in Tacoma, Washington, just south of Seattle. Her father had died of a heart attack in 2007 and her mother had died at her retirement home in Tacoma in March 2019 from the COVID-19 virus at the beginning of the pandemic. She had a normal upper-middle class upbringing and excelled at academics all through school. She was also a star track athlete in high school and went on to the University of Washington in Seattle on a full athletic scholarship. She had qualified for the US Olympic team for the 1988 Summer Olympics in Seoul, South Korea, for both the 400-metre and 800-metre track races, but tragically tore her Achilles tendon during training two months before the Olympics. That was the end of her track career, so she put all her efforts into her academic studies. She got her B.Sc. degree in Animal Physiology and Zoology in 1989, and then her M.Sc. degree in Genetics studying DNA bioassay techniques for tracing the geographic origins of endangered wildlife species.

She was then accepted at the University of Southern California to do her Ph.D. and continued with her M.Sc. research concentrating on DNA bioassay techniques specifically for the Sierra Nevada bighorn sheep. Sierra Nevada Bighorn Sheep were listed as a federally endangered subspecies in 2000, and as of 2016, only six hundred Sierra bighorns remained in the wild. They were also a prized trophy animal for poachers and wildlife traffickers, and the science of forensic wildlife biology and genetics was starting to be used for tracing the geographic origins of the confiscated trophy heads from poachers. In most cases, the origins of the trophy animals were from National Parks in the US or Canada.

After completing her Ph.D. in 1992, Kate spent two years at the University of Cambridge in England doing post-doctoral research with a team of researchers working on developing genetic bioassay techniques for tracing confiscated African elephant ivory to the elephant's geographic origin in Africa. She also got her first exposure to the fascinating world of international illegal wildlife trafficking and law enforcement. On returning to the US in 1994, she was offered a job at the United States Fish and Wildlife (F&W) Service Office of Law Enforcement. She also received training as a United States Fish and Wildlife Service special agent, with most of the same law enforcement powers as FBI special agents. The F&W Office of Law Enforcement investigated wildlife crimes, regulated wildlife trade, and worked in partnership with international, state, and tribal law enforcement agencies.

Kate had been in a short-term relationship with a fellow graduate student at the University of Southern California. The relationship did not last long, but she had gotten pregnant and had a daughter, Dianna, in 1992 while she was working on finishing her Ph.D. thesis. The father was not interested in sticking around so Kate carried on as a single mother. She had already been accepted to do her post-doctoral research at Cambridge University in England, so she packed up her new baby and they both moved to England for two years. She would often bring Dianna with her to the lab at Cambridge and would also take her to the daycare provided at the university for the research staff.

Kate's daughter, Dianna Beckett, was now twenty-nine years old and living in Portland. She was still single but had a serious boyfriend and was working as a graphic designer for an advertising company. Interestingly, two of John Benson' daughters were also graphic designers in Edmonton. Dianna had decided to not follow her mother into the family wildlife trafficking crime busting business and seemed to be happy with her life in Portland. Ashland and Portland were about a four-hour drive apart, so Kate was able to see Dianna quite often when she was home in the US.

Kate had previously heard of John Benson by reputation and had even spoken to him on the phone several times in 1992 when she was working on her Ph.D. at USC because their thesis research topics had been quite similar.

She had also seen him speak at a conference in 2001. However, she only first met him in person in 2004 at an international conference on wildlife trafficking and law enforcement in Lyon, France, sponsored by INTERPOL. They had both been invited to do presentations at the conference and were then on a discussion panel together. They had hit it off right away because of their common academic interests and similar jobs in forensic wildlife biology and law enforcement. They started a professional relationship via email and phone calls, often discussing cases they were working on or asking each other for advice about new forensic procedures being published in the literature. They also continued to see each other periodically at international conferences and meetings.

In 2010, they were jointly invited by INTERPOL's Wildlife Crime Working Group to work together as advisors on a new initiative named Operation Worthy. John and Kate were brought in ahead of the operation to assist in formulating a training program developed and delivered by the Wildlife Enforcement Directorate of Environment Canada's Enforcement Branch. One of the first training workshops was held in 2011 in Gaborone, Botswana, with sponsorship from the International Fund for Animal Welfare (IFAW). They brought together enforcement officers from the participating countries to update them on the latest search and seizure techniques, and to allow them to directly exchange information and expertise.

In 2014, John and Kate and their support people from Canada and the US were invited to become members of a larger team of international forensic wildlife scientists and wildlife law enforcement personnel to further support the member countries in the fight against illegal ivory and rhino horn trafficking and other environmental issues. The team's administrative headquarters was located within the INTERPOL Regional Bureau for East Africa in Nairobi, Kenya. The environmental crime team acted as an extension of INTERPOL's Environmental Security Unit located at its General Secretariat headquarters in Lyon, France.

Although John and Kate and their teams spent most of their time with INTERPOL working in Africa, they also worked on assignments in South America on occasion, operating out of the INTERPOL Regional Bureau in Buenos Aires, Argentina. One of the more notable operations was Operation Cage, which included national wildlife enforcement authorities, police, customs, and specialized units. While the operation focused primarily on the illegal trade of birds, several other fauna and flora were found, including elephant ivory, turtles, fish, and other live wildlife.

Operation Cage was launched in response to the growing illegal trans-border trade of captive-bred and wild birds and eggs, and the increasing involvement of organized crime networks in their transit from Latin America to Europe. More than 8,700 birds and animals, including reptiles, mammals and insects were seized and nearly 4,000 people arrested in an operation across 32 countries. John and Kate's expertise was mainly at the planning level, instructing the law enforcement agencies in various countries in the proper procedures in gathering wildlife forensic evidence that could then be used by government prosecutors. Their teams, including Denny Bear and Anna Dupree, would often accompany the local law enforcement personnel on raids and seizures and instruct them on proper scientific wildlife crime scene investigation procedures.

John and Kate were often in Nairobi working together at the INTERPOL Regional Bureau offices. Their relationship soon progressed from a professional one to also a romantic one. INTERPOL had several apartments and cottages in facilities close to the Bureau offices which had special security provisions and were reserved for visiting scientists and law enforcement personnel. Since they were there so often, they had their own permanent cottage which they could use as their home away from home. Their teams also had cottages or apartments they could use, but they were often away in the field working with the local wildlife enforcement agencies in various African countries. When John and Kate were travelling together at other locations in Africa and elsewhere in the world, they generally stayed together in hotels or whatever accommodation that was provided. People mostly treated them like they were a married couple, and they usually did not make any special effort to explain their relationship to anyone if it was not necessary.

Kate Beckett and John Benson had been a romantic couple off and on for the last ten years. Unfortunately, since they were both obsessed with their demanding careers and lived in different countries, they had trouble maintaining anything approaching a normal romantic relationship. However, they had come to an understanding about the demands of their careers and private lives and had decided that when they had a chance to be physically together, wherever in the world that might be, that they would live together as a couple if possible. When the time came to go back to their respective homes, families, and regular jobs, they would temporarily part ways until the next assignment brought them back together. So far it seemed to be working for them.

For considerable periods over the previous three years, when they were not at their respective home bases in Canada and the US, they had been operating primarily out of the Operations Coordination Centre at INTERPOL's Global Complex for Innovation in Singapore. They had been assigned to lead their respective Canadian and US contingents in INTERPOL's largest ever global enforcement activity named "Operation Thunderball." They had a similar living arrangement in Singapore, using one of INTERPOL's apartments reserved for visiting scientists and law enforcement people. These apartment buildings had special access and security provisions like dedicated elevators, electronic eavesdropping blocking devices, and bullet and soundproof windows. The world of global wildlife trafficking was a dangerous one, worth billions of dollars every year, so INTERPOL did not take any chances with their important strategists and planners.

After they had gotten off the phone with Kate Beckett, John thought about seeing her again after two months of being away from each other. These times apart, especially after being together so much in Singapore over the past three years, were getting harder. Now it looked like they might be getting involved in one of the highest stake's operations in their careers. He was not sure he was up to the task, but at least Kate would be by his side and maybe together they could pull it off.

CHAPTER 5

10:30 a.m. Thursday, February 25, 2021
RCMP K Division Headquarters, Edmonton, Alberta, Canada

Denny Bear stuck his head into John Benson's office door and said, "How's it going, John? What is so important that you have summoned me from my life of leisure at Slave Lake?"

"Hi, Denny, good to see you again. How was the drive?"

"It was okay, the roads were dry, so I made good time. While it was still dark after I had just left, I saw a moose at the last second on the side of the road just south of Slave Lake, but thankfully it didn't step out in front of me."

"That section of road is always dangerous for moose and deer collisions so I'm glad you didn't hit it," John said. "Why don't you put your stuff in your office and fire up your computer and I will send you a classified file named Operation Coyote. It should save us some time getting you up to speed. After you have finished reading the file, grab Anna and we can give Kate Beckett a call."

After Denny left, John could not help but reflect on how lucky he was to have had Dennis Bear as a friend and partner for the last fifteen years. They had been through a lot over the fifteen years and there was not a better person in the world you would want with you when the bad guys where shooting at you in the jungle, or anywhere else for that matter. Denny was forty-seven years old now. He was a member of the Driftpile Cree First Nation located south of Lesser Slave Lake in northern Alberta. His father was a chief of the First Nation like his father before him. When they were back home in

Alberta, he usually went back to his cabin on the south shore of Lesser Slave Lake, a two-hour drive north of Edmonton.

As a young teenager Denny loved to go hunting with his father and grandfather. He got his first hunting rifle at the age of fourteen and it was his most prized possession. He and his cousin Mike Giroux set up a shooting range in the forest and they would spend hours shooting at homemade targets. Denny had saved up some money and bought the best rifle scope he could afford in the sporting goods store in the town of Slave Lake, east of the reserve. Mike was a good shot, but Denny seemed to have a special skill for hitting the bull's eye almost every time from ever-increasing distances.

Both Denny and Mike also liked watching war movies on TV and talked about maybe joining the military when they were old enough. Denny had talked to the guidance counsellor at the high school in Slave Lake and he had given him some pamphlets about what was required to join the Canadian military. The one thing that was most important was to have graduated from high school. So, Denny and Mike, although not the best students, worked harder than ever to get through high school and get their diplomas. As soon as they turned eighteen and finished high school, they informed their parents that they were going to enlist in the military. They were both accepted, and in September 1992, went off to basic training in Quebec. They both immediately took to the military lifestyle and excelled at all the training exercises.

Both Denny and Mike's skill on the shooting range immediately got the interest of their instructors. Denny's marksman scores were always the best of anyone in his training class. In fact, they were the best of anyone his instructors had seen for quite a while. After their basic training was completed, they were asked if they would like to go into the specialized sniper training program. Once again, Denny completed the program as the best marksman in his training class, with Mike not far behind.

They both also trained as mountain warfare specialists and as paratroopers which included helicopter assault techniques. They were then assigned to the special forces sniper unit and got their first overseas deployment to Bosnia and Herzegovina in January 1994 with Canada's NATO peacekeeping forces. They served in Bosnia and Croatia on rotating deployments for several years and were also deployed to missions in the Central African Republic and Sierra Leone in the later 1990s. Denny and Mike's reputations as snipers grew not only in the Canadian Armed Forces, but in other country's forces as well, particularly the US Army and Marine Special Forces.

In 2001, Denny and Mike were included among the few dozen Canadian Special Forces troops who participated in the US military invasion of Afghanistan. They were followed in February 2002 by an infantry battle group (approximately 1,200 troops), sent to the southern Afghan province of Kandahar as part of a United States Army task force searching for insurgents in that area. The Canadians fought against al Qaeda and Taliban forces, and provided protection for humanitarian operations and for Afghanistan's new interim government. From 2003 to 2005, the Canadian battle group's mission focused on providing security in the Afghan capital, Kabul, and helping to disarm Afghan militia units under the command of local warlords. Despite occasional insurgent suicide bomber attacks, Canadians were mostly involved in patrolling, policing, and the stabilization of the new Afghan government.

Denny and Mike, however, as special forces snipers, were deployed mostly with the US Special Forces in forward bases in the mountains of Afghanistan searching for and killing senior Taliban and al Qaeda fighters. With Mike Giroux acting mostly as Denny's spotter, their kill success was usually the highest of all the special forces sniper teams. Their Aboriginal background and special forces training seemed to be particularly suited to operating in the mountainous terrain of Afghanistan. Their reputation grew and Denny became know as "The Ghost" in special forces circles. He always deflected credit though, and seldom talked about his missions with his fellow soldiers.

John Benson was very busy with his RCMP wildlife trafficking law enforcement duties at this time and managing his forensic lab but realized if he wanted to get more involved in international enforcement operations with agencies like INTERPOL, he needed some additional specialized field training in military combat tactics. He managed to persuade his superiors to let him go to Afghanistan in 2005 for three months and spend time with the Canadian Special Forces there. Most of his time in Afghanistan was spent at the Canadian base in Kabul and going out on routine patrols. However, he met Dennis Bear one day when he was back at the base in Kabul and since they were both from Alberta, they struck up a friendship. John talked with Denny about the type of wildlife trafficking enforcement work he was doing with the RCMP and the wildlife forensic lab in Edmonton and Denny was fascinated. He invited John to come with him on a few missions into the mountains and act as his spotter to give Mike Giroux a break. John was nervous about getting so close to the action, but during their time in the mountains waiting to get the shot at whatever bad guys they were after, they had a lot of time to talk about international wildlife trafficking and wildlife law enforcement.

Denny's latest enlistment term in the military was about to end in early 2006 and he and John agreed that Denny could join John's team if Denny were to quit the military and go through the RCMP basic training program. So, both Denny and Mike Giroux ended their military careers in January 2006 and applied to join the RCMP. They were both accepted and completed their training at the RCMP Training Academy in Regina in late 2006. Mike went on to become a RCMP special constable working close to home in the Slave Lake Detachment, and Denny joined John Benson's team at RCMP K Division Headquarters in Edmonton.

Since then, John and Denny had travelled around the world together on various INTERPOL operations. They had sometimes gotten themselves into some very tough spots, but had always managed to survive, often only because of Denny's military skills with his rifle. Denny was also a fast learner, and despite his lack of any formal university training in forensic wildlife biology, he seemed to have an innate understanding of the science involved. He and Anna Dupree often worked with local wildlife law enforcement personnel in the various countries they visited instructing them on forensic evidence gathering and wildlife crime scene processing.

As usual, John had brought Syd and Nelle into the office with him so they would not have to stay home alone and could mingle with the rest of the office and lab staff. Since they were great at looking hungry, there were strict rules about feeding them snacks, but they managed to get their share anyways. When they realized Denny was back in the office today, there was great excitement with much squirming and tail wagging until Denny had to give them the down signal, when they immediately dropped down on the floor and remained motionless beside him in his office until Denny gave them the up signal after he had read the Operation Coyote file.

Ever since they had first gotten the two dogs, the RCMP dog trainers had advised John and Denny that since Denny was going to be the principal dog handler on assignments, that they try to separate their "work lives" from their "off duty" lives. So, they seldom stayed with Denny when they were not working so they knew that when they were with him it meant that they were "on duty" and their innate instincts and training kicked in.

After about forty minutes, Denny and Anna came into his office with Syd and Nelle and sat down at John's small meeting table. Denny said, "Alright, I see now why this is more important than getting in a couple more days of fishing at the lake before the winter ice fishing season closes. So, what's the plan?"

"Anna and I spoke with Kate briefly yesterday afternoon and she filled us in on what she knew so far from the new COVID-21 Task Force. RCMP Commissioner Alden had called me earlier to fill me in and Kate had gotten her call directly from US Vice President Amanda Kincaid. It seems that they want us to work together heading up Operation Coyote and saving the world as we know it. I guess we should be kind of honoured to be given the job, but the bottom line is that failure is not an option. No pressure though, right?"

Looking a little overwhelmed by the whole situation, Denny said, "Wow, the stakes are a lot higher than breaking up some wildlife trafficking syndicate. Are you sure we are up for this?"

Smiling a little, John said, "I sure hope so because it seems a lot of powerful people are counting on us. So, why don't we give Kate a call and get her on a secure video link here in my office and we can get down to business. We would like to have a firm plan of action put together so we can present it at the task force meeting in Denver on Monday morning."

They waited for a few minutes while Anna went on her laptop and set up the secure video link. It always baffled John and Denny how she knew how to do that kind of stuff. It was just one of the many reasons why they appreciated her many contributions to the success of their team.

After the link was up and Anna had placed the call, John said, "Hi, Kate. I have Anna, Denny, Syd, and Nelle in my office as you can see. How is the reception on your end?"

"It is good, John. Hi, everyone. It is nice to see the gang back together again after the last couple of months. I have been quite busy since we talked yesterday afternoon, as you can imagine. I've spoken with Fish and Wildlife Law Enforcement. They have notified our field agents to stand by for further instructions about a possible new operation over the next few days. We also spoke with Larry Greer — the FBI agent in charge in Denver — and notified him that we will require some agents. He'll be at the task force meeting on Monday. We also had a brief discussion with General Shields of the US Special Forces about getting some snipers to participate in the field collection.

"It seems our main tasks over the next couple of days will be to determine how the field teams will be structured, how and where they will be deployed within seven US states and two Canadian provinces, what equipment they will need, and how we will go about controlling the information needed by the field teams and the various levels of supervisory personnel in all the different agencies involved. Am I missing anything, John?"

"Probably, but this should keep us busy for a while," he said. "I was thinking though, if we only need about one thousand coyote units at least initially, why don't we try to minimize the geographic area we will be operating in. There is no reason to operate in all seven states if we can maximize our efforts in fewer states, plus maintaining a certain effort in the two Canadian provinces. Why don't you get some of your people working on the coyote population demographics in the states having populations of Plains coyotes and see where we will get our best 'bang for the buck'. Plus, it would probably be best to operate in the less populous states if possible or at least the less populous areas of the other states. That would make it easier for the field teams to work without a lot of interest from the local landowners."

"That is an excellent idea, John," Kate said. "I'll get some of my biologists and statisticians working on that right away. Any ideas on how we should structure the field collection teams?"

"Here are some of my initial thoughts," John said, "and please, everyone, speak up if you disagree or have anything to add. We should take full advantage of the rabies testing and control guise and use only local state or provincial Fish and Wildlife vehicles for field transport of the field teams."

"Why is that important?" Denny asked.

"Because it will minimize concern by local landowners and media," Anna answered.

John continued, "The field teams in each state or province should be comprised of at least two Fish and Wildlife ground vehicles and one helicopter operating as a unit. The field teams should be comprised of a mixture of local Fish and Wildlife officers who know their areas, at least one agent from the Fish and Wildlife Office of Law Enforcement who has some training in forensic evidence gathering and wildlife crime scene processing. If possible, these will also be the people who do the on-scene biopsy procedure of the coyote brain removal. They have the added benefit of having advanced weapons training so could also help with shooting the coyotes if necessary. The other members of the team will be US Army Special Forces snipers who will be in both the helicopter and at least one of the ground vehicles. Of course, there will also be the helicopter pilots."

"That all sounds logical," Kate interjected.

"As for locating the coyotes, this time of year many of the female coyotes will either be getting ready to have their pups or will have already had them and will be in their dens. This will mean that most of the coyotes that we will encounter will be older males or younger unproductive coyotes, both male and female. The teams should avoid taking females with pups or obviously still pregnant females, if possible."

"What about actually killing the coyotes? How is that gong to happen?" Denny asked.

John replied, "We hopefully can rely on the local Fish and Wildlife officers to provide the expertise about the areas they work in and the more likely locations to find the coyotes. We can also use various techniques to bring the coyotes to the field teams, rather than randomly searching for them. Among other things, we could use bait stations and blinds to lure the coyotes to specific locations, and then shoot them. The bait stations could use wild game like deer or moose, or could use cattle, pigs, or sheep purchased from local landowners. I am sure there are probably also other ways of attracting the coyotes to fixed locations, but I will let the experts with Fish and Wildlife figure that out. Of course, to preserve the brain tissue, only body shots can be used, and preferably heart shots to take the coyotes down instantly. That is why the special forces snipers will come in handy."

"That sounds good," said Denny. "I will try to think of some other ways the teams can be as efficient as possible in hunting down the coyotes."

Anna interjected, "From the research I did this morning about rabies testing, and talking to John, we think that once the coyote is killed, the brain will have to be removed in the field within a maximum of thirty minutes, and placed in a cooler and transported via helicopter or truck to the designated collection airport in the region, and then transported via fixed-wing aircraft to the CDC lab in Fort Collins within a maximum of twelve hours from when the coyote brain was initially harvested. This process will have to be going on simultaneously with multiple teams, in multiple locations within multiple states and provinces."

Smiling at Kate on the monitor, John asked, "Any comments or questions?"

Kate said laughing, "I knew there must have been a reason Vice President Kincaid wanted you involved in Operation Coyote, even if you are a Canadian. It appears you may have organized a few operations before."

Smiling, John said, "Yes, Kate, I have, and you should know, since you have been there beside me almost all of the time, so don't seem so surprised that I had some ideas about how to put this operation together. Anyways, it looks like I have done most of the hard work so why don't you guys work out the details."

"Okay, John, I apologize for the Canadian jokes. Maybe you could stick around for a while to give us a hand with the details," Kate said smiling.

"Okay, I accept your apology, and I guess I would just have to go back to Operation Thunderball report writing anyways, so I might as well give you a hand. So how do we go about figuring out how many field teams we will need to collect a minimum of one thousand coyote brain specimens in two to three weeks and transport them all to the CDC in Fort Collins?"

"I'll get my biologists, statisticians, and GIS mapping people here at the lab on this right away so we can narrow down the areas of operation. We can have another video call tomorrow morning to start planning the logistics in more detail. Maybe you can reach out to your Canadian Fish and Wildlife people to do the same analyses? And we should see about putting together the equipment we'll need."

"Sounds good, Kate," said John. "Let's do the video link tomorrow morning at 9:00 a.m. our time since we are an hour ahead of you. In the meantime, we can chat on the phone today if we need to check in with each other."

Once they were disconnected from the call with Kate, John, Anna, and Denny divided up a list of Operation Coyote tasks they could work on for the rest of the day. Syd and Nelle went back to sleeping on their dog beds in John's office, assuming their services would not be needed at this point. Unless of course, they heard a bag of snacks opening or smelled something good coming from down the hall in the kitchen area. Every couple of hours they would get up and wander around the offices and lab area just to make sure there were no people there who they did not recognize. If they happened to come across a morsel of food from someone's lunch on an office floor or in the kitchen area, of course they thought it was their duty to dispose of it. And people seemed to like seeing them so why not cheer them up a little by letting them give them a pat or telling them how cute they were.

9:00 a.m. Friday, February 26, 2021
RCMP K Division Headquarters, Edmonton, Alberta, Canada

Syd and Nelle were standing by in their dog beds waiting for any instructions to go into action. They had enjoyed their evening yesterday going for a walk and then hanging out with Denny and John at the house. John, Anna, and Denny were gathered in John's office again with the video link operating with Kate in Ashland, Oregon. They were all looking a little tired and the gravity of the situation was starting to sink in.

Kate said, "Good morning, everyone. From the serious looks on your faces, I assume you are also realizing the size of the job we have ahead of us. I assume you had a chance to have a look at the analysis and maps I sent you last night that my team put together yesterday afternoon. It should really help focus our logistical planning for the operation. And I also received your Fish and Wildlife information for the similar data in Alberta and Saskatchewan. My team has also been busy contacting the state Fish and Wildlife senior people and alerting them about the people and resources we will be needing over the next few weeks for the rabies testing program.

"It seems weird to say this, but I updated the vice president of the United States yesterday afternoon about our progress, and she has contacted the governors in all of the states we will be operating in and informed them that they will be expected to facilitate any requests that we might be making of their state agencies in the next few days. The governors have all been briefed about the true nature of Operation Coyote and are willing to participate as required in the rabies testing cover operation. I have also contacted General Frank Shields and he has agreed to make as many special forces snipers available as we will need for the operation. We just must let him know the numbers and where they must be. How are things going on your end?"

"Speaking of a conversation that also has never happened before," John said, "I had a conference call with the prime minister and RCMP commissioner yesterday afternoon and updated them about our progress and the things we will need going forward. The prime minister was going to call the premiers in Alberta and Saskatchewan and brief them about Operation Coyote. The premiers are also going to alert the key people involved in their provincial governments with the same instructions to provide whatever we need for the operation."

"That sounds great, John," Kate said. "So, we basically have today and tomorrow to get a firm preliminary plan put together that we can present to the task force Monday morning in Denver. We will have some time to finalize some details on Sunday while we are flying down to Denver and on Sunday evening at the hotel. We should be ready by tomorrow afternoon to start contacting the state and provincial agencies involved to start deploying people and equipment to the locations we recommend. I know we both have people on our teams who can put together the technical presentation materials, so we do not have to worry about that part. We just have to figure out the details to give to them."

John said, "Okay, Kate, so let's start breaking it all down and figuring out the people and equipment details and the logistics of how we get everything done. How are you feeling about things on your end? We are definitely panicked a little here trying to get this all organized for Monday morning."

"I know, John, me too. The expectations about getting this right are really high. We can only do our best and then hope for some good luck for it all to come together. So, I guess we better get to work."

CHAPTER 6

10:00 a.m. Sunday, February 28, 2021
RCMP Hangar, Edmonton International Airport

John and Denny had met Anna at the office earlier in the morning with Syd and Nelle and finished packing the last few items of equipment they were likely to need over the next few weeks. Kate had informed them that the FBI were providing one of their planes in Denver for their team to use as a mobile tactical operations centre since they would be on the move daily and needed to be as efficient as possible. The plane was outfitted with all the latest communication and office equipment and even had sleeping quarters if they needed them. They had already sent most of the equipment and their personal belongings to the Edmonton airport yesterday and it was already loaded on the RCMP plane that they were using to fly to Denver.

They met Bill Shaw, the RCMP superintendent of K Division Headquarters, and John Clark, the CSIS station chief in Edmonton, at the RCMP hangar at the Edmonton International Airport and they all boarded the RCMP PC-12NG single engine turboprop plane, with seating for up to ten people, for the three-and-a-half-hour flight to Ashland, Oregon, to pick up Dr. Kate Beckett and Robert Carter, the US Fish and Wildlife Service director. Syd and Nelle were settled into their travel kennels and happy to be out on some sort of assignment again. They were veteran fliers and were used to all the commotion in airports all around the world.

They all settled in for the flight to Ashland and talked about Operation Coyote. John Benson filled in Bill Shaw and John Clark about the Operation

Coyote planning progress to date and they offered some suggestions about logistical and security details. John, Kate, Anna, and Denny had worked all of Friday and Saturday on the logistical details of Operation Coyote, and their people had put together a digital presentation and a briefing report for the task force meeting on Monday morning. John and Kate were planning on going through the overview of the plan with the attendees at the meeting and hoping to get the go-ahead right away. They had also contacted the heads of most of the government agencies who would be involved in the operation to give them the heads-up about what they might be needing from them.

The flight to Ashland went by quite fast and they had eaten the lunch that had been provided by the RCMP. They landed at the small Ashland Municipal Airport to pick up Kate Beckett and Robert Carter, and Kate's luggage and gear. Denny took Syd and Nelle out for a quick walk and to have a doggie bathroom break. John saw Kate come out of the small Ashland airport terminal building looking as beautiful as ever. He was always amazed at how someone so smart, fearless, and good at her job, could also be as beautiful as she was. He was a lucky man to have her as his best friend, lover, and colleague. As she was walking across the tarmac, John greeted her at the bottom of the portable stairway that had been rolled up to the airplane.

As they hugged and exchanged a quick kiss, Kate said, "Hi, honey. I missed you. Two months is too long to be apart. How was your flight so far?"

Looking at her and smiling, John replied, "It's great to see you again too. The flight has been fine. We had lots to talk about, so it went by quite fast. Too bad the plane is filled with all these important cops, otherwise we could have a better time on the flight to Denver."

Smiling back at him, Kate said, "I know, but we will be together now for the next month at least so there should be lots of time to get reacquainted."

When they were all back on the plane, introductions were made for those who had not met before and they took off for the almost four-hour flight to Denver. They all talked some more about Operation Coyote and more suggestions were made about the logistical details of the operation. Robert Carter, the director of the US Fish and Wildlife Service, was particularly helpful in committing F&W resources to the operation and reinforcing the rabies research and testing cover operation. He assured John and Kate that he would provide as many F&W federal law enforcement special agents as well as regular state F&W officers as they needed.

The plane landed at the Denver Airport and taxied over to the FBI hangar. A US customs agent came on board and looked at their Canadian passports and the credentials of all the people on the plane. He also checked the gun transport permits which included not only all their personal sidearms, but numerous sniper and assault rifles. He looked at them and said, "Wow, you guys expecting a war?"

When none of them said anything, he shrugged and said they were free to leave the plane. On the tarmac, pulled up to the plane, were four black Chevy Tahoe extended SUVs with tinted windows like you see in the movies. Several FBI workers from the hangar unloaded all the luggage and equipment and put their personal suitcases into one of the vehicles. The field equipment and the numerous gun cases they brought with them were left at the FBI hangar at the airport.

They all got into the other three SUVs with the drivers and left the airport in a convoy to go to the hotel, which was a little different from your ordinary hotel. The Denver FBI Field Office had rooms permanently reserved on the top three floors of a hotel about a block from the FBI office. A special elevator not available to the public, and with a permanent security guard posted outside, was used to access the three floors. There was no check-in procedure, and they entered the hotel through a service bay overhead door. They all got their room assignments from a nice FBI lady carrying a standard FBI sidearm. Denny (with Syd and Nelle) and Anna got their own rooms, but Kate and John got a nice suite reserved for couples. Denny asked if there was a park or off-leash dog area close by and headed off with Syd and Nelle for a little walk and another doggie bathroom break.

Kate and John went up to their suite, which was genuinely nice with a separate bedroom, two bathrooms, a small kitchen and dining area, and a living room with a large flat-screen TV. Kate and John had not been together for two months, so were happy to have some privacy and were looking forward to spending the night together. However, tomorrow was going to be a big day, and they still had some last-minute details they needed to add to their presentation to the task force based on discussions they had on the plane trip to Denver. They ordered room service dinner from the special FBI kitchen in the hotel, and then spent the evening going over their presentation and watching some news on TV, and then went to bed to get some rest for the coming day.

After a while, when they were lying in bed, Kate said to John, "I was talking to Denny and he said he still has that vacant lot next to his cabin at Slave Lake saved for you whenever you decide to start taking things easier or maybe even retire. Maybe we should start thinking about making some plans for when that might happen. We are not getting any younger and maybe we should start thinking about settling down to more of a normal lifestyle."

"I know, I have been thinking more about that lately too," John replied.

Kate said, "I know Denny is getting tired and is only still working with the team because he is afraid of what might happen to us if he let us go off by ourselves without him being there to watch our backs. He is starting to get more involved in reserve politics and since both his father and grandfather were chiefs of the First Nation, there are expectations that he will be as well some day. He also has his long-term girlfriend, Mary Woods, who says she will not marry him until he settles down and is not travelling around the world all the time."

After a few minutes, Kate turned on her side so she could look directly at John and continued, "I was thinking, after Operation Coyote is over, and we finish testifying at all the Operation Thunderball trials over the next year, maybe I could move to Edmonton and take over the forensic lab with Anna, and you could semi-retire and become an advisor or something. Maybe we could also finally get married and be together full time."

"Why, Kate Beckett, did you just propose to me?"

"Oh, John, stop trying to avoid this decision. It's not like we haven't talked about it before."

"I'm sorry, Kate. I know it is probably time to slow down and live a more normal life. And I would love to marry you and be together all the time. I just must decide if I can live without all the action and adrenaline rushes. And besides, I guess we have managed to survive a lot of bad situations, so I know we should stop pushing our luck. Okay, after we finish Operation Coyote, I promise I will start making plans to retire and start building that cabin at Slave Lake."

"I'm going to hold you to that, John, now let's get some sleep because we have a big day tomorrow, and a very busy few weeks coming up."

CHAPTER 7

9:00 a.m. Monday, March 1, 2021
Secure Boardroom, Denver FBI Field Office, Denver, Colorado

Besides the people on the RCMP plane from Edmonton, and the prime minister's chief of staff from Ottawa, various COVID-21 Task Force members had flown to Denver from Washington DC and Fort Collins. They were all convened in the large secure boardroom in the basement of the Denver FBI Field Office. As the host of the meeting, and the FBI agent in charge of the Denver Field Office, Special Agent Larry Greer acted as the meeting chairman. After everyone had gotten their coffee or other beverages and any of the assortment of pastries available on the side table, Larry Greer called the meeting to order.

"Thanks, everyone, for being here this morning. This is not a meeting any of us ever wanted to be attending; however, we all know the situation we are facing so, as always, we will do whatever has to be done. Although the COVID-21 Task Force has many things to do over the coming days and weeks, we are here today primarily to finalize and hopefully greenlight Operation Coyote. I will now turn over the meeting to Vice President Amanda Kincaid, the chairman of the task force."

Vice President Kincaid said, "Thank you, Special Agent Greer. I think most of you already know each other so I won't bother to go around the table and introduce each of you.

"I would like to welcome the Canadian contingent to the meeting here today as well. To my right are the Operation Coyote tactical team leaders, Dr.

John Benson, Dr. Kate Beckett, Anna Dupree, and Dennis Bear. Lying down behind Mr. Bear are Sydney and Nelle. I am told they like to attend briefing sessions, so they know what is going on firsthand.

"As you all know, Operation Coyote is the first critical phase of the effort to develop a new vaccine for the COVID-21 virus. Dr. Benson and Dr. Beckett and their teams have been working extremely hard over the last few days to develop a plan for tackling Operation Coyote and are here today to present their plan. They have provided a briefing report for us and have also put together a presentation to explain the basics of the operation. Included in the briefing report is a short biography of each of their team members, so I will not repeat that information. Suffice to say that, as you will see this morning, there was a particularly good reason the president and I chose Dr. Benson and Dr. Beckett and their team to run Operation Coyote. Also, many of you here have already worked with Dr. Benson and Dr. Beckett in the past and may have already spoken with them or someone from their teams over the past few days. I will turn the meeting over to Dr. Benson and Dr. Beckett now, and then we can discuss the kickoff of Operation Coyote."

Kate Beckett got up and went to the front of the boardroom where a large monitor was mounted on the wall. As the lights in the room were dimmed a bit, she said, "Good morning, everyone. Dr. Benson and I, and our teams in Edmonton and Ashland, have been working over the past few days trying to put a plan together for Operation Coyote. The briefing report you all received yesterday evening provides all the basics of the plan, but we have also put together a short presentation for you. I will go through the basics and the logistics for the US portion, and Dr. Benson will handle the Canadian portion.

"I have a series of slides that will illustrate the basics of Operation Coyote. These same slides are also included in the briefing report you were given yesterday evening. As you all know, the goal of Operation Coyote is to kill a minimum of approximately one thousand Plains coyotes, remove their brains, and deliver them to the CDC facility in Fort Collins over the next couple of weeks." As she spoke these words, she saw that most people in the room shifted nervously in their seats, realizing the stark reality of what Operation Coyote entailed.

"As you also know, Operation Coyote will be completed under the guise of an experimental rabies testing and control program initiated by the CDC, which is entirely plausible based on their mandate. Although certain senior people in various government agencies will know the true nature of Operation Coyote, the actual 'on the ground' people will not be told and will think they are carrying out a very high-profile and urgent experimental rabies testing program. The FBI and F&W Service have also developed a very plausible PR program which should keep the media, conservation groups, and the local landowners satisfied if questions are asked about why the field teams are hunting down and shooting coyotes. We will also try to keep the operation very compartmentalized on a state by state or province basis, so the extent of the whole operation is not evident.

"We adopted a conservative approach and have estimated we will need twenty twelve-person teams spread over six US states and two Canadian provinces. As you can see, the makeup of the teams is illustrated in the slide on the screen." Kate waited for a couple of minutes before continuing so people could absorb the information on the monitor.

Continuing, she explained, "As you can see, each team will operate with three different F&W trucks with one support helicopter. We have estimated that each team should be able to kill a minimum of three coyotes per day, in which case it would take sixteen or seventeen days to kill the required one thousand coyotes. Although we doubt it will take longer, it may take fewer days depending on the success of the teams. Once deployed in the various states and provinces, the teams will operate autonomously as much as possible after they are given clear instructions about the expectations for daily coyote kills and the protocols for the field autopsy procedures and the storage and transport of the coyote brains.

"We will rely on the local F&W officers in each jurisdiction to navigate the terrain and facilitate the efficiency of the operation. The special forces snipers will have the obvious duties of making the coyote kills, and the F&W special agents will be primarily responsible for performing the field autopsies and making sure the brain specimens are properly preserved and stored for transport back to the CDC lab in Fort Collins on a daily basis. The helicopter teams, in addition to air support for the ground teams, will be responsible for transporting the coyote brain specimens back to the base of operations in each jurisdiction. This next slide illustrates where these bases of operation will be located."

Again, Kate waited a couple of minutes for everyone to look at the information on the monitor before continuing.

"As you can see, there are six bases at airports in the US and two in Canada. At each of these airports, we will establish a base of operations using an existing vacant commercial hangar facility, or we will bring in a temporary structure like a trailer or industrial portable building. We will have government transport planes stationed at each airport base available to fly the coyote brain specimens daily to the CDC lab in Fort Collins. Depending on the logistics, it may be possible to have a single transport plane service more than one base. We have chosen smaller municipal or regional airports to serve as bases of operation to make it easier for the teams to operate. The deployment of the teams to jurisdictions was based on research we completed about current coyote population demographics in each state and province."

Kate paused here and looked around the room to see how people were doing with the information so far. She asked if there were any questions, and when no one indicated that they had a question, she continued.

"We have been instructed by the CDC in Fort Collins that to ensure the viability of the coyote brain specimens, the brains will need to be removed from the coyote within a maximum of thirty minutes after the coyote is killed. Obviously, there can be no head shots and the coyotes will need to be killed as efficiently as possible with heart shots if possible. Each field team will be outfitted with several field biopsy kits with bone saws and all the required surgical instruments, which will be generally used only once and then disposed of. The brain specimens will have to be placed in special refrigerated coolers for storage and transport. We have been instructed that to ensure the viability of the coyote brain specimens, they will need to be delivered to the CDC lab in Fort Collins within a maximum of twelve hours from the time they were removed from the coyotes. This will obviously require a high level of coordination with the twenty field teams and the eight different jurisdictions.

"We have already contacted the senior people in the state and federal agencies who will be involved in sourcing the field team personnel and have given them the heads-up about contacting and deploying their people to the particular operational base locations in each state and province. One of the senior F&W special agents on each team will be assigned to be the team leader and will be our primary contact person. They will be required to submit a daily report to our mobile command centre. The senior F&W people in each state and province will be instructed to set up the operational bases and have them ready to go by Wednesday of this week. All the equipment needed for the operation will be sourced and delivered to the operational bases by end of day on Wednesday as well.

"Dr. Benson and I and our team will be working out of an FBI command centre aircraft and we will be travelling from base to base on a regular basis to check on the field team progress and to troubleshoot as required. Dr. Benson, would you like to provide any additional information about the Canadian part of the operation?"

As Kate returned to her seat, John got up and came to the front of the boardroom and stood in front of the monitor.

"Thank you, Dr. Beckett, I think you have covered most of the basics of Operation Coyote. As you have seen, the Canadian part of the operation will be in southern Alberta and Saskatchewan and will function in basically the same way as in the US. The personnel involved; however, will be from the provincial F&W agencies, and the special forces snipers will be from the Canadian military. We will also use only one transport aircraft to service both the provincial operational bases. Since the distance to Fort Collins from the Canadian bases will be longer, we will use a faster plane to transport the coyote brain specimens.

"Dr. Beckett or I, or one of our team members have already spoken with many of you over the last few days, or members of your senior staff. I think we have got the ball rolling on numerous fronts already so hopefully we can get the green light to proceed this morning with Operation Coyote. If so, we would like to have the operational bases set up and the field personnel assembled by end of day Wednesday, and the teams ready to go on Thursday morning.

"Dr. Beckett and I, and our team can be ready to go as of tomorrow morning and will attempt to briefly visit each of the eight operational bases prior to Thursday morning. We can make sure that all the required equipment is assembled, and hopefully we will be able to meet and run through the operation with most of the field team leaders prior to them starting on

Thursday morning. I am sure that there will be some glitches to work out, but with the cooperation of the various government agencies involved, we can hopefully get them resolved as soon as possible. I think that is about all we have for our presentation so we would be happy to answer any questions you might have."

Special Agent in Charge Larry Greer said, "Thank you very much, Dr. Beckett and Dr. Benson. You have obviously been busy over the last couple of days. Maybe before we continue, we should take a short twenty-minute break if anyone needs to use the washrooms and replenish their coffee cups."

During the break, General Frank Shields went over to Denny Bear while he was getting a refill of his coffee and said hello. "Hi, Denny. I'm not sure if you remember me from Afghanistan, but we ran into each other a few times."

"Yes, General, I remember you, but I think you were a colonel then as I recall. Your men always spoke very highly of you."

"Yes, it was a wild time those first few years in Afghanistan. I know my men missed you after you and your spotter left in early 2006. I know you two completed a lot of very tough assignments and they are still telling some of the stories to the new guys coming into the special forces' sniper units. I suppose you know they called you 'The Ghost' back then."

"Yes, I know," Denny said. "But that was a long time ago. There was a lot of killing and I just had enough after a while. When I got the chance to work with John Benson, I knew it was something I wanted to do, and we have done a lot of good things over the past fifteen years."

"Yes, I know. I have heard some of those stories as well. It seems your military skills have also served you well in the international wildlife trafficking law enforcement business over the years."

Smiling a little, Denny said, "Yes, we have managed to get ourselves out of quite a few pretty tough spots over the years. It seems wildlife poachers and traffickers like their guns as well. Anyways, we are still around, and a lot of the bad guys are not, so that is good. I do not expect there will be any bad guys shooting at us in Operation Coyote, so that will be a nice change."

While they were talking, Denny noticed that most people were back in their seats, so he said, "It looks like the meeting is going to start again so maybe we better get back."

Special Agent in Charge Larry Greer had returned to the front of the boardroom and after everyone had settled back into their seats, he said, "Thanks, everyone. Does anyone have any comments or questions for Dr. Benson or Dr. Beckett?"

Robert Carter, the director of the US Fish and Wildlife Service said, "First I would like to commend Dr. Benson and Dr. Beckett and their teams for the great work they have done putting the plan for Operation Coyote together over the past couple of days. I have spoken with them several times in the past few days and have directed both the federal Fish and Wildlife Office of Law Enforcement and the various state F&W Services to start assembling the field personnel and equipment we will need. Of course, there are still some details to work out, but the F&W agencies should be ready to go by Thursday morning."

Commander of the US Army Special Forces General Frank Shields said, "I have also spoken with Dr. Beckett several times over the past couple of days. I have instructed the commanders of several army bases in the western US to assemble the approximately eighty special forces snipers required for Operation Coyote. Although they do not know the nature of the deployment at this point, they are all standing by and ready to go wherever we need them."

"The CDC lab in Fort Collins is also ready to start processing the coyote brain specimens when they begin to arrive later in the week," said Dr. Fred Pryor, the CDC deputy director, and the head of the CDC facility in Fort Collins. "We will be finalizing the coyote autopsy and brain specimen transport protocols with Dr. Beckett and Dr. Benson and their team and will be providing detailed instructions to be distributed to the field teams."

Going around the table, Caleb Miller the deputy FBI director was the next to speak. "The FBI through our office here in Denver and elsewhere in other field offices in the states involved in Operation Coyote, will be available to support the operation in any way that is required. We have outfitted one of our aircraft as a mobile tactical base of operations for Dr. Benson, Dr. Beckett, and their team to use for the duration of the operation. It is ready to go and is in the FBI hangar at the Denver Airport."

Bill Shaw, the RCMP superintendent of K Division Headquarters in Edmonton said, "The Canadian component of Operation Coyote is also ready to get started. The prime minister's office has contacted the premiers of Alberta and Saskatchewan and has briefed them about the operation and the people and resources that will be required in each province. I have also contacted the appropriate Fish and Wildlife Service senior people to let them know about the operation. We have also contacted General Ben Hartman, the commander of the Canadian Military Special Forces at the Canadian Forces Base in Edmonton to let him know about the upcoming requirement for approximately fifteen to twenty special forces snipers to be deployed for Operation Coyote."

After another few seconds when it was obvious no one else was going to be saying anything more, Vice President Amanda Kincaid returned to the front of the boardroom and said, "Thank you, everyone, for your very quick response to the preparations for Operation Coyote. I am sure there will be some issues that will arise working out the details in the next few days; however, I think we are in fairly good shape and I see no reason why we cannot get the field component of the operation up and running by Thursday morning as Dr. Benson has recommended. Please continue to work with Dr. Benson and Dr. Beckett as necessary over the coming days because, as you know, Operation Coyote is one of our highest priorities right now and is the key to our early response to the production of a new vaccine for COVID-21. Thanks again, everyone, and I will let you all get back to work now. I will schedule another meeting of the task force in a week or so to get an update about how the operation is progressing and to make any adjustments if necessary."

As the meeting was breaking up several people came over to Kate and John and congratulated them on all the work they had done so far getting Operation Coyote organized. Amanda Kincaid also came over and thanked them and then, smiling a little, asked Denny, "I noticed that Syd and Nelle were very attentive during the meeting. Do you think that they understood what was going on?"

Smiling, and a little nervous about talking to the vice president of the United States, Denny said, "Well, I don't know for sure how much they understood, but I have learned over the years to never underestimate how smart they are."

Amanda Kincaid replied, "I know what you mean. I am a dog person myself and own two border collies. It always seems that they can almost read my mind, or at least sometimes my mood, and can understand an amazing amount of what I say to them."

Feeling a little more comfortable, Denny said, "I have been working with Syd and Nelle for over eight years now, and some of the things they do still surprise me. They have taken down more bad guys than most policemen do in their careers and are as brave as any soldier on the battlefield."

"Well, it was nice meeting you and Syd and Nelle, and I wish you all luck in what we have asked you to do with Operation Coyote." Turning her attention to also include John, Kate, and Anna, the vice president said, "Please let me personally know if there is anything you need over the next few weeks to make sure that this operation succeeds. I know it is a big responsibility, but we all have confidence that you are the right people to do the job."

CHAPTER 8

9:00 a.m. Tuesday, March 2, 2021
Billings Beckett International Airport, Billings, Montana

John, Kate, Anna, and Denny had spent the rest of Monday after the task force meeting in Denver firming up details for Operation Coyote. They had to make sure that all the operational bases in each of the six states and two provinces were going to be fully stocked and up and running by Wednesday evening. They were hoping to briefly visit each of the operational bases before Thursday morning to meet the field team leaders and to make sure everything was ready to go.

They had gone to the FBI hangar at the Denver Airport in the afternoon and transferred all their gear to the FBI tactical plane that they would be using as their mobile command centre for the next three to four weeks. It was a twin-engine Beechcraft King Air 350ER, which would normally have seating for fifteen, but was reduced to seating for six, with the additional space converted to a mobile office and communications centre. It had a cruising speed of 350 miles per hour and could land and take off on runways as short as 4000 feet. There was also a small galley for food preparation and hammocks if they needed to sleep on the plane. Syd and Nelle had their travel kennels fastened to their own seats so they could be close to the rest of the team when they were flying from base to base.

Two FBI pilots were also part of the deal. Their names were Paul Judson and Lucy Boyette. They were both in their late thirties and had been flying FBI planes for the last ten years. They were also trained FBI agents based out of the Denver Field Office but could be almost anywhere in the US on any given day. They seemed like good people and they really liked Syd and Nelle, which was good because they would all be spending a lot of time together over the next few weeks.

John and the team had spent Monday evening at their hotel rooms in Denver, and had gotten up early to fly to Billings, Montana. During the flight they got a chance to check out all the cool equipment on the plane in a little more detail, make themselves some coffee with the Keurig machine, and sample the breakfast sandwiches provided by the FBI in the galley.

"This is a pretty sweet ride. Nothing but the best for the FBI, I guess," Denny said. "I think we should be able to survive okay for the next few weeks."

Gesturing with her arm around the interior of the plane, Anna said, "I think we have everything we will need for office work and communication with the field teams and all the government and law enforcement agencies."

Kate said, "There are even hammocks we can hang up if we need to get some sleep, although we should be able to stay in hotels overnight most of the time wherever we end up at the end of the day. It would be nice to eat a proper dinner every evening and get a good night's sleep. It would also be great to be able to go for a run and get a little exercise when we can."

"Yes, a run in the evenings whenever we have the time would be great after sitting in this plane for hours every day," replied Anna.

Anna and Kate were still both serious runners and a daily five- or ten-mile run was common for them. John's running days were behind him with his chronically sore knees. Denny never really liked running unless someone was chasing him but could still hike through the mountains all day if he needed to.

Since four field teams would be operating out of Billings, it was the largest of the bases. The state F&W Service had managed to rent a good-sized vacant hangar with a large, attached office space. The hangar was large enough to store the helicopters overnight if necessary, and even the transport plane to be used for the daily flights to Fort Collins. The four federal F&W special agents who were to be the team leaders had flown to Billings Monday evening and were waiting for John and Kate at the hangar when their plane arrived. Some of the forty-eight people to be deployed to the Billings base had already arrived as well, and the others were on their way. Hotel rooms at several hotels close to the airport had also been reserved for the next three weeks. It was decided to have each team stay at a different hotel so there would not be too many F&W trucks in the hotel parking lot every night.

John, Kate, Anna, Denny, and the dogs met the four team leaders in the small meeting room in the office part of the hangar. Syd and Nelle had enjoyed the plane ride in their own seats with the rest of the team. Things seemed to be getting more serious now so they thought that maybe they would be chasing after bad guys again soon. Introductions were made, and it was discovered that Kate already knew a couple of them, and the other two certainly knew Kate by reputation. Since Operation Coyote was to be carried out under the guise of a high priority rabies testing and research program, the meeting was conducted under that premise. They checked on the status of all the equipment to be delivered to the base and if there were any problems that needed to be addressed. Anna and Denny also went over the protocols provided by the CDC for the field autopsies and the storage and transport of the coyote brain specimens.

The team leaders were to start briefing their team members as soon as they all arrived at the base. They were also expected to develop a plan for deploying the field teams to different parts of the state based on the coyote demographic and population information Kate Beckett's team had put together. The teams were free to come up with a variety of ways to hunt for and kill the coyotes. The local F&W officers would be able to use their knowledge of the local geography and terrain to direct the teams to the highest probability locations for encountering the coyotes. John and Kate also suggested using bait stations with wild game or domestic livestock to lure the coyotes to locations where they could be easily killed by the snipers concealed in blinds. They finished the meeting and told them they would be back in a few days to check on how things were going.

3:00 p.m. Tuesday, March 2, 2021
Casper/Natrona County International Airport, Casper, Wyoming

After a one-hour stop at the operations base at the Dickinson, North Dakota Regional Airport, which was located a few miles south of the city, they continued to Casper, Wyoming. The Casper, Wyoming airport was a larger airport servicing the city of Casper, with a population of about 58,000, and the surrounding region. The operations base at the Casper airport was in a vacant aviation hangar on Fuller Street, a service road northeast of the airport terminal. The hangar also had an area with office space and a lunchroom where John and the team met with the three F&W special agents who were the field team leaders in Casper. Some of the other team members had already arrived and were busy unloading and organizing the equipment that had already been delivered.

John and the team went through the briefing routine again with the three team leaders and then did a little tour around the hangar and met a few of the field team members. As they were walking to go back to their plane which was on the tarmac just outside the hangar, a couple of older special forces guys came over to Denny and introduced themselves. They said that they had been in Afghanistan in 2005 and had been at a couple of the same forward bases with Denny and Mike Giroux, his spotter.

Denny said, "That was a long time ago and I am sorry, but I don't remember you, but it's good to meet some guys again from those days. I have been working with Dr. John Benson, the older guy walking to our plane over there, since I left the military in 2006. We work for the RCMP out of Edmonton, Alberta, and are involved mostly in forensic wildlife biology and wildlife trafficking law enforcement. Dr. Benson and Dr. Kate Beckett from the National US Fish and Wildlife Forensic Lab in Ashland, Oregon, are helping the Fish and Wildlife Service organize this rabies testing research operation."

Trevor Griffiths, one of the special forces snipers said, "We haven't been briefed yet about the whole operation and we just got here a few hours ago. We were just told yesterday to report here as soon as possible from our base at Fort Riley, Kansas. The army flew us here this morning, plus several other special forces' snipers at the base. So, Denny, it is great to see you again. You know, they still tell stories about you to the new recruits coming into the special forces' units. Most people think the stories have been exaggerated over the years, but we were there with you at some of those hellholes they called forward bases in Afghanistan and we know that most of the stories were true. You and your spotter had quite the reputation back in those days and I'm glad that we had the chance to meet up with you again."

Denny said, "Yeah, well, that was a long time ago, and I live a little quieter life now, although Dr. Benson and I do get ourselves into a little trouble occasionally. My spotter and cousin, Mike Giroux, has been an RCMP special constable for the last fifteen years and works in the area that we are from in northern Alberta. It's been great seeing you guys again and maybe we can have a beer together the next time we come to Casper."

As Denny was walking over to the plane, Trevor Griffiths said to his fellow sniper, "I have heard of Dr. John Benson and Dr. Kate Beckett. They are two of the most well-known INTERPOL wildlife trafficking law enforcement people from the US and Canada. They have helped organize some of biggest INTERPOL global wildlife trafficking takedowns in the last ten years. I wonder what they are doing here helping run this F&W Service rabies testing operation. And they have one of the most famous special forces snipers in the last twenty years working with them and are flying around in what looks like one of the FBI's mobile tactical planes. Maybe there is more to this Operation Coyote than what we are being told."

5:30 p.m. Tuesday, March 2, 2021
Rapid City Regional Airport, Rapid City, South Dakota

The Rapid City Regional Airport was also one of the larger airports with a base set up for Operation Coyote. The airport serviced Rapid City, with a population of approximately 68,000, and the surrounding region. The Ellsworth Air Force Base was located just northeast of the city and the Black Hills National Forest was not too far to the west. The state F&W Service had located the operations base in a vacant private hangar on Airport Road northwest of the airport terminal. John and his group again met with the three F&W special agents who were assigned to be the team leaders of the three field teams deployed to Rapid City. Things seemed to be progressing well and the team members who had already arrived were busy organizing the equipment and supplies in the hangar.

They had decided to stay overnight in Rapid City and booked some rooms at the Hampton Inn and Suites on Eglin Street in Rapid City. After the meeting at the base was over, and their plane was secured at the hangar, they borrowed one of the twelve-person passenger vans F&W had rented and drove the ten miles northwest on Highway 44 to the hotel. Everyone, including the two FBI pilots, got their own rooms, except John and Kate who booked a king studio suite. Denny also got a king suite so there would be more room for Syd and Nelle.

They got to the hotel at about 7:00 p.m. and got checked in. Kate and Anna decided to take Syd and Nelle for a run before they ordered dinner and settled in for the evening, so they looked at Google Maps and decided to run north of the city along Haines Avenue. Denny said he would drop them off with the van at the corner of Haines Avenue and Secondary Highway 214 and then pick them up in an hour at the same location. Haines Avenue had a few acreage developments but was mostly in the countryside and crossed Boxelder Creek which eventually flowed into the Cheyenne River east of Rapid City.

Denny dropped them off and then went to buy a few things at the grocery store to bring with them on the plane the next day. In an hour he went back to the same intersection and got there just as Kate, Anna, and the dogs were arriving back from their run. They all got back in the van all sweaty and looking quite tired. The temperature was only 45°F, but there was no snow on the ground anymore. They drove back to the hotel and decided to all just order room service and go to bed early. They wanted to get an early start because they planned to fly to Lethbridge and Swift Current first thing in the morning to check on the two Canadian operational bases.

Syd and Nelle were excited to get out for a run after being cooped up in hotel rooms and on the plane for the last few days. They were extremely interested in all the new smells they encountered along the road and even saw a few ground squirrels which they figured they could have easily caught if Anna had let them. However, they had learned their lesson about catching wild animals in Africa and now were careful to only catch them if Denny or Anna told them to. Who knew that mother warthogs were that protective of their babies? They had been hearing the word "coyote" a lot lately in the meetings and on the plane. They knew what coyotes looked like and were quite sure that they could chase one down and capture it if Denny told them to. No one was carrying any guns yet, but as soon as the guns came out, they knew that their part would be coming soon.

John and Kate ordered dinner and a bottle of wine from room service and had a nice romantic meal in their suite. John said, "So what do you think, will we make our start-up deadline on Thursday morning?"

After they refilled their glasses with wine, Kate answered, "I think so, things seem to be coming together pretty fast. I guess we will know for sure after we check the rest of the bases tomorrow."

"At least we are getting to spend time together again," John said, looking lovingly at Kate. "I missed not being with you for two months straight. Being apart is getting harder all the time. I have been thinking more about what we were talking about the other day and you are right about me slowing down. After Operation Coyote is over why don't we start making plans for you to move to Edmonton to help manage the forensics lab with Anna and maybe I can become a consultant or something."

"That sounds great, John. I was really hoping you would take me up on my offer. So, let's talk about it some more in that big king-sized bed over there. I can see you are looking a little tired. And bring the rest of the bottle of wine with you."

9:00 a.m. Wednesday, March 3, 2021
Lethbridge Regional Airport, Lethbridge, Alberta, Canada

They had all gotten up early and drove back to the Rapid City Airport and flew to Lethbridge in southern Alberta. The flight took two hours, and they arrived in Lethbridge at 9:00 a.m. They had skipped breakfast at the hotel and picked up coffee and breakfast sandwiches at the drive-through at a Tim Horton's. Everyone mostly napped on the plane since it was going to be a long day. Syd and Nelle did not see any guns yet, so they thought that they would probably be having a slow day again as well.

The operations base had been set up in a small vacant commercial hangar at the north end of Stubb Ross Road by the local Alberta F&W Service and they had also rented a large commercial trailer to be used as an office and meeting space. There seemed to be lots of activity already with team members organizing equipment and supplies. John and his team met with the two senior F&W team leaders in the meeting room area in the trailer. Since the base was in Canada the personnel comprising the team members were different from the US bases. The

F&W officers on the teams were from Lethbridge and Calgary, the snipers were from the Canadian Forces Base in Edmonton, and there were six RCMP officers who were also forensic biologists and worked for the wildlife law enforcement unit out of K Division in Edmonton, and a similar unit in Calgary.

John and Kate went over the operation in general again with the two team leaders, and then they called in the RCMP forensic biologists and Anna and Denny went over the specifics of the coyote autopsy procedures. Anna and John already knew most of the RCMP biologists, and all of them certainly knew John, Anna, and Denny by reputation. After the meeting, they checked out the hangar facility and introduced themselves to a few of the team members. They then all got back on the plane for the one-hour flight to Swift Current, Saskatchewan.

3:00 p.m. Wednesday, March 3, 2021
North Platte Regional Airport, North Platte, Nebraska

After the stop at Swift Current Municipal Airport, in southern Saskatchewan, and the flight south to North Platte, Nebraska, everyone was getting tired of sitting on the plane and were glad when they finally had the chance to stretch their legs and go for a little walk. Syd and Nelle were also happy to be able to go to the doggie bathroom and check out the new smells in Nebraska. The operations base was at the North Platte Regional Airport, which was off the Lincoln Highway east of the city of North Platte, population 25,000, and the North Platte River. It was located west of the small airport terminal on E. Lee Bird Drive in a good-sized vacant commercial hangar with a small office and meeting area. After the one-hour meeting with the team leaders, they got back on the plane for the short thirty-minute flight to the last of the eight bases at Sterling, Colorado.

4:30 p.m. Wednesday, March 3, 2021
Crosson Field Municipal Airport, Sterling, Colorado

The operations base was located at the Crosson Field Municipal Airport, west of the small city of Sterling, population 15,000, off Highway 28. The state F&W Service had rented a small commercial hangar and brought in a commercial trailer for office and meeting space. John and the team once again went through the briefing routine with the two F&W special agents. The base looked quite organized and all the team members had arrived. Two helicopters were sitting on the grass outside the hangar. The two team leaders said that they would give the teams their final briefings that afternoon, and that they should be ready to roll in the morning.

Once again, John and his team did a short tour of the hangar and met a few more of the team members, and then got back on the plane for the short twenty-minute flight to the Denver Airport. They had decided to spend the night back at the FBI hotel in Denver and then spend the next day at the Denver FBI Field Office where they could monitor the progress of the eight operations bases and troubleshoot any problems if they came up.

8:00 p.m. Wednesday, March 3, 2021
FBI Hotel, Denver, Colorado

They had arrived at the Denver Airport at about 6:00 p.m. and taxied over to the FBI hangar and secured the plane in the hangar. They had then been picked up by an FBI driver in a fifteen-passenger van with tinted windows and driven to the same FBI hotel they had stayed at previously and given the same rooms by the same FBI agent. Denny and Anna had decided to take Syd and Nelle for a walk and then go and get some dinner at a nearby restaurant. John and Kate decided to just stay in their hotel suite for the evening and order room service for dinner, plus a nice bottle of wine.

While they were eating dinner, John said, “So, that was quite the busy couple of days. I am tired. How do you think things are going so far?”

“Yes, I know, I didn’t realize how tired I was until we got settled in the hotel room. I hope I can stay awake long enough to finish dinner,” Kate said as she yawned a little. “I think things with Operation Coyote have fallen into place amazingly well given the time we all had to make it happen. I guess we will see over the next couple of days how things go with the coyote hunting and if our hunting success and time predictions will hold up. I like the idea of us working here out of the Denver FBI Field Office for the next couple of days so we can monitor all the operational bases. After a couple of days, we can do another round of visits to all the bases and see how they are all doing.”

After taking a few bites of her dinner, Kate continued, "Maybe we should send Denny and Anna to the Sterling base while we are here in Denver so they can get some field time on the ground and see firsthand how the teams are functioning. It is only a two-hour drive to Sterling from Denver. I'm sure Denny wouldn't mind getting his sniper rifle out of storage and Anna would like to try her hand at a coyote field biopsy."

"That is a great idea," John said. "They would just be bored sitting around the office here for the next two days anyways. They can take Syd and Nelle with them too. The dogs have been looking bored with all the plane travel and hotel rooms. I will give them a call right after we finish dinner and let them know.

"Now we better finish eating before we both fall asleep at the table." Giving Kate a little wink and gesturing to the adjoining bedroom, John said, "That big bed in there looks pretty comfy and we can continue our discussion while we finish the rest of the bottle of wine, unless we think of something else to do."

CHAPTER 9

10:00 a.m. Thursday, March 4, 2021
Denver Post Newsroom, Denver, Colorado

Cheryl Kaplan was a seasoned investigative reporter with the *Denver Post*, which had an average weekday circulation of over 400,000 and its website received close to two million online page views each day. She had covered the COVID-19 pandemic for the paper and had reported on the Colorado state and federal government responses to controlling the pandemic over the past year. She was often critical of the state politicians and especially the Trump White House's actions and did not have a lot of fans among the ardent Republican voters in the Denver region.

She was pleased that several COVID-19 vaccines were due to be available soon and her source at the CDC facility in Fort Collins had told her that the proposed date for the US and then worldwide rollout was going to be March 15th. She was therefore quite surprised to hear through her anonymous source at the CDC that a high-level unannounced meeting of several former members of the COVID-19 Task Force had convened at the Denver FBI Field Office on March 1st. The CDC source had also told her that Vice President Amanda Kincaid had also attended the meeting, as well as several top Canadian law enforcement people. She had also heard that the CDC facility in Fort Collins was dealing with a possible mutated strain of the COVID-19 virus.

She had been receiving routine email updates from the Denver public health media relations office about numbers of COVID-19 infections and hospitalizations since the pandemic had started in March 2019, and the numbers of both seemed to have suddenly increased over the past week. She had thought that it was just a coincidence, but when she started checking the case numbers around the US and in Europe, there were also numerous unexplained increases in infections, hospitalizations, and deaths. In several European countries, there were reports of numerous people being reinfected who had already had COVID-19. There were also several stories speculating that there was a mutated version of the COVID-19 virus causing the recent spike in case numbers.

Her calls to the public relations office at the CDC lab in Fort Collins had been dismissive and she was told that there was no information available about any new mutated strains of the COVID-19 virus. She was told, however, that a new rabies testing and control research program had recently been initiated by the CDC, and that they could send her some information about the program. She had told them to email her all the public information they had about the rabies research project.

When Cheryl Kaplan received the slick public relations digital brochures from the CDC, she read that the rabies research program was called "Operation Coyote" and was focussed on testing Plains coyotes in Colorado and several other adjacent states for the presence of rabies, which had apparently been increasing in prevalence in recent months in the coyote populations in the western US. This seemed entirely plausible to her so she thought she would dig a little deeper in case there was a story to be reported on for her paper. So, she called the media relations department at the Colorado Parks & Wildlife Headquarters office in downtown Denver and was told that yes, the state Wildlife Division was participating in the CDC rabies research program. When she asked them about which other states were involved in the research project, she was told about the five other states and the two Canadian provinces.

It seemed to be quite a large initiative by the CDC, plus six state governments and two Canadian provinces, and had received little if any public notification. She started calling the media relations departments of the Wildlife Service Divisions in each of the other five states and got a similar story from each one. When she asked who was managing the overall research program, she didn't get much concrete information until she happened to speak to a surprisingly talkative lady named Carol in the Casper, Wyoming F&W public relations office.

Carol had said, "My husband is a Fish and Wildlife officer, and he was just assigned to work at the new rabies research operations base at the airport along with almost forty other people from the state F&W offices, the federal Fish and Wildlife Service Office of Law Enforcement, and even about twelve US Army Special Forces snipers. My husband told me that some 'bigwigs' had flown into the operations base a couple of days ago in what looked like an FBI tactical plane. His team leader told him that they were the organizers and managers of the research program and that their names were Dr. John Benson and Dr. Kate Beckett. One of the US Army Special Forces' snipers assigned to his team told my husband that one of the other guys on the plane was a former Canadian Special Forces sniper who he knew from 2005 in Afghanistan. I guess the guy was one of the most famous snipers in Afghanistan back in the day."

Cheryl Kaplan said, "Thank you for the information, Carol, you have been very helpful." She was now definitely thinking that this was a much bigger operation than she had first thought and had been told by the media relations people she had been talking to. She Googled the names Dr. John Benson and Dr. Kate Beckett and what came up was not what she was expecting. They were both Ph.D. forensic wildlife biologists which made sense; however, they were also two of the most senior strategists and trainers from Canada and the US working with INTERPOL's International Wildlife Crime Group. This rabies research project seemed to well below their pay grade, if that was what Operation Coyote was all about, and she was beginning to have some serious doubts about that.

She decided to use her contact at the FBI Field Office in Denver to try to find out more about what was really going on with Operation Coyote. Her contact was an FBI special agent who was the sister of her best friend Kiera Bernstein, who also worked at the *Denver Post* as a news editor. She tried not to use this FBI contact unless she had no other options because she did not want Kiera's sister to get into any trouble with the FBI and jeopardize her job. Her name was Danielle and Cheryl decided to talk to her friend Kiera about what she had found out before she contacted her sister Danielle.

She texted Kiera and asked her if she would meet her for dinner after work because there was a potential news story she needed to talk to her about. Kiera told her no problem they could meet at their favourite bistro at 6:00 p.m. They met at Steuben's Food Service and Cheryl told Kiera about what she had found out about Operation Coyote so far, and that she suspected that the operation was not really about a rabies research program but had something to do with a new mutated COVID-19 virus being tested at the CDC in Fort Collins.

Looking a little surprised, Kiera said, "That sounds very scary if it is true. Alright, I will ask my sister if she has heard anything at the Denver FBI office where she works."

After they had left Steuben's, Kiera called her sister Danielle and asked, "Do you know anything about something called Operation Coyote and if it has anything to do with a new mutated version of the COVID-19 virus?"

After a long pause, Danielle said, "I cannot tell you anything about Operation Coyote because it is a national security issue. All I can say is that you are right in assuming that Operation Coyote is not about a rabies research program. I really cannot say anything else or I might get fired. I suggest that you try to talk to Larry Greer, the FBI special agent in charge, if you want to find out more. You need to careful, Kiera, publishing this story would be a big mistake. You really need to talk to someone higher up in the FBI than me before going any further with your investigation."

After Kiera had told Cheryl Kaplan about the conversation with her sister, Cheryl agreed to hold back on the story until she checked with someone in authority with the FBI. She called the Denver FBI Field Office in the morning and told the receptionist who she was and that she needed to speak with Larry Greer about Operation Coyote. The receptionist took her number and told her that someone from Larry Greer's office would call her back shortly.

In about an hour her cell phone rang and when she answered a female voice asked her if she was Cheryl Kaplan, the investigative reporter from the *Denver Post*. When she said that she was, she was told to hang on for Larry Greer, the Denver FBI special agent in charge. Larry Greer then got on the phone and said to Cheryl, "Hello, Ms. Kaplan, I understand you wanted to discuss Operation Coyote with me."

Cheryl said, "Yes, Special Agent Greer, I have been doing some investigative work on Operation Coyote and I have discovered that it is not actually about a rabies research program but is connected to a new mutated COVID-19 virus that is being tested by the CDC in Fort Collins. I was wondering if you could verify this information or if you had any other information you could provide."

After pausing for a few seconds, Larry Greer said, "Ms. Kaplan, I think we need to talk in person. Do you think you could come to the Denver Field Office this afternoon, say about 2:00 p.m.?"

Cheryl told him that she would be there.

11:30 a.m. Thursday, March 4, 2021
Office of Larry Greer, Denver FBI Field Office, Denver, Colorado

After receiving the call from Cheryl Kaplan, Larry Greer called John and Kate, who were working out of an office just down the hall from him. When they had arrived in his office and were seated at his meeting table he said, "We have a problem. I just got a call from a hotshot investigative reporter, Cheryl Kaplan, from the *Denver Post* who asked me if I could confirm that Operation Coyote was not actually about a rabies research program but is connected to a new mutated COVID-19 virus that is being tested by the CDC in Fort Collins."

Surprised, Kate asked, "How the heck did she figure it out so soon?"

Larry Greer answered, "I don't know exactly, but I had her checked out and she is one of the best investigative reporters in Denver. She has broken quite a few top stories over the past few years. She was apparently even in the running for a Pulitzer two years ago for a story she did on corruption and payoffs in the state senate. We need to take her very seriously. I asked her to come here at 2:00 p.m. so we can talk to her."

John asked, "What do you think we should tell her?"

"I think we need to tell her the truth and then appeal to her good judgement and patriotism to keep the story under wraps until Operation Coyote is completed. Maybe we can promise her the exclusive inside story when the time is right."

2:00 p.m. Thursday, March 4, 2021
Executive Boardroom, Denver FBI Field Office, Denver, Colorado

Cheryl Kaplan was intrigued that she had obviously hit a big nerve with Larry Greer and was anxious to hear what he had to say about Operation Coyote. She was not expecting what she was about to hear when she arrived at the Denver FBI building at 2:00 p.m. and was escorted up to the executive boardroom on the top floor of the building. Seated in the boardroom were two men and one woman. One of the men got up as she walked into the room and introduced himself as Larry Greer. He then introduced the two other people in the boardroom as Dr. John Benson and Dr. Kate Beckett.

Larry Greer said, "Ms. Kaplan, I have to congratulate you for some fine investigative work. My people checked you out and reviewed your work at the *Denver Post* and you have an extremely good reputation and have written some interesting and important stories. I understand you were even in consideration for a Pulitzer at one point. What we are about to tell you now about Operation Coyote can not be written about for several more weeks; however, when the time comes, we will give you the exclusive inside story about Operation Coyote, or at least the part of the story not restricted by national security protocols. Dr. Benson and Dr. Beckett have organized and are managing Operation Coyote so I will let them give you a brief synopsis of the operation."

Kate Beckett introduced herself and John Benson with a short biography and explained their current employment situation. She then explained about the origins of the COVID-21 mutated virus and what was at stake with Operation Coyote. When she had finished, she asked Cheryl Kaplan if she had any questions.

Looking quite tense and uncomfortable, Cheryl Kaplan said, "I was not expecting to be getting this much information, so I am a little overwhelmed right now. I never considered that the stakes with Operation Coyote would be this high and I understand that revealing the true purpose of the operation right now could be devastating for the country. Please forgive me for asking, but I am an investigative reporter and people threaten me quite often, so if I agree to delay publishing the story, how can I be sure that I will get the exclusive rights in a few weeks?"

"That is a fair question, Ms. Kaplan. I guess you will just have to take my word for it," Larry Greer answered. "Right now, other than the people in the need-to-know category, you are one of the few people who is privy to the real story around Operation Coyote. Making the details of Operation Coyote public right now would be a breach of national security and could endanger the lives of thousands or even millions of people. I would think that you do not want to be in any way responsible for that for the sake of a good story in your newspaper."

"You are right, Special Agent Greer," Cheryl replied. "I am an ethical, very patriotic person, even though I am an investigative newspaper reporter and sometimes have to disclose some very unpleasant and often illegal activities by otherwise respected people in positions of power and influence. I do not want to be in any way responsible for adding to the already horrific circumstances of the past year, so I agree to delay publishing any details about the true purpose of Operation Coyote until you give me the go-ahead to do so."

"Thank you, Ms. Kaplan. You are doing the right thing," John said. "Operation Coyote will hopefully be completed before the end of March and, if things go as hoped, we should know at that point if the new COVID-21 vaccine testing and development process is viable and progressing on schedule. If so, Dr. Beckett and I will be more than pleased to provide you with all the information you need to accurately tell the story about Operation Coyote."

"Alright then, I really appreciate your candid response to my questions about Operation Coyote and I wish you luck over the next few weeks as you complete your work. I will look forward to hearing from you towards the end of the month. If given the opportunity, I will do my best to do justice to telling the extraordinary story around Operation Coyote and the development of the new COVID-21 vaccine."

After Cheryl Kaplan left, Larry Greer said to Kate and John, "I hope we can trust her to keep the story under wraps until Operation Coyote is completed. We better review and beef up our security protocols at all levels if we want to avoid having this conversation with any other hotshot reporters."

CHAPTER 10

9:00 a.m. Thursday, March 4, 2021
Russian FSB Headquarters, Lubyanka Square, Moscow

The Federal Security Service of the Russian Federation (FSB) is the principal security agency of Russia and the main successor agency to the USSR's KGB (Committee for State Security). Its main responsibilities are within the country and include counterintelligence, internal and border security, counterterrorism, and surveillance, but it also works with the Russian Foreign Intelligence Service (RSV), the successor to the KGB's First Directorate, to conduct electronic surveillance abroad, among other things. It is headquartered in Lubyanka Square, Moscow's centre, in the main building of the former KGB. The operations and direction of the FSB is overseen by the president of Russia, Vladimir Putin. The current director of the FSB is Yuri Solatov, an old friend of Putin's from his days in the KGB.

The FSB Director, Yuri Solatov, was in his large office and sitting at the smaller of the two boardroom tables in the office area. Sitting across from him was Igor Larionov, one of the director's most trusted senior FSB agents. He was an expert in American affairs and had spent many years in the US as an undercover asset, and now ran a network of undercover agents in various areas of the US, a few of which had access to high level classified information in Washington, DC.

Yuri Solatov, the director of the FSB, said, "So, Igor, what can you tell me about the COVID-19 situation in the United States and the reports that there is a mutated version of the COVID-19 virus that was started by a US citizen and has spread to various other countries, including ours I presume?"

Igor Larionov explained, "Yes, Director Solatov, as you know the COVID-19 virus is mostly under control now, except for a few hot spots in some Third World countries. The COVID-19 vaccines are going to be available worldwide by March 15th and we are preparing for a widespread vaccination program here in Russia, using our own Russia-manufactured vaccine, as well as several other vaccines from other countries.

"Our health authorities were notified by the CDC in the United States on February 24th that they believed that there was a mutated version of the virus discovered in a US citizen, a medical doctor, and that she may have infected numerous people in the Denver, Colorado area and that she had also travelled to London, England to a medical conference while she was infectious and had infected several people at the conference. The CDC said that they were tracing all the people she had been in contact with and were trying to contain the spread of the mutated virus until they could do some more testing. Our health authorities have received a few more updates since then but have not gotten much information about the nature of the mutated COVID-19 virus or how it started.

"That was the official communication protocol from the US CDC sent out to numerous countries, including Russia; however, there have been a lot of things happening behind the scenes in the US that have not been disclosed to other countries. My assets in Washington, DC, have discovered that a new task force has been formed to handle what they are calling the COVID-21 virus, and it is chaired by the new US vice president, Amanda Kincaid. Apparently, there was a big meeting of the new COVID-21 Task Force in Denver, Colorado, on Monday, March 1st, attended by numerous big players from the previous COVID-19 Task Force.

"What was particularly interesting was that several directors from the Federal US Fish and Wildlife Service were in attendance, as well as the heads of several federal law enforcement agencies from both the US and Canada. The two other interesting attendees were Dr. John Benson, a very well-known RCMP forensic wildlife biologist from Canada, and Dr. Kate Beckett, also a well-known forensic wildlife biologist from the US Fish and Wildlife Service Office of Law Enforcement. They are both big-shot INTERPOL international wildlife enforcement senior planners and have worked on most of the big INTERPOL wildlife trafficking takedowns in the last ten years. So, one of the big questions is why are these two INTERPOL heavy hitters involved in the COVID-21 Task Force."

"Yes, Igor, that is interesting. Do you have any information about the how the virus mutation started and if the US is trying to develop a new vaccine for this COVID-21 mutated virus?"

Igor Larionov said, "If they are trying to develop a new vaccine, they are being very secretive about it, and my assets haven't been able to get much information about that yet. In our standard surveillance of US government communications, the term 'Operation Coyote' has been noticed quite a few times. Maybe it relates to why Dr. Benson and Dr. Beckett are involved in the COVID-21 Task Force. I have notified a few of my assets in the US to go to the Denver area to see what they can find out. I have also assigned a couple of my best undercover agents to locate Benson and Beckett and find out what they are up to."

"Thanks, Igor. Why don't we get together again on Monday morning and you can let me know what you have been able to find out. The US is still struggling to get their economy back on track so it would be nice to find a way to obstruct their plans for containing this new COVID-21 virus. The fact that it originated with a US citizen and would likely impact the US the most would definitely be good for Russia."

CHAPTER 11

6:00 p.m. Friday, March 5, 2021
FBI Hotel, Denver, Colorado

John Benson and Kate Beckett had spent the last two days at the FBI Denver Field Office talking with the team leaders from the eight bases in the US and Canada. There were a few problems with some of the equipment not arriving on time at a couple of the bases, but all the field teams were operational on Thursday morning as scheduled. The meeting with the investigative reporter from the *Denver Post*, Cheryl Kaplan, had been an unexpected event, but they were relieved that they had persuaded her to delay publishing her story for a few weeks until Operation Coyote was successfully completed. They were hoping that there would not be any other reporters smart enough to piece together the true purpose of the operation.

The reports from the team leaders at the end of the first day showed that they didn't get the overall daily quota of sixty coyote brain specimens; however, that was to be expected since it was the first day and there were still details to work out about how the teams would function in the different bases. However, the coyote brain specimen numbers in preliminary reports from the team leaders that second day had also fallen short with a total of only fifty-five. John and Kate were a little alarmed that they may have overestimated the number of coyote specimens that the teams could collect per day. They needed to figure out how to get things back on track and hope that the teams became more proficient in the next few days.

There were reports on CNN of unexplained outbreaks of new COVID-19 cases in several European and Asian countries. Several health officials were expressing concerns that there seemed to be a high number of reinfections of people who had already been infected with COVID-19 in 2020. Some of the news media pundits were speculating that the new infections may be from a new mutated version of the COVID-19 virus.

John and Kate had also been in contact with Vice President Kincaid and had briefed her about the status of Operation Coyote. They had also spoken with Dr. Fred Pryor, the deputy director of the CDC, and head of the Fort Collins lab. They had updated him about the status of the operation and let him know that things were a little behind schedule, but he should be expecting the delivery of between fifty and sixty coyote brain specimens Thursday evening at the CDC lab in Fort Collins. Arrangements had been made to pick up the brain specimens from the transport planes at the Northern Colorado Regional Airport located about thirteen miles south of the Colorado State University Campus, the site of the CDC facility, as they arrived from the bases every evening and take them to the CDC lab.

Three transport planes were being used to get the coyote brain specimens from the operations bases to the CDC lab in Fort Collins daily. One plane serviced the two Canadian bases, another picked up specimens from the bases in Billings, Casper, and Sterling, and a third plane picked up specimens in Dickson, Rapid City, and North Platte.

John had called Denny and Anna on Wednesday evening to let them know that they could spend a couple of days working out of the Sterling, Colorado base. They had gotten their gear together and driven the 120 miles to the base at Sterling on Thursday morning and had met up with the team leader, Kevin McClain, of one of the two teams working out of the base. They spent the rest of the day with Kevin and his team who managed to kill three coyotes. Anna had the chance to observe the autopsies of all three of the coyotes and was able to offer a few suggestions about the technique to the F&W special agent doing the autopsies.

They decided to set up a bait station for the next day that Denny and Anna would use. They set up the bait station on a state grazing reserve in an isolated area away from any private landowners. One of the local F&W officers on the team had shot a mule deer on Thursday evening and they then built a blind for Denny and Anna about five hundred yards downwind from where the deer was to be placed. Denny and Anna arrived at the site early on Friday morning with the dead deer and then got settled in the blind. They decided to bring Syd and Nelle with them, and the dogs settled down in the blind with them, as they had done many times over the years while they were on undercover operations. The only big difference was that usually they were hunting wildlife poachers, not coyotes. The dogs would often have to chase down and capture any of the poachers who decided to make a run for it. They were well trained and incredibly good at their jobs. They were both happy to be out working with Denny and Anna again, although they did not know that it was only coyotes being hunted.

As they were settled in the blind with their smaller calibre sniper rifles waiting for any coyotes to catch the scent of the dead deer which had been partially eviscerated to enhance the smell, Denny said, "It sure is nice to be back in the field again with you and the dogs. It's also nice that we don't have to worry about the coyotes shooting back at us."

"Yeah, it is nice," Anna said. "I was getting tired of all the office and lab work over the past couple of months. The two teams here at Sterling seem to be well-organized and have totally bought into the coyote rabies testing and research cover operation. The F&W Service has done a good job with the PR program. It all seems very logical and believable."

Denny said, "That's how it seems to me too. A couple of the older special forces' snipers said that they had heard of me and were wondering what I was doing here in the US on an operation like this. I told them that my boss, John Benson, was invited by the F&W Service to consult with them and the CDC on the operation and I was just along to help in whatever way I could. They seemed to be fine with that explanation."

They waited for a couple of hours and were getting quite bored and discouraged, when finally, a coyote came over a small ridge about two hundred yards from the deer and was sniffing the air and looking around. It then slowly began walking towards the deer looking quite nervous and continued to sniff the air. It would stop every twenty yards or so and look around and then carry on towards the deer. When it finally got to within about five yards from the deer, Denny shot it through the heart and it instantly dropped down dead on the ground. They had silencers on their sniper rifles so there was not even any gunshot sound. The dogs were very alert and waiting for the signal from Denny to go but Denny told them to stay down so they reluctantly obeyed.

Anna jumped out of the blind and walked over to the dead coyote and put it into a carrying bag and brought it back to the blind. She then left Denny and the dogs in the blind, in case any more coyotes showed up, and took the dead coyote over to where their truck was parked. Each truck was outfitted with a mobile autopsy station which could be laid out on the tailgate. There was a disposable plastic sheet which she laid the dead coyote on. There were also surgical instruments for removing the skin to expose the bone on the top of the skull. She then used a surgical bone saw to remove the top of the skull and expose the brain. She then removed the whole coyote brain including the cerebellum, hippocampus, and brain stem. She then put the whole brain in a sterilized plastic bag and placed it in a special transport cooler with several freezer packs.

Depending on the situation they could just leave the coyote carcass where it was shot to decompose naturally, or they could transport it back to the base to be disposed of in a veterinarian animal crematorium. Since they were in a remote location, Anna decided they could just leave the carcass where they were to decompose naturally. After she was finished, she went back to the blind to see how Denny and the dogs were doing.

They decided to wait in the blind for a couple of more hours, and then just before they were about to give up for the day, another coyote appeared over the same ridge and Denny was able to shoot it as well. Anna went through the same autopsy procedure and they then headed back to the base in Sterling with the two coyote brain specimens. They checked in with the team leader and dropped off the two coolers and then started their two-hour drive back to Denver so they could get there in time for a late dinner. Syd and Nelle had enjoyed their time in the field with Denny and Anna but were disappointed they were only hunting coyotes and did not need to chase down any bad guys. They were quite sure though that they could have caught one of those coyotes if Denny had needed them to.

They had called John and Kate and had agreed to meet them for dinner at a restaurant close to the hotel when they got back to Denver so they could talk about what had happened over the last two days. They arrived back at the hotel, unloaded their gear, had a shower, met up with John and Kate and then walked to the restaurant which was only a block away. They picked a table in a secluded part of the restaurant and were careful to keep their voices low and to not say too much about what had happened over the last couple of days. They went into more detail after dinner when they got back to John and Kate's suite and shared a bottle of wine.

While they were walking to the restaurant, they did not notice the black Jeep SUV with the tinted windows follow them and then park about half a block down the street. They also did not notice the two men from the SUV come into the restaurant and sit at a table across the room but with a good view of the four of them at their table.

7:00 a.m. Saturday, March 6, 2021
FBI Hotel, Denver, Colorado

John and the team had decided to spend the next two days travelling to all the operations bases again to see how things were going with the field teams. They planned to follow the same itinerary as the last time which meant that their first destination was Billings, Montana. They got all their gear into the FBI passenger van and left the hotel at 7:00 a.m. for the FBI hangar at the Denver International Airport.

As the FBI driver pulled the passenger van out of the service bay of the hotel, the same black SUV with the tinted windows pulled out from the curb down the street and started following the van. One of the occupants of the SUV called another employee of the security company who was driving a second vehicle, a silver Toyota RAV, and told him that they were on the move and gave him a description of the van and the licence plate number. He told him to pull in behind them and then take over as the lead vehicle when the van got onto the freeway to the airport. They were professionals and had done this tag-team surveillance routine many times before and were very seldom detected by the driver of the vehicle they were following.

The FBI passenger van drove to the security gate of the FBI hangar and then through to the hangar and parked on the tarmac beside the FBI Beechcraft King Air. John and the team got out of the van and started loading their gear on the plane. The two FBI pilots had arrived about an hour earlier and had gotten the plane ready for the flight. They had already filed a flight plan for the day with the Denver Flight Center with stops in Billings, Montana; Dickinson, North Dakota; Casper, Wyoming; and finally, Rapid City, South Dakota, where they would spend the night again.

The black SUV with the tinted windows had pulled into the parking area next to the FBI hangar with a clear view of the Beechcraft King Air and the FBI passenger van parked next to it. They noted the plane's registration numbers and watched as John Benson's team boarded the aircraft. One of the men phoned his boss and told him what was going on and the aircraft's registration numbers. His boss told him to drive over to the main airport terminal and wait for him to call back. He said that he had a contact in the Denver Flight Center and that he would find out if they had filed a flight plan. About thirty minutes later his boss called him back and gave him the flight plan and told them to book the next available flight to Rapid City.

9:00 a.m. Saturday, March 6, 2021
Billings Beckett International Airport, Billings, Montana

John, Kate, Anna, Denny, and the dogs met the four team leaders again in the small meeting room in the office part of the hangar. They discussed how things were going in general and how successful the four teams had been in the past two days since the operation had started. The team leaders said that all forty-eight of the team members had arrived at the base and that all the equipment and supplies had been delivered. The state F&W Service had also supplied a base manager to keep things organized at the hangar and watch over the equipment. However, the four field teams were having trouble reaching their quotas of three coyote brain specimens per day. Some had been slightly more successful, but a couple of the teams were struggling. There seemed to be some problems with mixing the teams with personnel from different agencies. They were trying to resolve the problems by reassigning some of the team members, but overall, they thought that the quota seemed to be achievable, even though they were behind schedule right now.

They also said that the PR material about the rabies testing and research program supplied by the F&W Service was very helpful, but a few landowners had still been reluctant to allow access to their properties until they had talked to someone in authority, even though they were supplied with the brochures and PR materials. The local newspaper had also run a short story about the rabies research project, which had caused a bit of a panic and prompted lots of calls to the local F&W office.

John and the team met the base manager, hired to keep everything organized, and got a short tour of the hangar and the facilities. Most of the field teams had already left for the day but the base manager gave them a list of all the people who had been deployed to the base with their backgrounds and the locations of where they had come from. John and the team thanked him for the tour and got back on the plane for their next destination.

5:30 p.m. Saturday, March 6, 2021
Rapid City Regional Airport, Rapid City, South Dakota

John and the team had gone through the same routine at the bases in Dickinson, North Dakota, and Casper, Wyoming, and had arrived at their last destination for the day in Rapid City. John and the team met with the three F&W special agents who were assigned to be the team leaders of the three field teams deployed to Rapid City. Things seemed to be progressing better there than at some of the other bases and the South Dakota state F&W Service had also assigned a base manager to keep the equipment and supplies organized in the hangar.

The field teams in all the four bases they had visited during the day were all in place and had been out in the field for the last three days. Overall, the coyote brain specimen quotas were not being met on a consistent basis, with some teams being more successful than others. There were also several supply and equipment problems. Two of the helicopters had broken down and had to be replaced. And the shipments of travel coolers to the bases in Dickson and Casper had been short, so they were in danger of running out if the replacement coolers were not delivered soon.

They had decided to stay overnight in Rapid City and booked rooms at the Hampton Inn and Suites again on Eglin Street in Rapid City. After the meeting at the base was over, and their plane was secured at the hangar, they borrowed the twelve-person passenger van again and drove to the hotel. Everyone, including the two FBI pilots, got their own rooms again, except

John and Kate who booked a king studio suite. Denny also got a king suite again so there would be more room for Syd and Nelle.

As they were driving in the van to the hotel, John, looking frustrated, said, "Well, it seems there are definitely some start-up problems at most of the bases. Maybe we were a little too optimistic about how well things would work. It didn't help that planning was so rushed getting the operation up and running. Hopefully, they will be able to get back on track and make up for the coyote specimens they should have had by now. I am not sure what else we can do except keep on top of things and trouble-shoot as soon as there are any problems."

"I think it was too much to expect that everything would run smoothly right from the start," said Kate. "We are dealing with a lot of moving parts here, so we just have to be as proactive as possible and not let things get too far off track."

They got to the hotel at about 6:00 p.m. and got checked in. Kate and Anna decided to take Syd and Nelle for a run again before they ordered dinner and settled in for the evening. They decided to run north of the city along Haines Avenue again. Denny said he would drop them off with the van at the corner of Haines Avenue and Secondary Highway 214 and then pick them up in an hour at the same location just as he had done the previous time they were there.

Scott Martin and Hector Martinez had taken an 11:00 a.m. flight from Denver to Rapid City, had rented a silver Mazda X3, and had parked on Airport Road northwest of the airport terminal at about 4:30 p.m. and waited for the King Air to arrive at the airport. The two men were former US military police officers, but now worked as security contractors for a company that did business with any foreign government agency that was willing to pay the extremely high fees for their discretion and willingness to handle sensitive and often illegal assignments. In this case the client was a Russian FSB agent by the name of Igor Larionov, although that was not the name that he had given their boss, Daniel Lavoy, when he told him what he needed his security company to do for him.

The King Air had arrived at about 5:00 p.m. and they watched it taxi over to a hangar just down the road from where they were parked. They drove a little closer to the hangar where they had a good view of the plane and noticed a twelve-person passenger van pull up to the plane on the tarmac. The pilots from plane and a couple of people from the hanger were unloading luggage from the plane including two dog kennels and putting it all in the back of the van. At about 5:30 p.m., the two pilots and the four people from the plane and two German shepherd dogs all got in the van and left the hangar. Scott and Hector followed the van into Rapid City to the Hampton Inn and Suites. They watched them all get out and unload their luggage and go into the hotel. The middle-aged guy who looked like he might be a Native American parked the van in the hotel parking lot and then went into the hotel.

Scott and Hector parked in the back area of the hotel parking lot with a good view of the van and the hotel entrance. At about 6:30 p.m. they saw the two women from the plane, the Indian guy and the two dogs come out of the hotel and get in the van again and drive out of the parking lot. Scott and Hector followed them to the corner of Haines Avenue and Secondary Highway 214 where the two women and the dogs got out and started running north along Haines Avenue and then the van left. Scott and Hector waited about five minutes and then drove north along Haines Avenue and passed the two women and the dogs running along the side of the road.

They noticed that Haines Avenue had a few acreage developments but was mostly in the countryside and crossed Boxelder Creek. They drove a few miles down the road north of Boxelder Creek and then parked and in a little while saw the two women coming towards them. The women and the two dogs then crossed to the other side of the road and started running south again. Scott and Hector waited for a while and then drove south and passed the two women and the dogs and parked again about a block from the corner of Haines Avenue and Secondary Highway 214. After a few minutes, the van came back, and the two women and the dogs got back in the van and Scott and Hector followed them back to the Hampton Inn and Suites.

Scott and Hector decided that they were probably going to be spending the rest of the evening and night at their hotel, so they left and got a couple of rooms at the Best Western Hotel next door. Scott called his boss and told him about what they had found out. His boss told him to follow them back to the airport in the morning to make sure they left on the plane again. His boss told Scott that he had gotten a copy of the flight plan for the next day from his contact at the Denver Flight Center and the plane was scheduled to go to Lethbridge and Swift Current in Canada, and then back south to North Platte, Nebraska; Sterling, Colorado; and then finally back to Denver at the end of the day. He told them just to stay put in Rapid City until he contacted them again in a couple of days. He said he needed to contact the client and let him know what they had discovered so far and find out what the client wanted them to do next. He told them to check out the hangar where the plane had landed while they were in Rapid City and maybe see if they could talk to a few of the people working there about what was going on.

After he was finished the call with Scott and Hector, the boss, Daniel Lavoy, previously a French citizen, but who had been living in Los Angeles for many years, called the client in Moscow on one of the many one-time-use burner phones he kept for private conversations. His company's name was World Security Services and most of the work it did was legal, although generally right on the edge. He supplied people, mostly ex-military, or ex-law enforcement, to take care of sensitive security issues that his clients, mostly military or government security agencies, did not want to appear in any official records. For his discretion and efficiency, he was able to charge considerably higher fees than most security companies. Some of his company's very specialized services were not legal but were also the most lucrative. Sometimes countries or corporations needed certain people to disappear or have unfortunate accidents. Daniel Lavoy also had people who worked for him who could make those types of things happen.

Daniel Lavoy, who was forty-seven years old and a fit six foot one, and spoke English with a slight French accent, told his client what the surveillance of Dr. John Benson and his team had discovered over the last couple of days.

Igor Larionov, who spoke almost flawless English with a slight New England accent, listened patiently while Daniel Lavoy explained what his men had found out about what John Benson and his team where up to, and then said, "Thank you, Mr. Lavoy. That is all interesting. Through some of my other sources, I have discovered that the operation they are working on is called Operation Coyote."

He then continued, "Apparently, Operation Coyote is supposed to be about a rabies testing and research program, but that is just a cover story. My people have discovered that the real reason for Operation Coyote is related to a new vaccine that is being tested by the CDC for a mutated version of the COVID-19 virus. We are still trying to get more details about the CDC vaccine program, but we know that Operation Coyote is connected in a big way, and not because of any rabies research and testing program."

After a brief pause Igor Larionov closed out the conversation by saying, "Mr. Lavoy, have your people in Rapid City try to find out some more details about Operation Coyote on that end and I will get back to you in a couple of days about what I want done next."

CHAPTER 12

7:00 p.m. Sunday, March 7, 2021
FBI Hotel, Denver, Colorado

John and Kate were back at their regular suite at the hotel in Denver. During the day, they had flown to Lethbridge, Swift Current, North Platte, Sterling, and finally back to Denver. They had left Denny and Anna and the dogs at the base in North Platte, Nebraska so they could spend a couple of days working with the field teams there. John and Kate had decided to spend the next couple of days at the Denver FBI Field Office again monitoring how the field teams at the eight bases were doing. They would then head out again in a couple of days, pick Denny and Anna up in North Platte, and do another tour of the bases.

"So, it's nice to be back in our Denver home away from home again," Kate said. "I ordered dinner and a bottle of wine from room service while you were in the shower — steak and a Caesar salad with a piece of cheesecake for dessert that we can split. It's going to be nice to be out of that airplane for a couple of days."

John said, "No kidding. It is a great little plane but a break from travelling in it is going to be nice. Anna and Denny and the dogs seemed happy as well to spend a couple of days at the base in Nebraska. Neither of them is particularly good at flying so much with not a lot to do except going to meetings. They were both excited when they got the chance to kill a couple of coyotes in Sterling the other day and then do the field biopsies. Hopefully, they can do the same at the North Platte base. We could use the extra coyote specimens. Things seem to be getting back on track at most of the bases, but

I am still worried that some of the teams are not making their quotas. Do you think we can still get the one thousand coyote specimens by the deadline?"

"I sure hope so. We will need some good luck that there aren't any more serious delays or problems with equipment or bad weather. There is only so much we can control, and then we just have to hope for the best."

When they heard a knock at the door Kate said, "That must be room service with dinner. Let's watch some news while we eat, I haven't seen what is going on in the rest of the world for days now."

John said, "Good idea, I wonder how the plans for the March 15th COVID-19 vaccine rollout are going? We should find out when and where we can get our vaccine shots. We can ask tomorrow at the FBI Field Office. Maybe they already have access to the vaccine since medical, first responder, and law enforcement personnel are supposed to be some of the first to be vaccinated."

On the TV, CNN was still reporting that there were numerous resurgences of reinfections of COVID-19, both in the US and elsewhere in the world. There were interviews with both the CDC Director Dr. Miriam Bateman, and the Director of the National Institute of Infectious Diseases, Dr. Stephen Favaro. They were both saying that the resurgences of reinfections were likely caused by a minor mutation of the COVID-19 virus, but that the new vaccine should bring things under control. There was no mention of Operation Coyote or the actual seriousness of the situation. John and Kate both hoped that the scientists could spin the story long enough until they could complete Operation Coyote.

Kate said, "I'm really beat again. Why don't we finish dinner and crawl into bed with the bottle of wine and finish watching the news and then maybe watch a movie if we can stay awake long enough."

Laughing, John said, "You know what usually happens when we get into bed with a bottle of wine, you can't keep your hands off me."

9:00 a.m. Monday, March 8, 2021
North Platte Regional Airport, North Platte, Nebraska

Denny, Anna, and the dogs stayed behind at the North Platte base Sunday afternoon and continued talking to the two team leaders about how they could help the field teams during the next two days. They had agreed that

Denny and Anna would spend Monday in one of the helicopters with one of the local F&W officers and try to do some coyote hunting from the helicopter. On Tuesday they would use a bait station and blind again like they did in Sterling, Colorado a few days before.

They had to leave Syd and Nelle behind at the hangar for the day with the base manager, but they seemed to like her, and she was a dog person which they could sense somehow. Denny and Anna left in the helicopter with the pilot and the F&W officer to fly around some of the more remote areas in western Nebraska hoping to see a coyote on the ground. Denny had his sniper rifle and Anna had an autopsy kit. After flying around for about an hour they finally spotted a coyote in a remote semi-forested area. The pilot maneuvered the A-Star helicopter over the now running coyote and Denny opened the backdoor window and rested his sniper rifle on the window frame. When he finally had an open shot, he took it and they saw the coyote stumble and then then fall over motionless in a few more yards. The pilot circled back and found an open landing spot not too far from the dead coyote.

Once they were on the ground and the helicopter had shut down, they all got out and walked over to the dead coyote. Anna had the portable autopsy kit and proceeded to lay everything out on the plastic sheet on the ground. She then completed the extraction of the coyote brain and put it in the cooler. They decided to relax for a little while and eat the lunches they had brought with them from the base. After lunch they went to a nearby F&W fuel cache and refuelled the helicopter and then went coyote hunting again. They managed to locate one more coyote and Denny shot it and they did the field autopsy again.

Later in the afternoon, after another refuelling stop, they decided to collect the two specimen coolers from one of the ground teams who had been operating close by and returned to the base at the North Platte airport. Syd and Nelle were excited when they saw Denny and Anna walk back into the hangar, even though they had enjoyed their day with the base manager. After talking with the other returning field team members for a while, Denny and Anna and the dogs went to their hotel in North Platte for the night. Together with the two coyote brain specimens that Denny and Anna had gotten, the other two field teams had gotten another five for a total of seven for the day.

After getting settled back at their hotel and having showers, Denny and Anna went for dinner at the restaurant in the hotel. Denny said, "That was a pretty awesome day, I haven't done any shooting out of a helicopter for quite a few years."

Anna said, "I know, that was a great day for me too. It reminds me of some of the days we spent in Kenya and Tanzania chasing poachers with helicopters and you shooting out the tires on their Land Rovers. At least today the coyotes didn't have guns and weren't shooting back at us."

Denny said laughing, "Yeah, it doesn't really seem fair, but I can't say that I miss getting shot at on a regular basis. I'm getting a little more worried about people shooting at me in my old age."

"The teams here seem to be doing better, and the coyote specimen numbers at all the bases seem to be back on track for the most part," said Anna.

"I hope things continue to improve," said Denny. "John and Kate have been pretty stressed the last couple of days. Hopefully, we can shoot a few more coyotes tomorrow and take the pressure off a little."

They finished their dinner and then went to Denny's suite to check on Syd and Nelle and watch some TV before turning in for the night. They had planned with the field team leaders to set up a bait station and blind for them for the next day to do their coyote hunting.

9:00 p.m. Monday, March 8, 2021
World Security Services Office, Los Angeles, California

Daniel Lavoy, the owner of World Security Services was in his home office at his gated estate in Los Angeles. He preferred to operate his business "under the radar" and didn't need a fancy office building because almost all his employees worked in various locations around the world and had no need to come into an office to do their jobs. He had a few trusted employees in Los Angeles - accountants and administrative people, who would come to work daily in the office bungalow on his estate. He also had a home and office in Marseille, France, which was a convenient location to manage many of his business endeavours in Europe, North Africa, and the Middle East. He was also able to travel on his French passport since he had dual US and French citizenship. Of course, he also had several other passports that he could use if required.

He had been in contact earlier in the day with his client in Moscow and had updated him on what new information he had been able to find out about Operation Coyote and the activities of Dr. John Benson and his team. His client had confirmed that it was consistent with the information he had gathered through his sources as well. It was apparent that Operation Coyote was a cover operation connected to the development of a new vaccine by the CDC for the new mutated COVID-21 virus. It was also apparent that if Operation Coyote could be disrupted in some way, it would have serious consequences for the development of the new vaccine.

Daniel Lavoy and his client discussed various alternatives about how that could be done and settled on one plan that could be implemented in the next few days. That would give the client time to develop some additional obstacles to the development of the new vaccine by the CDC.

Daniel Lavoy's next call was to Scott Martin and Hector Martinez in Rapid City and he filled them in on what he needed them to do.

7:00 a.m. Wednesday, March 10, 2021
FBI Hangar, Denver International Airport, Denver, Colorado

John and Kate had spent the last two days at the Denver FBI Field Office again monitoring the progress of the eight operations bases. There were still some problems with delivery of some of the equipment at a few of the bases, and two more helicopters had problems which took them out of operation for a couple of days. There were also a few PR flare-ups with some landowners, and the local F&W offices had to get involved. Operation Coyote was progressing, but they were still behind schedule. The eight bases had been fully operational for six days now, and they had only delivered a total of 330 coyote brain specimens to the CDC in Fort Collins, at least thirty specimens short of the expected quota.

They had arrived at the FBI hangar at the Denver airport at 7:00 a.m. and were about to take off to fly to North Platte, Nebraska, to pick up Denny, Anna, and the dogs, and then carry on to Billings, Montana. They intended to do the circuit of the four bases again today and end up again in Rapid City to stay overnight before flying up to Canada the next day and completing the tour.

The two FBI pilots, Paul Judson, and Lucy Boyette had arrived at the hangar at 6:00 a.m. and had the King Air ready to go. In addition to being excellent pilots, they were becoming part of the team and everyone enjoyed their company when they were off duty. They were also happy to keep Syd and Nelle entertained when John and his team were in meetings. They took off for the forty-five-minute flight to North Platte, and Denny, Anna, and the dogs were waiting for them when they got there. John and Kate had a short meeting with the two team leaders and then they all left for Billings, Montana. They then continued to the bases in Dickinson, Casper, and finally to Rapid City.

5:30 p.m. Wednesday, March 10, 2021
Rapid City Regional Airport, Rapid City, South Dakota

They booked rooms at the Hampton Inn and Suites again on Eglin Street in Rapid City. After the meeting at the base was over, they borrowed the twelve-person passenger van again and drove to the hotel. Everyone, including the two FBI pilots, got their own rooms again, except John and Kate, and Denny and the dogs, who booked the king studio suites again.

They got to the hotel at about 6:00 p.m. and checked in. Kate and Anna decided to take Syd and Nelle for a run north of the city along Haines Avenue again. Denny said he would drop them off with the van at the corner of Haines Avenue and Secondary Highway 214 and then pick them up in an hour at the same location just as he had done the previous two times they were in Rapid City.

Denny dropped them off at the intersection again and then left to go to the grocery store to pick up supplies and snacks for the plane. Kate and Anna started running north along Haines Avenue with Syd and Nelle close at their heels. After running for about twenty minutes, they had crossed Boxelder Creek and were in the countryside and they noticed a panel van with some sort of plumber business logo on the back doors parked on the side of the road and a man with a tire wrench kneeling by the back tire.

They looked at each other and decided to detour a bit into the ditch area to get around the van. They nodded hello as they slowly passed by the two men and the open side door of the van. Suddenly, both Kate and Anna felt very painful jabs on the sides of their necks, and then they got very dizzy and everything started to go black. Just before Kate blacked out, she heard a very loud yelp from one of the dogs.

Denny arrived back at the intersection at the designated time but could not see Kate and Anna and the dogs coming back towards him. He thought they must have decided to run a little further, so he just waited for another twenty minutes. He then tried calling Anna on her cell phone but there was no answer. He thought that was sort of strange so he decided to start driving north on Haines Avenue thinking that he would probably meet up with them. He drove north along Haines Avenue, past Boxelder Creek, and all the way to Elk Creek Road, which was about seven miles north of the Highway 214 intersection.

He was now getting quite concerned and decided to call John Benson. "Hi, John, I am on Haines Avenue to pick up Kate and Anna and the dogs and there is no sign of them here. Have you heard from them?"

John replied, sounding quite concerned as well, "No, I have not heard from them. Try checking the tracking app connected to the chips implanted under the skin in Syd and Nelle's necks. You remember that we sometimes used the app to locate the dogs when we sent them off to track down and capture poachers who had tried to run away."

Denny checked the app and it showed that the dogs were located about three miles to the south of where he was. He drove back south along Haines Avenue and the app showed he was getting closer until it showed that they were right beside him. He got out of the van and went down into the ditch area and he then finally saw the two dogs lying down on their sides, partially covered by some dead branches and grass.

Panicked, he rushed over to them and brushed the branches and grass off them and checked if they were still alive. They were both still alive and breathing very slowly. He then saw two cell phones lying beside them. He picked up the cell phones and then carried both dogs up to the van and put them inside. He then quickly tied a piece of cloth that was in the van to a post so they could locate the exact site again. He had previously noticed a veterinary clinic close to their hotel, so he started driving there while he called John again and told him what was going on. John said he would meet Denny at the vet clinic.

John was just coming across the parking lot looking very panicked as Denny pulled up to the vet clinic. They each carried one of the dogs into the clinic and were immediately directed to the observation area in the back where they put the dogs on two different tables. One of the vets came into the room and started checking the vital signs of Syd and Nelle. He said both their heart and breathing rates were very depressed, but they seemed to be unhurt otherwise.

He started checking the skin under their fur and finally found a puncture wound on each of their backs. He said to John and Denny, "It looks like they were probably tranquilized with a dart gun. I have some medicine that will bring them around sooner if you want me to use it on them."

John and Denny both said at the same time, "Yes, please give them some of the medicine. We need to find out what happened to the two women who were with them. They have both disappeared."

In a few minutes after the injection, both dogs started coming around and were mostly recovered in about ten minutes.

It was only then that they noticed a small plastic bag taped to the inside of Syd's collar which the vet had taken off when he had started his examination. Inside the bag was a note that said in capital letters,

"STOP OPERATION COYOTE NOW OR YOU WILL NOT SEE YOUR LADY FRIENDS ALIVE AGAIN — YOU WILL NOT FIND THEM SO DON'T BOTHER LOOKING — THEY WILL BE RELEASED UNHARMED WHEN OPERATION COYOTE IS PERMANENTLY STOPPED — WE ARE WATCHING YOU — FRIENDS OF THE ANIMALS."

John and Denny looked at each other with fear and alarm showing on their faces, and John said, "Oh my God, they have Kate and Anna. Let's drive back out to the spot you found the dogs and check if we can see anything there. While you are driving, I will call the Larry Greer at the FBI office in Denver and let him know what is going on and tell him to send an FBI forensics team here."

Larry Greer told him that he would contact the local FBI office in Rapid City and have them send their forensics team out to the site. The Rapid City FBI office was one of fourteen satellite offices or "Resident Agencies" of the Minneapolis FBI Field Office which covered the entire states of Minnesota, North Dakota, and South Dakota.

After a few more minutes the vet told them that Syd and Nelle seemed okay to leave and they all got back in the van and drove to the site on Haines Avenue where Denny had found the dogs. The cloth he had tied to the post was still there, so they knew they were at the exact location. They parked about twenty yards away and then cautiously walked around the area, careful not to disturb anything. They noticed some tire tracks and footprints in the soft gravel area on the side of the asphalt roadway. Some of the grass in the sloping area of the ditch had also been trampled down where they had probably dragged the dogs to the bottom of the ditch. They decided to call the state police office in Rapid City and tell them about the abduction and that they should send some police officers and a forensics team to secure the crime scene.

They waited for about twenty minutes for the first of several police vehicles to arrive, followed in about ten minutes by the state police forensic team van. John and Denny showed them their IDs and RCMP credentials and told the forensic team leader about what they knew had happened and that they had also called the FBI in Denver and that they would be sending the local Rapid City FBI forensics team to the site as well. John told the state forensics team leader that the FBI team would probably take over control of the crime scene when they arrived.

John and Denny watched as the South Dakota state police put up roadblocks and secured the scene with tape and set up lights because it was starting to get dark. The FBI crime scene forensics team, with some assistance from the state team, then began their work examining every inch of the area, taking pictures of all the tire tracks and footprints. They wanted to examine Denny's shoes to eliminate his footprints and took pictures of the tires on the van. John and Denny went back to the van to wait with the dogs since there was not much more they could do until the crime scene people had finished their work. Syd and Nelle were quite agitated, sensing that something was very wrong and wondering why Kate and Anna were not there with John and Denny. They remembered running with Kate and Anna, and then a man shooting something at them, but then could not remember anything after that until they were in the vet office with John and Denny.

While they were sitting in the van, they were getting more concerned by the minute. John phoned Larry Greer again to tell him about the note they had found in Syd's collar and sent him a photo of it from his phone, still leaving it in the plastic bag. He did not want to give it to the state police or FBI forensics people at this point until they had a plan of action.

Larry Greer said to John and Denny on speakerphone mode, "I will contact Caleb Miller, the FBI deputy director in Washington, who will probably contact Vice President Kincaid to tell her about what has happened. I will also get my people working on finding out anything they can about this supposed 'Friends of the Animals' group. It may just be a cover for something else more sinister. Just wait at the scene there while the forensics people are working, and I will call you back as soon as possible with instructions from my superiors."

9:30 p.m. Wednesday, March 10, 2021
About Four Miles East of Spearfish, South Dakota

Kate and Anna woke up in a room each lying on a bare single mattress that was lying directly on the carpeted floor. Other than being a little groggy, they both felt alright, except for the tenderness around the puncture wounds on each of their necks. They looked around the room and could see what they assumed was a window, but it had a large square of thick plywood covering it and was screwed into the window frame. They also saw the door which seemed to be made of solid wood, and the hole where the door handle should have been was also covered with a small square of plywood. The gap between the bottom of the door and the floor was about two inches wide. Other than the mattresses, there was no other furniture in the room. There was a small bathroom with no door that had a toilet and a small vanity and sink. They then noticed an envelop lying on the floor between the mattresses. They opened the envelop and started reading the letter inside which was written in all capital letters. It said,

"YOU ARE IN THE BASEMENT OF A PRIVATE RESIDENCE LOCATED IN THE COUNTRYSIDE FAR AWAY FROM ANY OTHER RESIDENCES. PLEASE DON'T BOTHER SCREAMING FOR HELP BECAUSE NO ONE WILL HEAR YOU. YOU ARE BEING DETAINED BY AN ANIMAL RIGHTS GROUP WHO KNOW ABOUT OPERATION COYOTE AND THAT YOU ARE IN CHARGE OF KILLING HUNDREDS OR PERHAPS THOUSANDS OF INNOCENT COYOTES FOR SOME GOVERNMENT EXPERIMENT. WE HAVE CONTACTED YOUR COWORKERS AND TOLD THEM TO IMMEDIATELY CANCEL OPERATION COYOTE. WE HAVE NOT ASKED FOR ANY RANSOM. WE DO NOT WISH TO HARM YOU AND YOU WILL BE RELEASED UNHARMED IF THE GOVERNMENT DOES WHAT WE HAVE ASKED. IF NOT, WE ARE PREPARED TO TAKE A MORE VIOLENT APPROACH TO REINFORCE THE SERIOUSNESS OF OUR DEMANDS. YOUR DOGS ARE ALIVE AND WERE NOT PERMANENTLY HARMED.

"WE ARE LETTING YOU STAY IN THE SAME ROOM TOGETHER AS LONG AS YOU DO WHAT WE SAY AND DO NOT CAUSE ANY TROUBLE. IF YOU TRY TO ESCAPE OR CAUSE DAMAGE TO THE ROOM, WE WILL SEPARATE YOU AND LIFE WILL BECOME MUCH HARDER FOR YOU. WE WILL BRING YOU FOOD ON A REGULAR BASIS AND PASS IT TO YOU UNDER THE DOOR. YOU CAN PASS THE USED PLATES BACK UNDER THE DOOR WHEN YOU ARE DONE WITH THEM. YOU CAN USE THE TOILET AS YOU NEED TO AND GET WATER FROM THE TAPS TO DRINK AND WASH IN THE SINK. WE HAVE MOUNTED A SMALL CAMERA ABOVE THE DOOR SO WE CAN SEE AND HEAR YOU AT ALL TIMES EXCEPT WHEN YOU ARE USING THE TOILET. PLEASE DO NOT TRY TO DAMAGE THE CAMERA OR THERE WILL BE CONSEQUENCES. THE LIGHT SWITCH HAS BEEN REMOVED SO THE LIGHTS WILL BE LEFT ON AT ALL TIMES. WE WILL PLAY MUSIC FOR YOU AND MAYBE TURN ON THE TELEVISION IN THE NEXT ROOM SO YOU CAN LISTEN TO PROGRAMS OF OUR CHOICE IF YOU BEHAVE AND DON'T CAUSE ANY PROBLEMS.

"YOU WILL NOT SEE US WHILE YOU ARE HERE BUT YOU WILL LIKELY BE ABLE TO HEAR US MOVE AROUND THE HOUSE. PLEASE DO NOT TRY TO TALK TO US. WE ARE NOT INTERESTED IN ANYTHING YOU MAY WANT TO SAY TO US ABOUT WHAT YOU ARE DOING AND WHY YOU ARE KILLING ALL THE ANIMALS. IF THE GOVERNMENT COOPERATES WITH US AND ACTS ON OUR DEMANDS YOU WILL BE RELEASED SOON.

"FRIENDS OF THE ANIMALS"

Kate and Anna looked at each other and then both got on the same mattress together and hugged each other and started to cry. After a few minutes they stopped crying and started quietly talking to each other.

With her arm around Anna's shoulders and holding her close, Kate said, "It looks like this is well-planned and thought out based on how we got here and how they prepared this room. We do not seem to have a lot of choices at this point but to do what they say so we can stay together. If we can believe what they say in the letter, they will treat us okay if we don't cause any problems."

Shivering a little and trying not to start crying again, Anna said, "I agree, let's just do what they say for now. I am sure that John and Denny will be doing everything they can to find us, and that they have contacted the FBI as well. I do not know if this 'Friends of the Animals' group is for real, but we must assume that there are a lot of law enforcement people working on our abduction already. Operation Coyote is way too important to let something like this shut it down."

Trying to not think about how much trouble they were in and how worried John and Denny must be, Kate said, "Yes, let's just wait and see what happens for a while. I see they took our watches, so we will not be able to tell what time it is. We will have to think of something to try to keep track of how long we are here. I know it must be well into the evening right now, so let's try to get some sleep."

Looking at Kate and trying to smile a little, Anna said, "We can try, but I have to admit that although I am trying to be brave, I am scared. I just hope that they do what they say and don't hurt us."

Smiling back at Anna, Kate said quietly, "I know, me too."

CHAPTER 13

8:00 a.m. Thursday, March 11, 2021
Room 310, Best Western Hotel, Rapid City, South Dakota

Scott Martin and Hector Martinez were in Room 310 of the Best Western Hotel in Rapid City. From the window in the room, they could see the parking lot and front entrance of the Hampton Inn and Suites. The van that John Benson and Denny Bear were driving was parked in the parking lot and several cars and SUVs had arrived this morning that looked distinctly like unmarked police vehicles, which was not unexpected. Scott and Hector had been busy over the last couple of days.

They had spoken with their boss, Daniel Lavoy, several times and were informed later Monday evening that he had sent two more of his employees to Rapid City, Ryan Miles and Helen Riggs, to investigate the short-term rental real estate market in the area. On Tuesday afternoon he told them that they had rented a partially furnished house on a secluded acreage for a month about four miles west of Spearfish, which was about forty-five miles northwest of Rapid City on Highway 90. One condition was that they needed immediate occupancy which was fine with the real estate management company since the house had been sitting vacant for a couple of months.

A rental agreement was signed by Ryan and Helen, who appeared to be a loving husband and wife from Minneapolis, who said they were writers and just wanted to get away someplace quiet to do some work and have a bit of a holiday, and maybe do some gambling at the casinos in nearby Deadwood. They signed the rental agreement as William and Amy Hanson. They said they preferred to pay in cash upfront, including the damage deposit, which was fine with the real estate agent.

They had moved in right away and then proceeded to do a few basement renovations with the materials they had purchased from the Home Depot in Spearfish to accommodate their expected house quests the next evening. The house was on five acres and was located at the end of a four-hundred-foot curved driveway so was not visible from the access road into the acreage development. The nearest neighbours were also not visible through the trees and were several hundred yards away. There was also a garage where they could park their rented SUV.

On Tuesday evening, Scott and Hector had stolen a white panel van from the one of the Rapid City Airport's long-term parking lots. They also stole a couple of magnetic signs from the side of a plumber's van parked behind a plumbing shop. They switched the licence plates on the van with a set they had stolen earlier from a similar-looking van parked on a side street a few blocks from the hotel.

On Wednesday morning they picked up a box at the UPS depot in Rapid City. In the box, shipped there by Daniel Lavoy's people in Los Angeles, were two tranquilizer pistols, one tranquilizer rifle, and several tranquilizer darts with the appropriate dosages for two 130-pound women and two German shepherd dogs. On Wednesday afternoon, at about 6:00 p.m., after seeing that John Benson and his team had arrived from the airport at the Hampton Inn and Suites, they drove the van north on Haines Avenue and parked on the side of the road a little way north of Boxelder Creek in an area that was secluded with no sightlines from any nearby residences. They put the magnetic signs on the back doors of the van, got all the tranquilizer guns ready, as well as the zip ties and cloth bags they could use as hoods if they needed them. They got out the tire wrench and waited for Kate and Anna to appear to the south.

As Kate and Anna and the two dogs got closer, Hector took out the wrench and pretended to be trying to tighten the tire lug nuts. Just as Kate and Anna were running by the open side door of the van, they each shot one of them in the side of the neck with the tranquilizer pistols. Scott then immediately grabbed the rifle and shot tranquilizer darts into the backs of both the dogs. The tranquilizing chemicals worked fast, and they quickly loaded Kate and

Anna into the van and shut the side door. They then dragged the two dogs down to the bottom of the ditch and covered them partially with some dead branches and grass. Before they left, Scott taped the small plastic bag with the note inside that was sent with the tranquilizer guns to the collar of one of the dogs.

As instructed, they then drove the van to the acreage west of Spearfish. When they got there after almost an hour of driving, they were met by Ryan Miles and Helen Riggs on the driveway of the garage and were told to drive the van into the garage. Kate and Anna were both still out cold from the tranquilizer drugs and they carried them down to the room in the basement that had been prepared for them. Scott and Hector then left with the van and drove it back to Rapid City and returned it to the long-term parking lot at the airport.

After they had unloaded all the tranquilizer guns and other equipment into their rental vehicle, they carefully wiped everything down and vacuumed the floor and seats with a portable vacuum cleaner to remove any trace evidence that they had used the van. They repaired the wiring harness from when they had originally hot-wired the van and put back the original licence plates. They then walked over to where they had left their rental vehicle and went back to their hotel.

Once they were back in their hotel room, they called their boss to let him know what was going on. Daniel Lavoy thanked them for the good job they had done, and then he called his client in Moscow to fill him in on the progress of the assignment.

10:00 a.m. Thursday, March 11, 2021
FBI Satellite Office, Rapid City, South Dakota

John and Denny were at the FBI satellite office in Rapid City in the office of the Deputy Agent in Charge Phil Cooper, reviewing the crime scene forensic reports. Unfortunately, there was almost no useful information in the reports. The tire tracks were from a quite common brand of tire used on numerous models of pickup trucks, SUVs, and panel vans. The shoe prints were from a common brand of running shoe. There were no fingerprints or trace evidence from fibres or any other materials. Basically, there was nothing in the forensic reports that helped to identify the vehicle used or the abductors.

The FBI and state police had done interviews with all the people living in the closest residences and none of them had seen anything. One resident who lived on an acreage about one mile north of the scene said that he vaguely remembered driving by a white van parked on the side of road but hadn't paid much attention and didn't see anybody at the van. He said he thought there was some sort of sign on the back doors of the van that could have had the name of a plumbing business on it.

The only communication about the reason for the abduction was from the note left in the plastic bag taped to Syd's collar. They had not received any other instructions or demands. They had spoken to Larry Greer, the FBI special agent in charge in Denver, and he told them that the FBI had done a thorough investigation of domestic ecoterrorism groups with any connection to the "Friends of the Animals" group claiming to be responsible for the abduction. Although there were several similar groups known to the FBI, there were no records of activities attributed to the Friends of the Animals group. So far, there were no clues about where Kate and Anna were being held.

Larry Greer told them that the vice president had called an emergency meeting of the task force in Washington for that morning to discuss the situation and would be getting back to him before noon Denver time. For now, Operation Coyote would continue until they were told otherwise by the task force.

Although John and Denny were totally focussed on finding Kate and Anna right now, John was also worried about the fate of Operation Coyote. John didn't know if he would be able to go on with the operation if something happened to Kate and Anna. Even though he was trying to appear in control of the situation, he had never been this scared. He knew that Denny was feeling the same way, but because of their training, they were both trying to focus on the problem, and not let their emotions overwhelm them.

11:00 a.m. Thursday, March 11, 2021
About Four Miles East of Spearfish, South Dakota

Kate and Anna had finally managed to sleep for several hours next to each other on the same bed. They had woken up at what they thought was the morning and saw that there was a tray on the floor with two bananas, two apples, and two granola bars on two paper plates. They also noticed that there were two red plastic cups on the vanity in the bathroom. They each filled a plastic cup with water and ate the food. They then put the banana peels, apple cores, granola bar wrappers, and paper plates onto the tray and pushed it back out under the door. A few minutes later they heard footsteps, and someone picked up the tray and they then heard footsteps going up the stairs. They heard someone talking upstairs but could not make out what they were saying.

They settled back on one of the beds and Kate said, "Well, I guess so far so good. Nothing bad has happened and they fed us like they said they would. I wonder what is happening with John and Denny."

Anna said, "I'm sure they have mobilized the entire FBI and are doing all the things we would normally do in an investigation. These people seem like they are professionals though, so I do not suppose that they would have left many clues about what they are doing. I think we should expect to be here for a while."

They heard some footsteps coming down the stairs again and then a few tattered paperback books and magazines from several years ago appeared on the floor from under the door. They then heard some soft classical music coming from what must have been a television in the next room.

12:30 p.m. Thursday, March 11, 2021
FBI Satellite Office, Rapid City, South Dakota

Feeling tired and stressed from not getting much sleep the night before, John and Denny were still at the FBI office in Rapid City and had spent the morning looking at the forensic evidence as it was analysed but it did not help much so far. They were also talking to the FBI agents in both Rapid City and Denver about information they were gathering about ecoterrorism groups in the region; however, there was no information about a "Friends of the Animals" group so far.

Larry Greer had called back and said that the FBI deputy director in Washington, Caleb Miller, had told him that the available COVID-21 Task Force members had met briefly in Washington and decided to let Operation Coyote continue and see what the FBI investigation turned up by the end of the day before making any decisions about suspending the operation.

Finally, they got some good news at about 1:00 p.m. The FBI were reviewing all the local Rapid City police reports from the last twenty-four hours and happened upon a phone-in complaint from a plumbing company named One-Stop Plumbing and Heating about the magnetic signs being stolen from their service van on Tuesday evening when it was parked behind their shop. The plumbing shop owner had apparently just called the police station to report that someone had found the two magnetic signs in a Dumpster and had called to tell him because his business phone number was on the signs. The FBI immediately called the plumber to find out where the signs were and that they would be sending a forensics team over immediately to pick them up since they may have been involved in a recent crime.

The forensics team picked up the magnetic signs at the plumbing shop and asked the owner and his assistant if they could take their fingerprints so they could eliminate them if they happened to find any other prints on the signs. They agreed and the signs were then brought back to the lab and analysed for prints and any other trace evidence. As expected, there were several sets of prints belonging to the plumbing shop owner and his assistant. However, there was also a partial index fingerprint and a full thumbprint on one of the corners of one of the signs. When they ran the prints through the database, the name Scott Martin came up. When they ran a search on Scott Martin in their various databases, they discovered an individual with an interesting and troubled past.

Scott Martin was thirty-two years old and grew up in Sacramento, California. He was a high school football star and got an athletic scholarship at Sacramento State University. He was a good wide receiver but was not very motivated. During his third year at Sacramento State, he got caught in a cheating scandal and lost his scholarship and dropped out of university. He then enlisted in the US Army and after basic training got into the US Army Military Police School. He finished his training and was then posted to Fort Hood in Texas. After about a year at Fort Hood he was deployed to Afghanistan.

During his second tour in Afghanistan, he was caught, along with several of his fellow MPs, skimming money from payments meant for the Afghan villagers for cooperating with the US military. Because the US Army wanted to keep the skimming operation quiet, they offered him and his fellow MPs a deal. A short three-month stay at the military jail at Fort Hood and a quiet court martial and discharge from the army. He took the deal and got out of the Fort Hood jail on July 15, 2018.

His employment records were quite sketchy after that, with the only employer of note being a security company in San Francisco named Atlas Security Services in 2019. Since then, his occupation on his income tax return for 2019 was listed as private security contractor with a home address in San Francisco. He had not filed his 2020 income tax return yet. Two of his fellow MPs, who had gotten the same deal from the US Army, were Hector Martinez and Ryan Miles.

The FBI immediately sent out a team of agents with pictures of Scott Martin, Hector Martinez, and Ryan Miles to the various hotels in the area and were surprised when the reception person at the front desk at the Best Western next door to the Hampton Inn and Suites said she recognized the pictures of Scott and Hector. However, they had checked out of the hotel at 9:00 a.m. and had registered under the names Tim Sullivan and John Lopez. They had not filled in the section of the hotel registration form about the vehicle they were driving. Calls to all the car rental agencies in the Rapid City area did not locate any records of vehicles rented by Scott, Hector, or either of their aliases.

3:00 p.m. Thursday, March 11, 2021
Country Inn & Suites, Billings, Montana

Scott Martin and Hector Martinez had checked out of the Best Western Hotel in Rapid City at 9:00 a.m. and had driven five hours to Billings, Montana. They had checked into the Country Inn & Suites on Main Street, just east of the Billings Beckett International Airport using different aliases and IDs, and again forgot to write down the type of vehicle they were driving and the licence plate number. Their boss, Daniel Lavoy, had told them to get out of Rapid City because things would be getting too hot for them there, and to go to Billings so they could observe the activities at the Operation Coyote base there. They needed to keep track of what was happening with Operation Coyote and whether the demand to shut down the operation was being followed.

After checking into the hotel, they drove over to the airport and located the Operation Coyote hangar. They pulled into an adjacent parking lot and watched as various F&W trucks and helicopters returned to the hangar. It was obvious that it was business as usual at the base for the day. They returned to the hotel and called Daniel Lavoy in Los Angeles to let him know.

Scott Martin and Hector Martinez had spent a lot of time together in hotel rooms the last couple of years. They had first met each other at the US Army Military Police School at Fort Leonard Wood in Missouri during their twenty weeks of training to become MPs. They had both been posted to Fort Hood and then Afghanistan. They had ended up in the army after quite different life paths.

Scott was the handsome high school football star. He was like many young men whose life seemed to have peaked in high school, always looking for the easy way to get the things he assumed he was entitled to. He came from an affluent upper-middle class family and was always given special treatment. He was a good but not great university football player. He got kicked off the Sacramento State University football team and lost his scholarship for paying people to take exams and write term papers for him. He quit university and joined the US Army and then became an MP.

Hector Martinez grew up poor, the son of Mexican migrant farm workers in southern California. Because he was born in California, he was a US citizen. After barely getting through high school, he joined the US Army. After several years of service, he decided to apply to the US Army Military Police School where he met Scott Martin and Ryan Miles.

After a year at Fort Hood in Texas they were all sent to Afghanistan. After a couple of tours, they were assigned to a team of MPs in charge of delivering cash payments to Afghan villagers. Seeing an opportunity to make a little extra cash, Scott Martin and his fellow MPs, Hector Martinez, and Ryan Miles, began skimming a few thousand dollars from each delivery. Since there was a lot of money being paid out to Afghan villagers at the time, record keeping and audits by the US Army were quite slack. However, an investigation by the army into missing funds eventually caught up with them, and they were all quietly kicked out of the army and spent a minimal three months in the military jail at Fort Hood. When they got out, they found that job opportunities were limited, and they eventually all ended up working for Daniel Lavoy at World Security Services.

Daniel Lavoy liked hiring ex-law enforcement people. They tended to be very well trained and by the time they got to him, they did not usually have a lot of good employment options and were willing to do the types of assignments his clients requested. He paid them very well and they understood that some of things they would be doing would be illegal, but only if they got caught, which almost never happened. Because his clients generally paid very well for his company's services, he was able to supply his employees with the best tools and equipment available to do their jobs, including the ability to provide excellent alternative forms of identification. He also had a particularly good team of lawyers in case they encountered any legal problems while completing their work assignments.

The other person on the Operation Coyote team, Helen Riggs, was an ex-San Francisco police officer. After graduating with a degree in criminology from San Francisco State University, she joined the San Francisco Police Department. After five years she passed the detective's exam and was assigned to the drug enforcement unit. Unfortunately, she got caught up in an ongoing drug cartel police payoff operation in her unit, and she and several of her fellow detectives got busted by internal affairs and were kicked out of the police department. She eventually ended up working for Daniel Lavoy at World Security Services as well.

The four employees of World Security Services who were assigned to the Operation Coyote file did not think of themselves as criminals. They were professionals at what they did and had come to accept the moral ambiguities of their situations. They generally did not know or care who the client was when they were assigned a file to work on. They had lines they would not cross such as knowingly taking someone else's life unless their own lives were in peril. They also did not condone any gratuitous or unnecessary violence. However, Daniel Lavoy did have other people in his employ who were not as concerned with the adherence to laws or moral standards.

6:00 p.m. Thursday, March 11, 2021
FBI Satellite Office, Rapid City, South Dakota

John and Denny had spent the day at the FBI office in Rapid City helping with the investigation. Other than finding the fingerprints of Scott Martin and verifying that he and Hector Martinez were likely responsible for Kate and Anna's abduction, they had truly little else to go on. They had been unable to locate Scott and Hector after just missing them at the Best Western Hotel and assumed that they were no longer in Rapid City. They also believed that Scott and Hector were probably working with others who were directly in charge of hiding Kate and Anna, assuming they were still alive.

They had come up with the idea of trying to locate possible sites where Kate and Anna were being held. They decided to have FBI agents contact all the real estate management companies within a one-hundred-mile radius of Rapid City in the hope that they would stumble on a suspicious transaction. So far, nothing had turned up.

Larry Greer from the Denver FBI Field Office had been in contact with his superiors in Washington during the afternoon, and at the end of the day the COVID-21 Task Force had decided to shut down Operation Coyote for the next day to give the FBI some time to figure out what was going on and hopefully locate Kate and Anna. Operation Coyote was already not going well and was behind schedule with a total of only 425 coyote brain specimens delivered to the CDC in Fort Collins. The need to suspend the operation now for one or two days, or more, put the whole operation in jeopardy, as well as the development and testing of the COVID-21 vaccine.

John and Denny decided to take the dogs for a walk and try to unwind a bit after a hard day worrying about Kate and Anna and working in the FBI office. They were extremely frustrated with how little they had accomplished so far. They were also worried that Operation Coyote had been suspended, putting who knows how many lives at stake. It was obvious they were dealing with professionals who were not going to make very many mistakes. The fact that they had been able to find the one good thumbprint on the corner of the magnetic plumbing business sign was the only mistake the abductors had made so far. And it was only dumb luck that they had even located the sign in the first place.

As they were walking the dogs John said, "I will never be able to forgive myself if something happens to Kate and Anna. We should have never let them go running by themselves without any protection. I don't know what I was thinking."

Shaking his head, Denny said, "I know, boss. I just let them go off by themselves. I could have easily followed them with the van and kept an eye on them. We have been doing this for ten years all around the world with them, busting some bad people with guns and we have never had anything like this happen. Operation Coyote should have been easy with no one shooting at us. We must be getting too old for this, letting our guard down after usually being so careful."

After walking the dogs in silence for a while longer, John said, "I guess it won't help beating ourselves up at this point. We just have to come up with a way to find them."

8:00 p.m. Thursday, March 11, 2021
About Four Miles East of Spearfish, South Dakota

Kate and Anna had spent the day reading the old paperbacks and magazines that their captors had passed under the door, listening to the classical music from the TV in the next room, and doing a few exercises on the floor in their room. Lunch was a banana, apple, and peanut butter sandwich. Dinner was a ham and cheese sandwich, some raw baby carrots, and two chocolate chip cookies for each of them served on paper plates with no cutlery.

After they had finished their dinner and had passed their dinner tray back under the door, a note was slipped under the door. It said,

"WE ARE GOING TO BE GIVING YOU A CELL PHONE AND A LETTER WHICH WE WANT ONE OF YOU TO READ WHILE THE OTHER MAKES A VIDEO. WE WILL BE WATCHING AND LISTENING SO DO NOT TRY TO MAKE A CALL OR TEXT WITH THE PHONE OR SAY ANYTHING THAT IS NOT IN THE LETTER. AFTER YOU HAVE FINISHED READING THE LETTER YOU WILL IMMEDIATELY PASS THE CELL PHONE AND LETTER BACK UNDER THE DOOR. IF YOU DISOBEY IN ANY WAY YOU WILL BE SEPARATED AND YOUR LIVES WILL BECOME VERY UNPLEASANT."

After a few minutes, a cell phone and letter were passed under the door. They read the short letter together and then Kate said she would read it while Anna videoed her with the cell phone. Kate sat on the edge of one of the mattress and Anna sat across from her on the other mattress. Kate then started to read the letter while looking at the cell phone.

"THIS VIDEO IS MEANT FOR JOHN BENSON AND THE UNITED STATES GOVERNMENT. MY NAME IS KATE BECKETT AND ANNA DUPREE IS HERE WITH ME AND IS VIDEOING ME. WE DO NOT KNOW WHERE WE ARE BUT WE ARE BEING TREATED WELL AND HAVE NOT BEEN HARMED SO FAR. OUR CAPTORS BELONG TO A GROUP CALLED FRIENDS OF THE ANIMALS. THEY DEMAND THAT YOU STOP KILLING THE COYOTES AND THAT OPERATION COYOTE BE CANCELLED IMMEDIATELY. MEMBERS OF THEIR ORGANIZATION ARE WATCHING AND WILL KNOW IF THE OPERATION CONTINUES. IF OPERATION COYOTE IS NOT CANCELLED ANNA AND I WILL BE TORTURED AND POSSIBLY KILLED. MORE VIOLENCE WILL THEN TAKE PLACE AGAINST OTHER PEOPLE PARTICIPATING IN OPERATION COYOTE. PLEASE DO WHAT THEY SAY."

After Kate was finished reading the letter, they did what they were instructed to do and passed the cell phone and letter back under the door. After a few minutes, after they had heard someone walking back up the stairs, they sat close together on one of the beds holding hands to try to stop them from trembling and Kate quietly said, "Do you think we did the right thing by reading the letter?"

With her voice quivering and tears in her eyes, Anna said, "I don't know but it seems like we didn't have much of a choice. They have all the power right now and we have none. I think we should just do what they say. If they separate us, we will be in a much worse situation."

Brushing a tear away from her own eye, Kate said, "Yes, I agree. The fact that we have not seen them or even heard them speak to us, means that we cannot identify them, and they could still let us go at some point. They do not seem to be violent and are not asking for any money which is good. We just have to assume John and Denny and all the resources of the FBI are out there looking for us."

8:00 a.m. Friday, March 12, 2021
Walmart Parking Lot, Rapid City, South Dakota

Helen Riggs had driven from Spearfish to Rapid City early in the morning with the burner cell phone that had been purchased in Los Angeles. She was parked in the far northwest corner of the Walmart Super Center in south Rapid City off East Stumer Road. She was sure that there were no surveillance cameras in this part of the parking lot and was also sure there were no other businesses or residences close enough to be able to record her vehicle. She had John Benson's cell phone number and was ready to send the video that Kate and Anna had made the night before.

She pushed the send button and then immediately shut it off and wiped it down with some alcohol-based hand sanitizer. She then put some gloves on and got out of the silver SUV and put it in front of the rear tire and drove over it several times. She then gathered up the broken phone and drove a few miles north on 5th Street until she saw a Dumpster in front of an apartment construction site. As she drove by the Dumpster, she tossed the broken cell phone into it. She then stopped at a Safeway to pick up some groceries and made the one-hour drive back to the house outside of Spearfish.

8:30 a.m. Friday, March 12, 2021
FBI Satellite Office, Rapid City, South Dakota

John and Denny were back at the Rapid City FBI office early Friday morning after trying, mostly unsuccessfully, to get some sleep at the hotel the night before. They had to bring Syd and Nelle to the office because there was nowhere else to leave them. However, the dogs were used to being in law enforcement offices, so they just settled down on the floor of the small boardroom that John and Denny had converted into a temporary office. At a little after 8:00 a.m. John heard his cell phone ping and he noticed that he had a message from an unknown caller with a video attached. He opened the video and was shocked as he watched as Kate read the letter. He immediately sent the video to the FBI email account he was using and brought it up on the sixty-inch monitor mounted on the wall. He and Denny watched it again and then called Phil Cooper, the deputy agent in charge, into the boardroom so he could watch it as well. John and Denny were relieved to see Kate and hear that Anna was there in the same room with her. Kate looked stressed but otherwise unharmed.

Phil Cooper asked John for his phone and then called one of his best tech guys in to see if they could figure out where the message had come from. He then said to John, "So at least we know they are alive and looking fairly good considering what they have been through. If we can believe what Dr. Beckett is reading, it seems that they are also being treated alright so far. So, the only demand the Friends of the Animals are making is that we shut down Operation Coyote. That seems a little strange since they could be making lots of other demands as well about other animal rights issues like factory farming, which is one of the usual targets of these types of groups. So why specifically target Operation Coyote?"

With relief showing on his face, John said, "You have no idea how happy I am to see that Kate and Anna seem to be doing okay and have not been abused or hurt. I agree with you, Phil, it does seem strange that they have only targeted Operation Coyote. Coyotes are killed all the time by ranchers and farmers and just for fun by recreational hunters. They are not one of the wild animals that animal rights activists are generally concerned about, and the public view them mostly as nuisance animals that come into urban areas and kill their pets and get into the garbage. Maybe there is something else going on here with the targeting of Operation Coyote. Also, the people who claim to be members of Friends of the Animals seem to be much more sophisticated than the usual animal rights activists."

"I agree as well," Denny said. "I think this could be about some bigger issue and may not have anything to do with killing several hundred coyotes over six US states and two Canadian provinces. I think we should broaden our investigation to include foreign agencies who might have something to gain by shutting down Operation Coyote. I am specifically thinking of the Russians or the Chinese."

"Yes, that makes a lot of sense," Phil Cooper said. "I will call my superiors and let them know about the video and our thinking about what might be going on. Maybe it is time we contact our friends at the CIA and NSA and bring them into the investigation. In the meantime, we need to find Dr. Beckett and Anna Dupree."

10:00 a.m. Friday, March 12, 2021
Country Inn & Suites, Billings, Montana

Scott Martin and Hector Martinez had driven to the Operation Coyote hangar at the Billings airport first thing in the morning and watched from the adjoining parking lot. Although there were quite a few people at the hangar, none of then were leaving in the F&W trucks and the four helicopters were all parked on the tarmac outside of the hangar. They left and went for coffee and then came back at about 9:30 a.m. and the situation was still the same. The four helicopters were still there, and ten F&W pickup trucks were parked in the parking lot outside the hangar.

Scott and Hector went back to their hotel and called their boss, Daniel Lavoy, in Los Angeles and told him that it looked like the Operation Coyote base in Billings had shut down for the day. After the call, Daniel Lavoy called his client in Moscow to let him know that Operation Coyote seemed to have been suspended for the day. His client thanked him for the information and congratulated him for the job he was doing so far.

5:00 p.m. Friday, March 12, 2021
FBI Satellite Office, Rapid City, South Dakota

John and Denny had spent the day at the FBI office in Rapid City helping the FBI agents contact real estate management companies in the Rapid City region. After they had struck out with all the larger agencies, they started calling the smaller independent agencies and property management companies listed online. Finally, at the end of the day one of the agents came across a woman who ran a small, two-person property management company in Spearfish.

When he asked her if she had rented any houses in the last few days, she told him about the nice writer couple from Minneapolis, William and Amy Hanson, who had rented a house for a month on an acreage about four miles west of Spearfish. She said that they had paid in cash upfront for both the rent and damage deposit. When the agent sent her photos of Scott Martin, Hector Martinez, and Ryan Miles, she said that she had never seen the other two, but the photo of Ryan Miles was William Hanson, the husband of the couple she had rented the house to. He got the exact address of the acreage and then went to tell his boss, Deputy FBI Agent in Charge Phil Cooper.

After congratulating the junior FBI agent, he called John and Denny into his office and said, "We finally caught a break. My agent just talked to the owner of a two-person property management company in Spearfish who on Tuesday rented a house on an acreage about four miles west of Spearfish to a young married couple from Minneapolis, William and Amy Hanson. The owner just identified the husband of the couple as being Ryan Miles, good friend of Scott Martin and Hector Martinez. It looks like we have probably found where Kate and Anna are being held. Now we just have to figure out how to get them out of the house unharmed."

John and Denny looked at each other and then spontaneously hugged, which was not something they did very often, being macho policemen. John said to Phil and Denny, "Thank God, finally some good news. Let's go and get them out of that house."

Phil Cooper called the leader of the Tactical Unit and told him to get his team ready for a house breaching and hostage rescue operation later that evening in Spearfish. He told him there would be an operational briefing in one hour in the main meeting room in the basement. He then called his analyst team and told them to get the most recent digital aerial photos of the acreage subdivision west of Spearfish. In ten minutes, an aerial photo from Google Earth dated from two days ago appeared on the sixty-inch computer monitor in the boardroom with the house of interest identified with a digital flag.

The residence was in a subdivision about four miles west of Spearfish off Hilltop Road. The subdivision access road was named Timber Ridge Road and the acreage driveway of interest was the first on the right, approximately one hundred yards from the intersection with Hilltop Road. The acreages were all about three to five acres and the residences along Timber Ridge Road were all well spaced from each other. There was variable pine tree cover throughout the subdivision.

The acreage of interest had a curved gravel driveway about four hundred feet long. It ended at a paved parking area in front of a one-story house that looked to be about 1500 square feet. Immediately beside it was an oversized garage with a short walkway to the side door into the house. There was quite dense pine tree cover between the house and Timber Ridge Road to the south and it extended for about two hundred feet down the gravel driveway before ending in an open grassy area surrounding the house. It looked like there would be several alternatives to getting the Tactical Team to the house undetected.

7:00 p.m. Friday, March 12, 2021
Briefing Room, FBI Satellite Office, Rapid City, South Dakota

The eight-person Tactical Team had assembled in the briefing room with several of the analysts and other FBI agents. Phil Cooper, John, Denny, and Syd and Nelle joined them. Phil Cooper brought up the aerial photo of the acreage subdivision on one of the large computer monitors, and a map of the Spearfish area on another monitor. He also brought up photos of Ryan Miles, Scott Martin, and Hector Martinez, as well as Kate Beckett and Anna Dupree. He explained that they believed that Ryan Miles also had a female partner who had not been identified yet but who was likely in the house as well. He said that he suspected that Scott Martin and Hector Martinez were probably not in the house, but they could not be sure at this point.

He brought up an enlargement of the acreage of interest on another monitor and there was a discussion about alternatives to breaching the house, subduing the captors, and rescuing Kate and Anna. Once they had decided on a general plan, Denny said, “I would like to be part of the breaching team. I think we should use Syd and Nelle to subdue the captors as we go into the house. They are trained for this and have done it successfully many times. And besides, they need some payback after getting jumped and tranquilized by these guys.”

The Tactical Team leader said he did not have any problems with that. He said that they often use dogs in these types of operations, and it was usually the best way to get to and subdue the suspects as quickly as possible. They had decided to first send a couple of tactical team members close to the house with a high-powered directional microphone to see if they could pick up some conversations from the house before they executed the breach after the captors had hopefully gone to bed for the night. Although they had no way of knowing for sure, they assumed that Kate and Anna were probably being held in one of the basement bedrooms.

10:30 p.m. Friday, March 12, 2021
About Four Miles East of Spearfish, South Dakota

The Tactical Team, as well as John, Denny, and the dogs, and about ten other FBI agents had all made the one-hour drive to Spearfish and had assembled in the local Spearfish police station parking lot. Two of the Tactical Team members had been dropped off at the subdivision with the high-powered directional microphone and were in place about one hundred feet from the back of the house. The microphone was transmitting a conversation from the house which the rest of the FBI team could hear over their communication devices.

A male who they assumed was Ryan Miles said, "Should we finish that movie? Looks like they are asleep downstairs. I wonder why they always sleep together on the same mattress?"

Helen said, "I'm pretty tired but I should be able to stay awake long enough to finish the movie. Did you hear from Scott in Billings?"

"Yeah, he phoned an hour ago while you were in the shower. Nothing happened at the base today. Hector said the F&W trucks were parked for the day and none of the helicopters took off."

"And Los Angeles?" Helen asked.

"I called Lavoy to check in and let him know that everything's good on our end. I wonder how much longer they'll want us here?"

Helen said, "I assume they don't want us staying here much longer. There must be plenty of law enforcement looking for them by now. I think Daniel Lavoy and the client will come up with some other plan to disrupt the operation in a day or two and we can get out of here and let the ladies go back to their lives. Now let's finish this movie so I can go to bed and get some sleep."

After about an hour of mostly TV program conversation, and car chase and gunfire sounds, Ryan and Helen turned off the TV and said good night to each other. After about thirty minutes of silence the two Tactical Team members returned to the access road and got picked up and returned to Spearfish to rejoin the rest of the team.

The surveillance had proved to be highly informative. They now knew that only Ryan and Helen were in the house and that Kate and Anna were in a bedroom in the basement. They also now knew that Scott Martin and

Hector Martinez were in Billings and that the guy calling the shots was named Daniel Lavoy and was in Los Angeles.

2:00 a.m. Saturday, March 13, 2021
About Four Miles East of Spearfish, South Dakota

The eight-person FBI Tactical Team and Denny and the dogs had driven about two hundred feet up the driveway to the house, parked the Tactical Team vehicle behind some trees, and then had walked the rest of the way to the house. Four team members went to the front door. The other four, as well as Denny, Syd, and Nelle went to the side door across from the garage.

Syd and Nelle were outfitted with canine bulletproof vests. They knew the routine, run into the house when Denny gave them the signal after the door was removed, and search for bad guys and take them down until Denny came in and told them to stand down. They had done it many times in all kinds of situations, but the basic routine was always the same. This was their job, and they were good at it. Sometimes the bad guys would try to shoot at them, but they were generally moving too fast and they would almost always miss. A couple of times the bullet went into their vests, but they were able to knock the bad guys over anyways and then Denny was there to help them.

One of the Tactical Team agents put small explosive devices on the door where the hinges were and another one beside the deadbolt. The other team members did the same with the front door. They then set off the explosives at the same time and both doors blew off their hinges. Denny gave Syd and Nelle the "Capture" command and they ran into the house and down the hallway to the bedrooms. At almost the same time, the doors to two bedrooms opened, and Syd and Nelle ran into each bedroom and knocked over the person who had opened the door. They were both holding a gun but did not get a chance to fire any shots before they were on their backs with one of their arms firmly held in the dog's powerful jaws. Denny and the other Tactical Team members were right behind them anyways and Denny told the dogs they could stand down with the "Release" command, which they did immediately.

John had come into the house right behind the Tactical Team and then he and Denny, Syd, and Nelle rushed downstairs and banged on the bedroom door with the lock on it. They yelled, "It is okay, it's John and Denny, we are going to get you out of there."

One of the Tactical Team members came down with a bolt cutter and cut the lock off and John opened the door to find Kate and Anna standing on the other side in tears. John and Denny rushed in and they all had a group hug. Syd and Nelle were jumping up on Kate and Anna and joining in on all the excitement.

With tears streaming down her face, Kate said to John, "You have no idea how glad I am to see you. I was so scared that I may never see you again."

Now holding Kate in a tight embrace, John said. "I know, me too. You are safe now. Your watchers are in custody upstairs. Syd and Nelle took them down."

Kate and Anna looked at Syd and Nelle who were now sitting down looking at their humans who were all together again with what could be interpreted as doggie smiles on their faces. Anna and Kate both kneeled down and hugged the dogs and Anna said, "Thanks, girls, we both knew we could count on you."

Upstairs, Ryan Miles and Helen Riggs were in handcuffs, lying facedown on the living room floor. Kate and Anna came upstairs with John and Denny and the dogs and looked at them lying on the floor. Kate said to John, "They actually treated us quite well and I think they would have let us go eventually."

Looking at them lying on the floor, John said, "Well, I guess we don't have to speculate about that anymore. They will be spending some time in captivity themselves for a while. Why don't we get back to Rapid City and let the FBI finish things up here?"

John introduced Kate and Anna to Phil Cooper and told him they were going back to their hotel in Rapid City and that they would come into the FBI office in the morning to wrap things up and have Kate and Anna give their statements. Phil told them that would be fine, and that an FBI team in Billings had also taken Scott Martin and Hector Martinez into custody at the Country Inn & Suites.

Denny drove the SUV they had borrowed from the FBI back to Rapid City with Anna next to him in the front. John and Kate were snuggled against each other in the back seat. Syd and Nelle were lying down in the back area of the SUV, happy that all their humans were back together again. When they got back to the Hampton Inn & Suites in Rapid City, Anna asked Denny if she could sleep in his room with him and the dogs. John and Kate went to their room and fell into bed still in each other's arms.

10:00 a.m. Saturday, March 13, 2021
Briefing Room, FBI Satellite Office, Rapid City, South Dakota

They were all gathered in the briefing room in the basement of the FBI office with Phil Cooper. Denny had gone out earlier in the morning and picked up breakfast to bring back to the hotel for everyone and they had all eaten together in John and Kate's suite. Denny had even gotten an extra order of bacon for Syd and Nelle, which was a treat because they did not get to eat people food very often. While they were eating, Kate and Anna told John and Denny more about their time in the basement room at the acreage. Although it was not something they would ever want to do again, it could have been a lot worse and they had not been harmed physically in any way, except for the tranquilizer darts. Even so, being forcibly deprived of their freedom, and fearing for their lives was a very unpleasant experience.

Phil Cooper filled them in on what had happened since they had last seen each other the previous night. They had brought Ryan Miles and Helen Riggs back to the FBI office in Rapid City in separate vehicles and put them in separate interrogation rooms. They told them about Scott Martin and Hector Martinez also being in custody in Billings, Montana. As is often done, they offered the first one to cooperate a deal. Helen Riggs was the first one to take them up on their offer in exchange for details about her employer.

An FBI Tactical Team in Los Angeles had raided the offices of World Security Services and the home of Daniel Lavoy at 8:00 a.m. that morning. Unfortunately, Daniel Lavoy was not there. A search of flight records at nearby private airports had turned up a report of a private jet owned by a subsidiary of World Security Services departing at 6:00 a.m., destination unknown. The FBI notified the French authorities, and a similar raid was carried out at the estate of Daniel Lavoy in Marseilles. He was not there either.

However, with the assistance of a very open-ended search warrant from a sympathetic federal judge in Los Angeles, some interesting World Security Services company documents and electronic files were now in the possession of the FBI. In addition, several key Los Angeles employees of World Security Services were now in custody and providing some interesting information about the business dealings of the company. So far, no one seemed to know who the actual client was for the Operation Coyote file.

Phil Cooper had notified his superiors in Washington about the events of the last few hours and they had notified the COVID-21 Task Force. The Operation Coyote team leaders at all the eight bases had been notified and told to resume Operation Coyote activities.

John and the team decided to fly back to Denver and relax for the rest of the weekend and then resume work on Operation Coyote on Monday morning. Larry Greer in the FBI office in Denver informed John that he would be assigning an FBI security detail to John and his team who would fly in a separate plane and accompany them everywhere until the completion of Operation Coyote. Considering the events of the last few days, John did not object.

Cheryl Kaplan, the investigative reporter with the *Denver Post*, had been keeping track of events with Operation Coyote as best she could since her meeting at the Denver FBI office. She had not heard about the abduction of Kate Beckett or Anna Dupree because the FBI had managed to keep it out of the news, but she did get a notification from one of her sources in the Los Angeles FBI media relations office that there had been a raid at the offices of World Security Services.

She didn't immediately connect it to Operation Coyote; however, after doing some web searches about the company, she became suspicious that maybe there was a connection of some sort. She was committed to holding off on publishing the Operation Coyote story until she received the go-ahead from the FBI, but the whole story seemed to be getting better and better.

CHAPTER 14

4:00 p.m. Saturday, March 13, 2021
Vista Mar Marina, Panama City, Panama

Daniel Lavoy had gotten a phone call at 3:00 a.m. from his contact at the FBI office in Los Angeles telling him that she had seen an internal FBI notice that the Rapid City FBI had raided the house in Spearfish, South Dakota, and arrested Ryan Miles and Helen Riggs. There was also a notice that Scott Martin and Hector Martinez had been arrested in Billings, Montana. The notice also said that the FBI in Los Angeles were in the process of getting a warrant to search the offices of World Security Services.

Daniel Lavoy, being a good businessman, had anticipated that this might happen at some point given the type of business he was in, and had made contingency plans to carry on elsewhere. After he finished the call, he woke up his girlfriend, Emilie Portier, and told her to pack a couple of bags because they were leaving in one hour. He then called his trusted second-in-command, Eric Boucher, and told him about the phone call and that he should go to the office and gather the files and documents that had been stored in anticipation of this eventuality, and then meet him at the nearby private airfield where the corporate jet was kept.

He also told him to call their pilot and tell him to get the plane ready to leave in one hour. He then called his executive assistant, Gabrielle Caron, and told her what was going on and that she should gather all the original business and personal files that she kept in the safe in her house and meet them at the airfield. He quickly packed his own bags and opened his safe and emptied the contents into another small suitcase. He and Emilie then left for the airstrip and met the others. The plane left at 6:00 a.m. for the six-hour flight to Tocumen International Airport in Panama City, Panama.

Several years ago, Daniel Lavoy had purchased a three-bedroom penthouse condominium in the exclusive neighbourhood of Coco Del Mar northeast of the old Panama City centre through a Panamanian-registered company with no apparent connection to Daniel Lavoy or World Security Services. The company had also purchased an eighty-foot yacht, the Sunseeker 80, which had three full beam double suites plus additional accommodation for a small crew. The medium-sized luxury yacht was kept at the exclusive Vista Mar Marina located about fifty miles southeast of Panama City.

A married couple, Joseph, and Marie Fillion, originally from Marseilles, were the caretakers of the Panamanian properties. Joseph was also a certified ship's captain, trained in the boatyards of Marseilles, and Marie was a chef, trained at one of the prestigious culinary academies in Paris. Joseph had gotten into some trouble with the French Customs Service for transporting what they said were illegal goods in his charter boat and they had to relocate suddenly to Panama City, with the help of Daniel Lavoy, an old family friend and business associate.

Daniel Lavoy, Emilie Portier, Eric Boucher, Gabrielle Caron, and the Fillions were all on board the Sunseeker 80 yacht moored in its slip at the Vista Mar Marina. They were enjoying a few drinks on the sundeck prior to being served dinner by Maria Fillion and discussing, in French, the events of the last twenty-four hours. They did not know if they would ever be going back to the US but were prepared to continue with their lives in Panama for the time being. Daniel Lavoy had his lawyers in Los Angeles looking into the absurd accusations by the FBI who apparently had not found too much of importance in his office or residence. He had considerable money stashed in several Panama City banks, as well as in several banks in Zurich, Switzerland, and still had his most trusted and valuable employees with him. He also still had his considerable work force spread out in various locations around the world.

Daniel Lavoy reluctantly called his client in Moscow to discuss the recent events concerning Operation Coyote.

After listening to what Daniel Lavoy told him about the happenings in South Dakota and Los Angeles, Igor Larionov said, "Mr. Lavoy, I am disappointed to hear that your plan to disrupt Operation Coyote was not successful. I will have to discuss these events with my superiors. Please wait to hear from me for further instructions. My superiors are considering some less subtle forms of interference with Operation Coyote and we might still have the need for your company to provide the services of people with different more specialized skill sets."

CHAPTER 15

8:00 a.m. Sunday, March 14, 2021
Russian FSB Headquarters, Lubyanka Square, Moscow

The FSB Director, Yuri Solatov, was sitting at the smaller of the two boardroom tables in his office. Sitting across from him again was FSB Agent Igor Larionov.

As he held up a small stack of papers, Yuri Solatov said, "So, Igor what can you tell me about this Operation Coyote situation in the United States? The reports say that the operation you had going with this World Security Services company was shut down by the FBI."

Igor Larionov said, "Yes, the FBI were apparently able to locate the house in South Dakota where the two women were being held, who were part of the team running Operation Coyote, and release them. The World Security Services workers holding them were all arrested as well by the FBI. The owner of World Security Services, Daniel Lavoy, and his key employees were able to flee to Panama City, but he assures me that he is still capable of completing the assignment of disrupting Operation Coyote. He says he will just have to go to Plan B, whatever that turns out to be when we give him the go-ahead to continue."

"So, Igor, do you have any ideas about what Plan B might involve?"

"I think the field portion of Operation Coyote is too far advanced now to bother with, so the next point of attack could be the CDC lab facilities in Fort Collins, Colorado. This could disrupt the ability of the CDC to process the coyote brain specimens and test and develop the new vaccine."

Yuri Solatov said, "Yes, that seems to be the logical next step. Any ideas of how that could be done?"

"I asked some of our science people and they said that the best way would be to contaminate the coyote brain specimens or the CDC lab facilities in some way, or to physically damage the lab facilities and obstruct their ability to test and develop the new vaccine."

"Alright, that sounds like a reasonable approach," Yuri Solatov said. "As long as the trail doesn't come back to Russia. Contact this Daniel Lavoy and tell him to come up with a Plan B. And that whatever happens with Plan B, Russia can not be implicated in any way, or World Security Services could cease to exist."

"Yes, Director Solatov, I will let you know what Mr. Lavoy comes up with for Plan B before we give the go-ahead to proceed."

2:00 a.m. Sunday, March 14, 2021
Vista Mar Marina, Panama City, Panama

Daniel Lavoy woke up at 2:00 a.m. to his private cell phone ringing on the small table beside the bed in the master suite of the Sunseeker 80 yacht. He recognized the phone number on the screen as being from his client in Moscow which was eight hours ahead of Panama City time. He still did not know his client's real name or which Russian agency he worked for, but Daniel assumed that it was for the best. The client's money was deposited on a regular basis into one of Daniel's Swiss bank accounts so that was all that mattered.

The client told him about wanting Daniel to figure out a Plan B for disrupting Operation Coyote involving the CDC facilities in Fort Collins. He told Daniel that he would call him back in twenty-four hours to find out what Daniel had come up with.

5:00 p.m. Sunday, March 14, 2021
Vista Mar Marina, Panama City, Panama

Daniel Lavoy and the other World Security Service's employees on the Sunseeker 80 yacht had spent much of the day discussing Operation Coyote and possible scenarios for a Plan B. Daniel Lavoy also had several other active operations going on in various other countries and he had to make sure everyone knew they were still in business, although he didn't mention where he was or what the exact circumstances were pertaining to the physical corporate operations of World Security Services. Best to keep the circle small at this point.

All the company's financial matters were handled digitally so there was no need to send out "change of address" notifications to his clients or employees. The company already had accountants and lawyers in Panama City so business would carry on with minimal disruption. They also had "friends" in several Panamanian law enforcement agencies so they would likely hear about any US government inquiries into World Security Services. Daniel Lavoy was still always a little surprised about what people would do for a little extra money in their bank accounts every month.

After exploring several possibilities for Plan B, they finally agreed on one that seemed to have the best chance of success. It involved the pilots of the aircraft that were transporting the coolers with the coyote brain specimens from the eight Operation Coyote bases to the CDC facility in Fort Collins daily. At some point in the next few days, there would be what seemed to be a legitimate switch in pilots in one of the planes, and one of the transport coolers would have something added to its contents besides the coyote brain specimen. Once the cooler was transferred to the CDC lab facility, Plan B would be executed.

Daniel Lavoy had been able to find out that three transport planes were being used to get the coyote brain specimens from the operations bases to the CDC lab in Fort Collins daily. One plane serviced the two Canadian bases, another picked up specimens from the bases in Billings, Casper, and Sterling, and a third plane picked up specimens in Dickson, Rapid City, and North Platte. The planes and pilots all belonged to the same private company that supplied additional aircraft support to the FBI on an "as needed" basis in the western US. The company was named Western Flight Services and its head office was in Denver, Colorado.

CHAPTER 16

7:30 a.m. Monday, March 15, 2021
FBI Hotel, Denver, Colorado

John, Kate, Anna, and Denny were all having room service breakfast together in John and Kate's suite. Syd and Nelle were quietly watching them. The dogs had been extra vigilant since they had all returned to Denver from Rapid City. They knew their job was to protect their humans and they felt that they had let them down. At least they had helped capture the bad guys who were hiding Kate and Anna. Syd knew she had bitten the bad man extra hard on the arm before Denny had a chance to give the stand down command. Nelle had done the same with the bad woman.

Domestic dogs are still instinctively pack animals. However, most of them live solitary lives with their owners or maybe in small groups of two or maybe three dogs. Working police or military dogs are trained to bond with their handlers who become the "alpha male" in the pack. They are trained to obey the alpha male no matter what, and to even sacrifice their lives if needed to get the job done. In the case of Syd and Nelle, Denny was the alpha male, and the rest of the team were members of their pack. They had been trained to obey Denny's commands no matter what else was happening around them. If he gave them the signal to lie down and be quiet, they dropped down and remained motionless until he gave them the command to get up. The world could be blowing up around them and they would not move. They instinctively knew that theirs and Denny's lives might literally depend on it.

Their primary job was to pursue and take down or subdue bad people. Sometimes that meant being the first to rush into a building or room and subdue whoever was there. They always assumed whoever they encountered was a bad guy. Generally, Denny and other police or soldiers were right behind them, so Syd and Nelle just had to get to the bad guys and get them on the ground, usually begging for them to stop biting them on the arm or leg.

In the case of poachers, if they were outside, they often tried to get away when they saw Syd and Nelle, wearing their Kevlar dog vests, running full speed at them. Since most poachers were cowards, and not usually well trained, they generally ended up dropping their weapons and curling up on the ground begging for mercy. Often, when Denny arrived at the scene, Syd and Nelle would just be lying on either side of the poacher, growling whenever the poacher moved from his fetal position. Denny would then give them the signal to stand down and tell them what good dogs they were. That was usually enough reward for them, but quite often they got one of the special treats that Denny carried in his pocket.

The team had arrived back in Denver from Rapid City in early morning on Saturday. Since then, they had been mostly relaxing, catching up with the world news, checking in with their families at home, and checking in with the eight Operation Coyote bases. The bases had all shut down for last Thursday and Friday but had been operating over the weekend again. Operation Coyote had been operating for nine days to date and a total of 505 coyote brain specimens had been delivered to the CDC in Fort Collins, still at least thirty-five specimens short of the expected quota. This meant that, given the average daily collection rate, and without any further delays, it would take at least another eight or nine days to get up to the target one thousand coyote brain specimens, if they did not have any further delays. There was also the danger that the longer the operation went on, the higher the chance that another reporter would find out what was really going on and break the story. They didn't want the panic that would cause in the US and everywhere else in the world.

They had been informed by the FBI that the offices of World Security Services in Los Angeles and Marseille had been shut down, but the owner of the company, Daniel Lavoy, had apparently been tipped off about the imminent raid of his offices, and had fled the country with several of his key employees and most of the important company documents and files. No one seemed to know where he had gone but the FBI and CIA were trying to track him down. Somewhere in Central America or the Middle East, in a country that did not have an extradition treaty with the US, seemed to be the best bets. In the meantime, it was assumed that there could still be additional attempts to disrupt Operation Coyote, so vigilance had been increased at all the bases and at the CDC facilities in Fort Collins. It was also assumed that a foreign government was behind the activities of World Security Services, and all evidence pointed to Russia.

While they were eating breakfast, John said, "It's been nice getting some rest and regrouping for the last couple of days. It seems everything is back up and running at the bases so maybe it is best that Kate and I stay here in Denver and try to figure out ways we can ramp up the specimen count. Denny and Anna, what would you like to do for the next few days?"

Denny looked at Anna and then said, "We have been talking about things and if you and Kate are staying in Denver, we think we would just as soon get out in the field again and do some coyote hunting with the dogs. We thought maybe we would get Paul and Lucy to fly us up to Casper and we could work out of the base there for a few days, or until you needed us here again. We could really use the extra coyote specimens, and there is not that much we can do to help in Denver."

Kate and John both nodded and Kate said, "That sounds like a good plan. That part of Wyoming is beautiful, and you can help with the coyote kill count rather than sitting around here getting bored. Syd and Nelle would enjoy it too. Why don't you let Paul and Lucy know that they should go out to the airport and get the plane ready and I'll give one of the team leaders in Casper a call to let them know they should expect you later this morning. We will also call the FBI office here when they are open so they can book your hotel rooms at one of their preferred hotels in Casper. Unfortunately, you will probably have to put up with our FBI protective detail while you are in Casper."

Anna said, "No problem, better safe than sorry. Maybe we will teach them something about coyote hunting and forensic biology while they are with us. We will check in every evening with you to see how things are going. I guess we should get ourselves packed and get out to the airport."

Syd and Nelle sensed that some big decision had just been made that involved them and were very alert when Denny told them to come with him to go back to their room. They were even more exited when they saw Denny start packing his field gear and getting a couple of his gun cases out of the closet. That usually meant the fun was about to start and that their services would be needed sometime soon. Denny made a couple of phones calls and finished packing and then they met Anna, and Paul and Lucy, the pilots, downstairs and they all got into the big SUV with the tinted windows and were driven to the FBI hangar at the airport. Another SUV with tinted windows followed them to the airport and then a man and a woman, Meagan and TJ, their FBI protection detail, who they had met yesterday at the hotel, got in another smaller airplane parked beside the King Air. After everything was loaded into the King Air, they all took off on their next adventure.

Back at the hotel in Denver, John and Kate finished their second cups of coffee and watched the news about the worldwide rollout of the COVID-19 vaccine. There was a big story on CNN about a suspected mutated version of the COVID-19 virus and reports from several countries of a significant increase in people apparently being reinfected with the COVID-19 virus, and a spike in the number of deaths. The news put even more pressure on John and Kate to get Operation Coyote back on track and try to reach their quotas and meet the overall deadline.

The team had all gotten their COVID-19 vaccine shots the day before at the FBI office. At about 10:00 a.m., they walked over to the FBI office to spend the day talking to the team leaders at the eight field bases, and the FBI agents in the office providing support for Operation Coyote. At least the reports from the CDC in Fort Collins were encouraging, and they seemed to be on track with their COVID-21 vaccine development and testing.

8:00 p.m. Monday, March 15, 2021
Vista Mar Marina, Panama City, Panama

Daniel Lavoy had spoken with his client in Moscow again at 2:00 a.m. Panama City time that morning and he told him about the Plan B option that they had settled on and the client agreed that it sounded like it had a good probability of success. He said he needed to check with his superiors and would call him back in a few hours. Igor Larionov called Daniel Lavoy back at 6:00 a.m. Panama City time and told him that he could proceed with Plan B. He also warned him that another failure would probably damage their business relationship, especially if there were any suspected connections to Russia.

Daniel had spent much of the day working out the details of Plan B with Eric Boucher and Gabrielle Caron. They had sent a couple of their senior US employees, Tom Blakely, and Derek Andrews, to Denver to investigate the aviation company Western Flight Services and the pilots working on Operation Coyote. The company was one of the larger private aviation and charter companies working out of the Denver Airport. They had about ten planes of various sizes and about thirty pilots on staff.

Tom and Derek had then driven up to the Northern Colorado Regional Airport south of Fort Collins where the three Operation Coyote transport planes landed every evening with their cargo of coolers containing the day's coyote brain specimens. They had noticed that all the Western Flight Services planes at the Denver hangar had the same logo and colour pattern and were easy to identify. They were parked on a service road at the Fort Collins airport with a clear view of the runway so they would be able to see the three planes as they arrived during the evening. They were particularly interested in observing the procedures for unloading the coolers from the planes and transporting them to the CDC facilities on the campus of Colorado State University.

Tom Blakely and Derek Andrews were both former police officers, Tom with the Houston Police Department, and Derek with the Miami Police Department. As with many of the employees of World Security Services, they had to end their police careers prematurely before they were eligible for their pensions. In both of their cases it was because of alleged issues with payoffs from drug dealers. They were both amateur pilots while working as police officers and had decided to get their commercial pilot licences at the urging of their employer, World Security Services. Daniel Lavoy always found it to be good business to have employees with multiple skill sets.

They knew from Eric Boucher that one of the planes serviced the two Canadian bases at Lethbridge, Alberta and Swift Current, Saskatchewan. Another picked up specimens from the bases in Billings, Montana; Casper, Wyoming; and Sterling, Colorado; and a third plane picked up specimens in Dickson, North Dakota; Rapid City, South Dakota; and North Platte, Nebraska.

The three planes all arrived within about an hour of each other between 9:30 p.m. and 10:30 p.m. There were two Cessna Grand Caravans and one Cessna Denali. The Cessna Grand Caravans were popular commercial, mid-sized, single turboprop aircraft that could be outfitted for passenger service with seating for ten to fourteen passengers, or for freight service, or some combination of both. The Cessna Denali was a faster plane, also a single engine turboprop with a cruising speed of about 330 miles per hour. It could also be outfitted to carry from six to nine passengers, or just freight, or a combination of both. They assumed that the Cessna Denali was being used for the Canadian bases and the two Cessna Grand Caravans were being used for the US bases. Coincidently, Tom Blakely and Derek Andrews had previously both flown these two models of aircraft.

The planes all taxied to the same location along Aviator Avenue, a service road where there were numerous private and small commercial hangars. A Mercedes-Benz Sprinter white cargo van with no markings or logos was parked on the tarmac to the side of Aviator Avenue. As each plane taxied to a stop beside the van, two workers in white coveralls unloaded the coolers from the plane into the van. This was repeated as each of the three planes arrived and then the van left.

The planes then all taxied to a nearby hangar and parked on the tarmac. They noticed that each plane had two pilots. Although Tom and Derek already knew where the van was probably heading, they followed it to the gated entrance of the CDC facilities on the campus of Colorado State University in Fort Collins. They assumed that this was probably the established routine that took place each evening. They then went to their hotel near the airport for the night. They would come back to the airport early the next morning to see when the pilots returned and when the three planes left for the day to start their routine all over again.

CHAPTER 17

7:30 a.m. Tuesday, March 16, 2021
FBI Hotel, Denver, Colorado

John and Kate had spent the previous day at the Denver FBI office and were eating room service breakfast in their hotel suite when John said to Kate, "You are looking a little more relaxed this morning. Are you starting to feel better about your ordeal at the house in Spearfish?"

Kate paused for a few seconds and then said, "The adrenalin rushes and anxiety seem to be finally subsiding, but I still can't stop thinking about what might have happened if you and the FBI hadn't found us so soon. I know we have been in some tight spots before, but we always seemed to be in control of the outcome. This was different, Anna and I were at the complete mercy of our captors. Even though we were not physically harmed, the threat was always there if we did not cooperate and do exactly what they told us to do. Even though we are seasoned law enforcement professionals and have probably witnessed more violence than most people do in our profession, this was personal and very real. I think it might help if I talked to one of the FBI staff psychologists and see if I can get things into perspective. I think Anna should too when they get back to Denver."

John said, "I am sorry that you and Anna had to go through that trauma. I hope you know that I am always here for you as well. I agree that it would probably help to talk to a professional FBI psychologist. They are trained specifically for this type of thing and know the pressures that law enforcement people are under to just suppress the trauma and get on with their jobs. Unfortunately, we have seen the bad results of that kind of thinking too many times."

Kate got up and gave John a big hug and said, "I am happy that you are here with me right now. Let's get ourselves ready now and go to the FBI office. If we can get the specimen numbers up, we will only have a few more days left, and Operation Coyote should be over, and we can go back home."

When they got to the FBI office there was a new testing routine going on. They needed to stand in line and have their temperature taken and were handed a surgical mask that they were required to wear if they wanted to go into the building. When they got to their temporary office on the same floor as Larry Greer, they stopped at his office and asked him what was going on with the new screening procedures and the masks. Larry said, "One of my senior agents just tested positive for the COVID virus again, even though he had already had it last August. We had to send him home, plus all the other agents on his immediate team until their tests came back. It is scary having this thing hitting close to home again. We haven't had to wear masks for months now."

5:00 p.m. Tuesday, March 16, 2021
Casper/Natrona County International Airport, Casper, Wyoming

Denny and Anna had spent the day hunting coyotes out of a blind set up by the F&W Service in a semi-forested hilly area about thirty miles southeast of Casper. They had used a dead mule deer as bait and had managed to kill two coyotes during the day. Their FBI, two-person protection detail, Meagan Fisk and Trevor Jordon (TJ), had come out with them for the day and had parked about one mile away along the access road into the area where the blind was located. They had already spent quite a bit of time with Meagan and TJ since leaving Denver the previous day and were becoming friends. As Canadians and working together for the RCMP and INTERPOL for the last ten years in wildlife trafficking law enforcement, Denny and Anna had lots of good stories to tell. Meagan and TJ had both grown up in big US cities and their law enforcement experience so far had been considerably different.

They were both in their mid-thirties. Meagan had grown up in San Francisco in a good working-class family. She had attended San Francisco State University after high school and gotten a four-year degree in criminology.

She had started taking karate lessons in high school and then competed in tournaments all around California, eventually getting her black belt. While at San Francisco State University she was on the SFU Gators volleyball team. In her senior year in 2008/2009 she was the first-string setter and captain. They had their best year for a long time with a record of 20–11 and went on to win the NCAA Division 2 West Championship. After university she was accepted into the FBI training academy and after completing the training program, was assigned to the Denver Field Office.

Trevor Jordan (TJ) grew up in San Bernardino, an eastern suburb of Los Angeles. His family had emigrated from Trinidad to the US and had done quite well owning a small community sporting goods store. TJ was a star high school basketball player and was recruited by the University of Southern California and offered a full scholarship. At six foot four inches, he was a little short to be a forward, however he became a star first-string point guard with a talent for sinking three-pointers. The NBA scouts were keeping an eye on him, but unfortunately, in his senior and draft year at USC, he tore both the ACL and MCL in his right knee in a huge collision with an opposing player. After that, the scouts lost interest since he would be out of commission for most of the following year. After graduating, also with a degree in criminology, he applied to and was accepted into the FBI training program. After a couple of years working in the Seattle FBI office, he was transferred to Denver.

TJ and Meagan had met about three years ago when they had both been assigned to the FBI detail responsible for protecting witnesses or other victims of criminal activity while investigations were ongoing. They had developed a romantic relationship but tried not to let it interfere with their professional responsibilities. Larry Greer, the Denver FBI special agent in charge, was aware of their relationship, but chose to ignore it if it did not affect their jobs. Sometimes, it even came in handy, such as with their current assignment protecting Denny and Anna in Casper, Wyoming.

They could not get enough of hearing about the crazy things Denny and Anna had done all around the world. Sitting in a blind hunting coyotes seemed quite safe to the two FBI agents, given the usual things Denny and Anna did. They told Meagan and TJ stories about taking down some of the biggest elephant ivory and rhino horn trafficking ringleaders in Africa like "Shetani", which meant "The Devil" in Swahili and a Chinese woman known as the "Queen of Ivory". One of the best stories was about how Anna and Denny had gone undercover in 2018 to help take down the African wildlife trafficking operations of the one of the most notorious Italian Mafia families. That one had almost cost the lives of all of John Benson's team, with only Denny and Anna's skill with their sniper rifles, and the heroics of Syd and Nelle, saving them all in the end. At one point, Meagan jokingly said, "Someone should write a book about all your adventures." Anna replied, "Yeah, maybe some day John will, if he ever decides to retire."

Little did they know that hunting coyotes was just what Denny and Anna needed to be doing right then. Anna was also trying to cope with the trauma of her abduction and confinement. She needed to be in as much open space as possible. She also needed to be doing her job and to be in control of her situation. Denny was being supportive of her as well, just letting her talk though things and tell him about the experience. He had seen too many of his fellow special forces' comrades try to supress the trauma of seeing death and suffering every day. He also had to deal with his own demons after so many years of taking other people's lives, even though they would have done the same to him given the chance.

After each coyote kill, Anna had called Meagan and TJ and told them to come to the F&W truck so they could watch as she did the field biopsy. Being city people, they had never observed a forensic wildlife biologist at work and had no end of questions about wildlife crime scene investigations and how they differed from the crime scene investigations that they were usually involved in. They gained a new appreciation for the importance and complexities of wildlife forensic science.

Denny and Anna decided to spend a few more days in Casper hunting coyotes unless they were needed back in Denver. With a few suggestions from Denny and Anna the teams in Casper had increased their daily coyote kill numbers. Most of the teams at the other bases were also finally increasing their numbers.

9:00 p.m. Tuesday, March 16, 2021
Vista Mar Marina, Panama City, Panama

Daniel Lavoy and his people had spent the day on the yacht taking care of business. Gabrielle Caron had been busy finding out more about the daily operations of Western Flight Services and how their pilots were assigned jobs.

She had called the head office in Denver posing as a potential client from a law firm in Denver that had a large class action lawsuit trial about to start in Phoenix and needed to transport lawyers back and forth between the two cities for several weeks.

She had managed to find out the name of the dispatcher who assigned jobs to their thirty full- and part-time pilots. The dispatcher also kept track of how many hours the pilots had flown in any given week so that they did not violate any aviation regulations. She also had the salesperson she talked to email her the bios of the company pilots who were qualified to fly executive charter flights with mid-sized aircraft like the Cessna Grand Caravan and Cessna Denali, the two most popular aircraft in the company's fleet for transporting client executives.

There were ten pilots on the list who regularly did charter flights using the two Cessna aircraft. The salesperson told Gabrielle that none of the pilots would be available for the next few days because they were all working on another big job. However, she told her that there was going to be a shift change on Friday evening so four of the pilots would be available again after their required two days off. She also told Gabrielle the names of the four pilots who would be available on the upcoming Sunday if Gabrielle needed to book a flight. Gabrielle thanked the salesperson for the information and said she would get back to her after she talked to her boss.

CHAPTER 18

9:00 a.m. Wednesday, March 17, 2021
FBI Field Office, Denver, Colorado

Larry Greer, the Denver FBI special agent in charge, had called John and Kate into his office after they had arrived for the day. He said, "I think we may have caught a break in locating Daniel Lavoy, the owner of World Security Services. The NSA had been checking cell phone calls to the Los Angeles area from likely countries that he may have gone to for the twenty-four-hour period after he left the US in his corporate jet. They came across a couple of phone calls originating from the Tocumen International Airport in Panama City, Panama between 2:00 and 3:00 p.m., the likely time his jet would have arrived.

"The phone calls were traced to a number in Los Angeles which belonged to a woman named Bonnie Moore. The FBI in Los Angeles were notified, and they paid Bonnie Moore a visit and asked her if she had recently been in contact with anyone from Panama City. She said she didn't think so, but her boyfriend, Jason Cassidy, who was a commercial pilot, had called her on Saturday afternoon to let her know that he had to fly his boss and a few other people from the company to another country for a meeting and would be away for a week or so. When asked what company her boyfriend worked for, she said she did not know the company's name, only that it was some sort of big-time security services company. She said her boyfriend did not talk much about his work. She said, 'He seemed to be always on standby, and would often need to fly his boss, Daniel something, somewhere on short notice.' She said she had not heard from her boyfriend again since the call on Saturday.

"Since the FBI in Los Angeles did not know if Daniel Lavoy had any contacts in the Panamanian National Police force, but assumed he probably would, they contacted the INTERPOL Sub-Regional Bureau in San Salvador, El Salvador. They told them what was going on and why they were trying to locate Daniel Lavoy. The INTERPOL people said that they would send a few field agents to Panama City to see what they could find out without alerting the Panamanian police at this point. They also said they would do some digging for any records of corporate transactions in Panama City that may involve World Security Services or Daniel Lavoy. They will give us an update sometime later today."

John said, "Kate and I have worked on assignments in South and Central America on occasion, operating out of both the INTERPOL Regional Bureau in Buenos Aires, Argentina, and the INTERPOL Sud-Regional Bureau in San Salvador. The most recent operation was Operation Cage which was launched in response to the illegal transborder trade of captive-bred and wild birds and eggs, and the involvement of organized crime networks in shipping them from Latin America to Europe. We got to know quite a few of the people in the San Salvador INTERPOL Bureau office. Kate and I both have credentials as INTERPOL field agents, and we would love to be a part of any apprehension operation if they are able to locate Daniel Lavoy in Panama City."

Larry Greer said, "Probably not my call, but if they locate Daniel Lavoy and his people, I assume we will want to have an FBI presence, so I'm sure you could probably tag along. Besides, you two definitely have a personal score to settle with Mr. Daniel Lavoy and whoever his client is."

10:00 a.m. Wednesday, March 17, 2021
Northern Colorado Regional Airport, Fort Collins, Colorado

Tom Blakely and Derek Andrews had arrived back at the airport at about 9:00 a.m. and had parked their rental SUV on a side street with a clear view of the three Western Flight Services' planes tied down to the tarmac in front of one of the hangars with a small sign on the overhead door saying "Property of the Center for Disease Control, Fort Collins, Colorado" with a telephone number to call for assistance.

At about 10:00 a.m. they saw three vehicles pull into the small parking area in front of the hangar, and two people get out of each vehicle and go to the planes. They unfastened the tie-down straps securing the planes to the rings on the tarmac and proceeded to do their standard pre-flight walk-arounds to make sure everything looked okay. A fuel truck then came and pumped aviation fuel into the tanks of each plane. At about 11:00 a.m. the pilots all got into their respective planes and taxied out to the runway and, one-by-one, took off for the day.

No one else seemed to be at the hangar, so Tom and Derek drove their SUV over to the parked vehicle that the two pilots flying the Cessna Denali had arrived in, and Tom quickly used a door lock opening tool to open the front passenger door. He looked in the glove compartment and found the vehicle registration document and took a picture of it. He then put it back in the glove compartment, locked the door again, and they drove back to their hotel. When they got back to the hotel, Tom emailed the picture of the vehicle registration with the name and address of the vehicle owner, Joshua Stewart, to Gabrielle Caron, Daniel Lavoy's executive assistant.

They spent the rest of the day watching movies on TV and ordering food from room service. At 8:30 p.m. they went back to the airport to wait for the arrival of the three planes with the day's batch of coolers. It was pretty much the exact same routine again, and when the pilots had secured their planes for the night, they all got back in their respective vehicles and drove to the same hotel, the nearby Embassy Suites by Hilton Hotel and Conference Centre. Tom Blakely then emailed the name and address of the hotel to Gabrielle Caron. They were all using untraceable burner cell phones but also switched to new phones every day just to be safe.

4:00 p.m. Wednesday, March 17, 2021
FBI Field Office, Denver, Colorado

John and Kate were back in Larry Greer's office at 4:00 p.m. after spending the day monitoring the activities at the eight operations bases. Larry Greer said, "I just got a call from the INTERPOL office in San Salvador. They had been doing searches of databases trying to find any links between World Security Services or Daniel Lavoy and any properties or businesses in Panama. They came across the records of several transactions between Daniel Lavoy's law firm in Los Angeles and a law firm in Panama City. When they checked the public records of real estate transactions filed by the Panama City law firm, they found that a condo had been purchased by a numbered company whose president was listed as Eric Boucher, Daniel Lavoy's second-in-command at World Security Services. A search for other transactions completed by this numbered company, turned up a record of the purchase of a medium-sized luxury yacht, an eighty-foot Sunseeker 80 model.

The INTERPOL field agents checked out the condo, and it appeared that no one was staying there. They are now trying to locate where the yacht might be moored in the Panama City area, but so far have not been able to find it. If Daniel Lavoy and his people are not staying at the condo, it seems likely that they would be staying on the yacht somewhere in the Panama City area. Hopefully, they have not gone on a cruise somewhere along the Central American coastline."

Looking excited, Kate said, "That is great news. At least we have found out where they have gone. Now we just must hope they are cocky enough to be relaxing on their fancy yacht, thinking they got away scot-free."

"Yes, that is what we are hoping," Larry Greer said. "The INTERPOL agent said that they are checking all of the high-end marinas in the Panama City area and will let us know as soon as they locate the yacht."

8:00 p.m. Wednesday, March 17, 2021
Hampton Inn and Suites Hotel, Casper, Wyoming

Denny and Anna were just finishing dinner at the hotel restaurant in Casper with FBI agents Meagan and TJ. They had another productive day coyote hunting and had managed to kill another two coyotes. The F&W had set up another bait and blind location about ten miles from the previous location the day before. They were becoming good friends with Meagan and TJ and they were all enjoying the open spaces and the lack of any other duties to worry about. Syd and Nelle were also enjoying their time with Denny and Anna in the field, although there was not much for them to do except nap in the blind.

Anna and Denny had talked with John and Kate before dinner and had gotten an update about INTERPOL tracking Daniel Lavoy to Panama City. They said that they were waiting to hear if the INTERPOL agents were able to find the location of the yacht he apparently owned there. If they did, and it was confirmed that Daniel Lavoy and his people were still there, John said that he and Kate would try to go to Panama City with the FBI to be there to observe the apprehension by the INTERPOL agents and the Panamanian police. John told them that Operation Coyote was finally back on track and getting closer to wrapping up, and if things continued as scheduled, the one thousand coyote brain specimen goal should be reached on Sunday, March 21st.

John said that Denny and Anna might as well stay in Casper and continue to hunt coyotes for the next couple of days and then plan to return to Denver on Saturday. John said that he and Kate might be heading down to Panama City as soon as Friday if they located Daniel Lavoy there. He said he would let Denny and Anna know as soon as they heard anything.

10:00 a.m. Thursday, March 18, 2021
Northern Colorado Regional Airport, Fort Collins, Colorado

Tom Blakely and Derek Andrews had arrived back at the airport at about 9:30 a.m. and had parked their rental SUV on the same side street again with a clear view of the three Western Flight Services' planes tied down to the tarmac in front of the CDC hangar. At about 10:00 a.m. the same three vehicles arrived back in the small parking lot and the six pilots went through the same pre-flight routines. The three planes took off again for the day around 11:00 a.m.

They went back to their hotel and Tom emailed Gabrielle Caron that the planes had left for the day and that they were back at their hotel. In a few minutes she emailed back that they were to be prepared to take over on Saturday morning for the two pilots who were flying the Cessna Denali aircraft to Canada and back. She told them to continue their surveillance of the pilots and the aircraft to make sure that the routine did not change.

2:00 p.m. Thursday, March 18, 2021
FBI Field Office, Denver, Colorado

Kate and John were spending the day again at the Denver FBI office monitoring the progress of Operation Coyote. Some of the bases had reported that their teams had exceptionally good days with additional coyote kills. Everything was finally on track for reaching the one thousand specimen target by end-of-day Sunday. The CDC in Fort Collins were also on schedule with the COVID-21 vaccine development and testing.

At 2:00 p.m. Larry Greer had gotten a call from the San Salvador INTERPOL Bureau Chief Carlos Sanchez, who told him that their agents had located the World Security Services' yacht moored in a slip in the exclusive Vista Mar Marina located about an hour's drive south of Panama City, in the district of San Carlos, West Panama Province. They had sent a surveillance team to the marina and had observed six people on the yacht. They had emailed several photos to Larry Greer of the yacht taken with a high-powered telephoto lens, as well as photos of the occupants of the yacht, one of which was confirmed to be Daniel Lavoy, based on photos recently confiscated from his home and office in Los Angeles.

The other people identified on the yacht from the photos were Eric Boucher and Gabrielle Caron, both senior employees of World Security Services, and Emilie Portier, apparently the current girlfriend of Daniel Lavoy. There were two other people on the yacht, a man and a woman who so far had not been identified in any of the South or North American INTERPOL databases. However, INTERPOL was expanding the search to include several European databases and were hopeful that their identities would turn up soon.

The report from the INTERPOL field agents said that the Vista Mar Marina was located within the Vista Mar Golf, Beach, and Marina resort complex at kilometre 92 of Highway #1, south of Panama City. The resort was quite large and had an eighteen-hole golf course, numerous types of on-site accommodation including bungalows and condos, plus several restaurants and bistros. The marina had a man-made causeway and L-shaped breakwater, creating a sheltered area with three main docking areas, each designed to accommodate different sized boats. The Pinnacle 80 yacht was moored at the furthest of the three docks, along the inside of the main breakwater and designed to service the larger boats. Larry Greer brought up the latest Google Earth images on the sixty-inch monitor mounted on the wall of his office so they could see the layout of the resort and marina.

Carlos Sanchez called back at 3:00 p.m. and on speakerphone with Larry Greer, John, and Kate said, "Hi, John and Kate. It's good to talk to you again. I guess it's been a couple of years since you were last here in San Salvador working on Operation Cage."

John said, "It's good to talk to you again too. Yeah, I guess it was back in 2018 before we started working on Operation Thunderball in Singapore. I guess Larry Greer has already given you an update about why we are after the occupants of the yacht moored at the Vista Mar Marina south of Panama City and why we need INTERPOL's assistance. Unfortunately, we can not give you all the details about the operation we are working on here in the US, but the owner of the yacht, Daniel Lavoy, was behind the recent abduction of Kate and Anna Dupree, and we believe he is still actively working for a foreign government to interfere in the national security of the US and Canada.

"As you know, the FBI have issued an international warrant for Daniel Lavoy's arrest and extradition back to the US, including anyone with him and employed by his company, World Security Services. We were able to rescue Kate and Anna unharmed, and the FBI raided his home and office in Los Angeles. The French authorities also raided his home and office in Marseilles. Unfortunately, he was tipped off about the raid and fled in his private jet to Panama City. We are grateful for your cooperation and assistance in tracking him down in Panama City."

Carlos Sanchez said, "Yes, Daniel Lavoy and his company World Security Services have also been on INTERPOL's radar for several years now. His company has been involved in quite a few activities in various countries that if not illegal, are certainly very questionable, including the brokering of firearms sales to anti-government rebel groups and supplying mercenary forces to train and fight with anti-government organizations. We think he also has an assassin-for-hire contingent in his company, but so far, we have not been able to prove anything for sure. We know that his company has been hired by various countries not exactly friendly with the US and western Europe to do their dirty work for them. So anyways, INTERPOL would be more than happy to assist the FBI in taking this guy down.

"I have a two-person undercover surveillance team stationed on a boat in the Vista Mar Marina with a good view of Daniel Lavoy's yacht. I also have several agents on a Panamanian National Border Service boat anchored not far from the marina entrance to keep an eye on the yacht in case they decide to leave the marina. We have decided not to involve the Panamanian National Police so far because we think that Daniel Lavoy probably has informants within the police force who would notify him if anything was happening concerning him.

"INTERPOL mostly works with the Panamanian National Border Service and I know I can trust the people who usually assist us with the operations we run in Panama. We have instructed them to keep the surveillance of Daniel Lavoy under wraps for now. Assuming we will be planning for the apprehension of Daniel Lavoy and his people in the next couple of days, we will only be using INTERPOL and National Border Service agents for the operation. I assume the FBI would also be interested in observing the apprehension operation in Panama, and hopefully taking Daniel Lavoy and his people into custody for extradition back to the US."

"Yes, you are right," Larry Greer said. "The FBI would definitely like to be there when Daniel Lavoy and his people are apprehended. John and Kate would also like to be there in their official capacity as INTERPOL field agents. If you think you can be ready on your end, we would like to execute the apprehension Saturday night, around 2:00 a.m. when they are asleep on the yacht. We can fly down to Panama City on an FBI plane early Friday morning and meet up with your agents in the afternoon to finalize the operation for Friday night, or technically Saturday morning, I guess. Does that sound doable for you on your end?"

"Yes, that should be doable on our end. I will work with my INTERPOL people and the National Border Service people to finalize the logistical details of the operation over the next twenty-four hours. The INTERPOL agent in charge of the operation in Panama City will be Lukas Romero. If you let me know when your FBI plane will be arriving at the Tocumen International Airport in Panama City on Friday, I will have Lukas Romero there to meet you and then take you to San Carlos to meet up with the rest of the INTERPOL team. We would also be happy to supply one of our INTERPOL prisoner transfer aircraft to transport Daniel Lavoy and his people back to Los Angeles. Of course, INTERPOL would also welcome the assistance of FBI agents during the transport of the prisoner's back to the US.

"I will contact the office of the director of the Panamanian National Border Service and ask them to authorize the participation of their personnel in the apprehension and extradition process. Through your US Consular Services in Panama, the FBI will need a US federal judge authorized to issue warrants of arrest in extradition cases and present a complaint on oath, as provided by the statutes of the United States.

"The judge will also have to provide a duly authenticated copy of the US warrant of arrest, and of the depositions or other evidence on which the warrant was issued. I'm sure you have all done this numerous times before, but we need to make sure we have all the legal documentation for the extradition in place if we want to avoid any delays in Panama and can immediately transport Mr. Lavoy and his crew back to the US before his Panamanian lawyers have a chance to work the legal system. Once Mr. Lavoy is back on US soil, it will be a done deal."

"Thanks, Carlos," said Larry Greer. "Yes, we have gone through this extradition process before, but we all know that lots of things can go wrong, especially on the short timeline we are operating under. We really appreciate your help, and we will have our FBI legal people start to get things in order immediately. We will arrange for our flight to Panama City on Friday morning and let you know the details as soon as possible."

"Alright then, let's touch base again at the end of the day to see how things are going and we can also talk again on Friday after you get to Panama City."

After the call ended, sounding excited, Kate said, "I can't believe the person responsible for my and Anna's abduction could be in custody in a little over thirty-six hours from now. We should call Denny and Anna and let them know what is happening."

6:00 p.m. Thursday, March 18, 2021
Hampton Inn and Suites Hotel, Casper, Wyoming

Denny and Anna had returned to the hotel in Casper after another successful day of coyote hunting in the same general area they had been for the previous two days. They had both showered, and Denny had fed Syd and Nelle, and they were in Denny's suite talking about the phone call they had just received from John and Kate. They had told Denny and Anna about the recent developments in Panama City and that they would be flying there early the next morning with the FBI. They had also decided that Denny and Anna would spend two more days in Casper and then fly back to Denver on Saturday afternoon in case anything needed to be done with Operation Coyote over the weekend while John and Kate were in Panama City.

Anna said, "Wow, that was really good news. I wish we could be there too when they arrest Daniel Lavoy, but I understand that we need to stay here to take care of things with Operation Coyote. Just a few more days now and we should all be able to go back home."

"Yeah, I know. It would be great to be in Panama City to watch the takedown," said Denny. "Anyways, let's go to dinner and we can talk about it some more."

CHAPTER 19

10:00 a.m. Friday, March 19, 2021
Northern Colorado Regional Airport, Fort Collins, Colorado

Tom Blakely and Derek Andrews had arrived at the airport at about 9:30 a.m., as they had been doing for the last three days and had parked their rental SUV on the same side street again. At about 10:00 a.m. the same three vehicles arrived back in the small parking lot and the same six pilots went through the same pre-flight routines. The three planes took off again for the day around 11:00 a.m.

As they had done the last three days, they went back to their hotel and Tom emailed Gabrielle Caron again that the planes had left for the day and that they were back at their hotel. In a few minutes, she emailed back that the plan for them to take over on Saturday morning for the two pilots who were flying the Cessna Denali aircraft to Canada and back was being finalized and that they should stand by for further instructions.

She also emailed that they should expect that a contractor who sometimes did very specialized projects for World Security Services, would be delivering a package to them in a carry-on bag on Saturday morning at their hotel before they left for the airport. They were to take the carry-on bag with them on the plane and put the package into one of the coolers they would be picking up on Saturday at one of the two Canadian Operation Coyote bases. She said they did not need to know what was in the package, but that they should handle it very carefully.

Gabrielle Caron had previously managed to find out the name of the Western Aviation Services dispatcher, Erin Wells, who assigned jobs to the pilots. The dispatcher also kept track of how many hours the pilots had flown in any given week. Tom and Derek had found out the name of one of the Cessna Denali pilots, Joshua Stewart, and that he and the other pilots were staying at the Embassy Suites by Hilton Hotel and Conference Centre near the airport. With that information, Gabrielle had managed to find out that the name of the other Cessna Denali pilot was Jay West. She intended on texting Joshua Stewart on his cell phone at the hotel on Friday evening when they had returned from their day of flying, posing as the dispatcher, Erin Wells.

The content of the text would be that he and Jay West were going to be assigned to another flying job for another client starting later Monday morning. However, to keep their weekly flying hours within the regulations, they would need to take Saturday off and just hang out at the hotel. They could fly the Cessna again on Sunday before coming back to Denver for the new job starting later Monday morning. The text would also say that she had assigned two of the company's new part-time pilots to fly the Cessna Denali on Saturday to the two Canadian bases and back to Fort Collins. The two new pilots had been told to just go to the CDC hangar at the Fort Collins Airport on Saturday morning at 9:30 a.m. as usual and meet the other four pilots and then fly the Cessna Denali for the day.

7:00 a.m. Friday, March 19, 2021
Denver International Airport, Denver, Colorado

John, Kate, Larry Greer, and the head of the Denver FBI office's tactical assault team, Tim Sullivan, and his second-in-command, Adam Donahue, had boarded the FBI's Cessna Citation CJ3 corporate jet at 7:00 a.m. at the Denver Airport for the six-hour flight to Panama City, which was one hour ahead of Denver time, so the estimated arrival time at the Tocumen International Airport was about 2:00 p.m. Panama time. The plan was that Tim Sullivan and Adam Donahue would participate in the apprehension of Daniel Lavoy and his crew on the yacht, and then accompany the INTERPOL agents on INTERPOL's prisoner transport aircraft to return them back to Los Angeles.

The Cessna Citation had seating for seven passengers, so the flight was quite comfortable and there was a good supply of coffee, beverages, sandwiches, and snacks provided by the FBI aviation services.

During the flight they discussed the plan for later in the evening to apprehend Daniel Lavoy and his people on the yacht. INTERPOL had identified the other two people photographed on the yacht using a French facial recognition database as Joseph and Marie Fillion. They were French citizens who were wanted by French authorities on charges of smuggling firearms from Marseilles to various North African countries.

It was thought they had been affiliated with World Security Services in Marseilles but had disappeared while they were on bail awaiting trial in France. They had obviously ended up in Panama City working for Daniel Lavoy and probably taking care of his interests there. People at the INTERPOL headquarters in Lyon, France, were currently planning to have them extradited back to France from Panama, assuming they were apprehended on the yacht as well.

The INTERPOL agent in charge of the operation in Panama City, Lukas Romero, had emailed them an outline of the plan he and the Panamanian National Border Service agents had put together for boarding the yacht. Several teams would converge on the yacht simultaneously at 2:00 a.m. when hopefully the occupants would all be asleep, or at least in their suites or cabins. One team would come into the marina by boat to block any attempt for them to start up the yacht and try to leave the marina. Another team would come by vehicle down the causeway and then onto the dock where the yacht was moored. A third team would approach the yacht from the water in a Zodiac-type boat. A total of eighteen agents would be involved in the operation. They hoped to overwhelm the occupants of the yacht before they had any time to react or get to any weapons that they might have on board. It seemed like a solid plan.

The Cessna Citation touched down at the Tocumen International Airport at 2:20 p.m. Panama City time. The FBI pilot taxied the plane over to an unmarked hangar apparently owned by the Panamanian National Border Service. As they approached the hangar the large overhead doors opened, and a ground crew person directed the plane to a spot inside the hanger.

The pilot shut down the engines and the overhead doors closed again. The co-pilot opened the door of the Cessna and a stairway was rolled up to the aircraft by one of the workers in the hangar. Everyone got up and proceeded out the door and down the stairs. They were met by Lukas Romero, the INTERPOL agent in charge, and his driver, Miguel Flores, another INTERPOL agent on the team. There was also a senior agent of the Panamanian National Border Service, Roberto Cruz, who was the leader of the Border Service team members. Everyone introduced themselves and Lukas said they could all go to the meeting room in the hangar where they could relax for a while and go over the plan for later that night.

4:00 p.m. Friday, March 19, 2021
Sunseeker 80 Yacht, Vista Mar Marina, San Carlos, Panama

Daniel Lavoy had spent the last two days on the yacht talking to, texting, and emailing his numerous employees in various countries, primarily in Europe and the Middle East. He had also been speaking with his lawyers in Los Angeles and Marseilles to get updates on the status of the investigation into World Security Services by the US and French authorities. As far as the lawyers knew, there was not too much happening with the investigation, and the FBI were still reviewing the documents and files that they had confiscated from his office in Los Angeles. However, they all knew that the documents and files that had been left behind in the offices in Los Angeles and Marseilles, were not of much importance, and that all the critical company documents and files had been taken with them to Panama City, and were safely stored in the condo in Coco Del Mar. The lawyers also said that there did not seem to be any "red flags" indicating that the FBI had any idea that Daniel Lavoy was currently in Panama City.

Daniel Lavoy and Gabrielle Caron had worked out the plan to substitute Tom Blakely and Derek Andrews on Saturday as the pilots of the Cessna Denali aircraft being used to transport the coyote brain specimen coolers daily from the two Canadian Operation Coyote bases. They had contacted an explosives expert, Edward Plummer, who had worked for World Security Services on numerous occasions in the past to prepare a compact, but powerful explosive device that could fit into one of the coyote brain specimen transport coolers. The device was to be detonated remotely using a cell phone.

Edward Plummer had been watching the activities at the CDC facilities in Fort Collins for the past several days. He had managed to "borrow" a facility access swipe card from one of the maintenance workers while they were on lunch break and had done a little tour of the interior of the loading dock area. He noticed that two workers in white coveralls were using a golf cart-type of vehicle to transport six travel coolers at a time from a large walk-in freezer located just inside the loading dock, down a hallway to another area of the facility. When the door to the walk-in freezer was open, he noticed that there was what looked like several hundred travel coolers stored on shelves. He assumed that when the van that was transporting the travel coolers from the airport every evening arrived at the CDC facility, the coolers were just taken into the walk-in freezer and put on the shelves until they were to be transported to another area in the facility. The detonation of an explosive device within the confines of the walk-in freezer would likely either destroy or contaminate the contents of all the coolers stored there.

Daniel Lavoy also had several conversations over the past few days with his client in Moscow. He had updated the client about how Plan B was progressing, and his client seemed to be satisfied that they were on the right track.

5:00 p.m. Friday, March 19, 2021
Hampton Inn and Suites Hotel, Casper, Wyoming

Denny and Anna had returned to the hotel in Casper after another successful day of coyote hunting. They had both showered, Denny had fed Syd and Nelle, and they were relaxing in Denny's hotel suite watching the daily news on TV before going down for dinner with FBI agents Meagan and TJ. They had decided to spend Saturday doing one final day of coyote hunting before flying back to Denver on the King Air in the evening. They had gotten a text from Kate earlier saying that she and John had arrived in Panama City with the FBI agents and were meeting with the INTERPOL and Panamanian National Border Service agents in a Border Service hanger at the airport. She said they were all going over and finalizing the plans for apprehending Daniel Lavoy and his people on the yacht later that night.

Anna said, “It looks like everything should be over with Operation Coyote in couple of days now. We might even have extra specimens if the teams keep up the kill rates that they have been getting the last few days. I hope things go alright down in Panama City tonight. It seems that they have a good plan and have all the bases covered.”

As he was scratching the top of Nelle’s head Denny said, “I hope so too. I wish we were all there together, but John said that they would text us as soon as they had Daniel Lavoy and his people in custody. They should probably be back in Denver later in the day on Saturday sometime so we will see them then and they can give us the play-by-play of how it all went down.”

CHAPTER 20

2:00 a.m. Saturday, March 20, 2021
Vista Mar Golf, Beach, and Marina Resort, San Carlos, Panama

John and Kate had spent the rest of afternoon and into the evening at the Panamanian National Border Service hangar at the airport with the FBI agents and some of the INTERPOL and Border Service agents. Food had been delivered to the hangar for dinner and they had finalized the last-minute details of the upcoming operation. At about 9:00 p.m. they all left the hangar in several unmarked SUVs for the two-hour drive south on Highway 1 to San Carlos and the Vista Mar Golf, Beach, and Marina Resort. At about 11:00 p.m. they stopped in the then deserted parking lot of the local Retroxvolq Shopping Mall, which was located just off the highway about one mile north of the main entrance into the Vista Mar Resort.

The six assault team members with the Zodiac boat had gone to a public boat launch located about one-and-a-quarter miles north of the marina in the Boca De Teta residential neighbourhood. The Panamanian National Border Service assault boat with the six agents on board was also standing by close to the Vista Mar Marina entrance.

Lukas Romero, the INTERPOL agent in charge, Miguel Flores, Roberto Cruz, the senior agent with the Panamanian National Border Service, and the two FBI tactical team members, Tim Sullivan and Adam Donahue, and one other INTERPOL agent were in one of the extended SUVs in the shopping mall parking lot. In a second extended SUV were two other INTERPOL agents, one of whom was the driver, plus John, Kate, and Larry Greer. They were all waiting until they had heard on the two-way radio from the team in the Zodiac that they were launched and proceeding to the Vista Mar Marina entrance. A Panamanian National Border Service prisoner transport van had stopped a couple of miles further north along the highway at a service station and was waiting until they heard that Daniel Lavoy and his people were in custody before they proceeded into the Vista Mar Resort.

At 1:30 a.m. they heard from both the Zodiac crew and the assault boat crew that they were in place outside the entrance to the marina. The two SUVs then proceeded to the main gated entrance to the Vista Mar Resort and had the security guard open the gate for them. They then had one of the INTERPOL agents stay with the security guard at the small entrance building so he would not alert Daniel Lavoy on the yacht about the SUVs coming onto the resort property.

They drove down Vista Mar Boulevard, the main access road into the resort, for about one and half miles until they got to the entrance to the marina. They had taken a swipe card for the lock on the marina gate from the security guard at the main entrance and opened the gate so the SUVs could drive through and down to the beginning of the far dock where the Sunseeker 80 yacht was moored. It was now 2:00 a.m. and everything was noticeably quiet in the marina. All the agents from the SUVs assembled on the dock and got their weapons ready. Lukas Romero radioed the agents in the Zodiac and the boat that they were ready to go. In a couple of minutes John and Kate heard the Zodiac outboard and the assault boat engines coming through the entrance of the marina. John, Kate, and Larry Greer had agreed to hold back at the SUVs until the operation was over and the occupants were all subdued and in custody.

The go order was given, and the INTERPOL, Border Service, and FBI agents moved down the dock and over the gangway going onto the yacht. At the same time, the assault boat pulled up immediately alongside the yacht and the Zodiac pulled up along the stern and the agents boarded the yacht as well. John and Kate heard some bangs and shouting coming from the yacht as the doors to the cabins were kicked open and people were ordered out of bed and then handcuffed. After a couple of minutes, it was all over, and Lukas Romero came up on deck and waved to Kate, John, and Larry that it was alright to come over to the yacht.

As they were walking to the yacht from where the SUVs were parked, they saw that the agents from the Zodiac were all getting back into the boat, and that three men and three women, all in handcuffs, and all in shorts and T-shirts, were each being escorted by an agent over the gangplank and onto the dock. Once on the dock they were each helped down onto their knees and told not to move.

As Kate and John walked up to the group of six all kneeling in a line on the dock, Lukas Romero came up to them and said, "I think there is someone here you would like to meet." He directed them over to the first man in the line of kneeling captives and said, "Dr. John Benson and Dr. Kate Beckett, I would like you to meet Mr. Daniel Lavoy."

Daniel Lavoy, who was looking forlornly down at the dock, suddenly jerked his head up as he heard the names of John and Kate, and looked at them and said, "What the hell. How did you find us down here?"

Looking directly down at Daniel Lavoy in handcuffs and kneeling on the dock, John said, "I would like to introduce Dr. Kate Beckett to you, one of the two the women you had abducted in South Dakota, and held captive in a basement bedroom, and then threatened to kill if we didn't do what you wanted."

With a slightly sarcastic-looking smile, Kate said, "Hello, Mr. Lavoy, it is really a pleasure to meet you in person." She then walked up to him and kicked him in the testicles as hard as she could.

As he fell on his side groaning in pain, Lukas Romero came over to him and helped him up again onto his knees and said, "Please be more careful stepping down onto the dock, Mr. Lavoy, you could really hurt yourself. Fortunately, it looks like you only fell on your testicles this time and you do not seem to have any other injuries."

As they were walking back down the dock to the SUVs, John and Kate looked at each other and smiled, and John said, "Remind me to never piss you off in the future. I think Mr. Lavoy will remember meeting you for quite some time."

Laughing, Kate said, "I would never kick you in the balls, maybe just break one of your arms so you could still perform your manly duties."

Smiling, John said, "Good to know."

As they arrived back at the SUV, the Panamanian National Border Service prisoner transport van pulled up and the six prisoners were escorted into the van by the Border Service agents. Several INTERPOL and Border Service agents with forensic crime scene analysis training stayed behind on the boat to confiscate all the documents, computers, firearms, cash, and anything else of interest, and then transport it all back to the airport hangar. Kate, John, Larry Greer, and the rest of the agents all got back in the SUVs for the two-hour drive back to the airport. Lukas Romero informed them that another team of agents had raided the penthouse condo in Coco Del Mar, and although there was no one there, they found numerous boxes that looked to contain some interesting documents. The boxes were also all being brought back to the hangar.

Since it was about 3:30 a.m. at this point, and no one had gotten any sleep that night so far, most people napped in the SUVs on the two-hour drive back to the Border Service hangar at the airport. When they got there at around 6:00 a.m., there was coffee and breakfast waiting for them in the big meeting room. All the vehicles parked inside the hangar, including the prisoner transport van. The prisoners were escorted one-by-one to the bathroom, and then were returned to the van under guard, to wait for the arrival of the INTERPOL prisoner transport plane to return four of them back to the US. In the bathroom, they were made to change into orange prisoner coveralls and were given prisoner slippers to wear on their feet.

Joseph and Marie Fillion were to be extradited back to France to face the charges still pending against them there. Both the yacht and the corporate jet, as well as the penthouse condo would be seized by the Panamanian National Border Service and eventually sold to help fund their work.

As they were sitting in the meeting room finishing breakfast and exchanging INTERPOL war stories, Lukas Romero came over to John, Kate, and Larry and said, "One of the agents in the prisoner transport van who also speaks French said he overheard Daniel Lavoy say to one of the women in French, 'At least it looks like they don't know about Plan B.' The agent said he told them to be quiet after that, so they did not say anything else."

John said thanks for the heads-up and then said to Kate and Larry Greer, "Maybe we shouldn't be celebrating too soon. It sounds like they probably still have something else in the works. We better try to figure out what Plan B might be. I'll give Denny and Anna a call to let them know what is going on."

Larry Greer said, "I'll give my people in Denver a call as well to let them know that there could be a Plan B about to happen to try to obstruct the completion of Operation Coyote."

At about 8:00 a.m. the INTERPOL prisoner transport plane arrived and taxied into the hangar. Daniel Lavoy, Emilie Portier, Eric Boucher, and Gabrielle Caron were taken from the van and escorted into the prisoner transport plane. Four INTERPOL agents, plus Tim Sullivan and Adam Donahue, the two Denver FBI tactical team members, also boarded the plane for the flight to Los Angeles. All the materials confiscated from the boat and the condo had also been loaded onto the plane. Kate and John noticed that Daniel Lavoy was moving very slowly with his legs slightly apart and with a pained look on his face. As he glanced back at them while he was making his way slowly up the stairs into the plane, they both smiled and gave him a sarcastic little wave.

The plane taxied back out of the hangar and proceeded to the runway, and after about fifteen minutes was given clearance by the control tower for takeoff. Everyone breathed a sigh of relief when the plane was in the air before there had been any chance of interference from Panamanian government officials. The FBI agents had all the required extradition paperwork on board so hopefully they would not have any trouble at the Los Angeles end. Joseph and Marie Fillion were to be held at the hangar for a few more hours while a flight back to France on another INTERPOL plane was arranged.

Since things were under control in Panama City, John, Kate, and Larry said their goodbyes with heartfelt expressions of thanks to the INTERPOL and Panamanian Border Service agents and boarded the FBI Cessna Citation CJ3 for their own six-hour flight back to Denver.

11:00 a.m. Saturday, March 20, 2021
Northern Colorado Regional Airport, Fort Collins, Colorado

Tom Blakely and Derek Andrews had arrived at the airport at about 10:10 a.m. and had parked their rental SUV beside the other two vehicles in the parking lot of the CDC hangar. The went out to where the three Western

Flight Services' planes were tied down on the tarmac. The other four pilots had arrived just before them and Tom and Derek introduced themselves and told them that they had just driven up from Denver so that they could replace the two Cessna Denali pilots for the day. The other four pilots said that they had already heard that they were coming from Jay West. They all then proceeded to do their pre-flight checks and waited as the aviation fuel truck came over and filled up the tanks of the three planes.

Tom Blakely and Derek Andrews had met Edward Plummer in the parking lot at their hotel just before they left for the airport. As they had been told, Edward Plummer had given them a medium-sized carry-on travel bag to take with them. He told them that after they had picked up the coolers from the bases in Canada, they were to take the package out of the travel bag and put it into one of the coolers. He told them that although they should handle the package very carefully, it was quite safe to have it in the plane with them.

After the fuel truck was finished, the six pilots got into their respective aircraft and one-by-one, taxied to the runway, and took off for the day. Tom and Derek were pleased that the plan had gone off without a hitch so far. They did not anticipate any other problems during the rest of the day. When they returned with the coolers later that evening, they would just taxi to the spot where the CDC cargo van was always parked and the coolers would all be unloaded from the plane into the van, including the one containing the package from Edward Plummer. They would then taxi back over to the CDC hangar and secure the plane for the night. After that they would disappear from the Fort Collins area.

1:00 p.m. Saturday, March 20, 2021
INTERPOL Prisoner Transport Plane Somewhere Over Northern Mexico

The INTERPOL Bombardier Challenger 650 prisoner transport plane was somewhere over northern Mexico, about one and a half hours from Los Angeles. The Challenger 650 had been in the INTERPOL fleet for about six years and was used for several types of jobs but was one of the primary aircraft used to transport prisoners or detainees to destinations around the world. It would normally have seating for up to nineteen passengers, but the seating capacity had been reduced to a maximum of fourteen to provide extra space for the detainees and the INTERPOL agents accompanying them. The seats that the detainees sat in had a heavy chain with a metal ring on the end attached to the floor in front of the seat. The handcuffs that the detainees were wearing were attached to the metal ring.

The mood on the plane was very subdued and any discussion between the detainees was forbidden. The four INTERPOL agents and the two FBI agents talked among themselves a little, but the flight was generally quiet. When Daniel Lavoy had asked to go to the bathroom, one of the INTERPOL agents unlocked his handcuffs from the metal ring and took him to the bathroom. The door to the bathroom was left open while he did his business.

While Daniel Lavoy was in the bathroom, Emilie Portier, Daniel Lavoy's girlfriend, leaned over to the female INTERPOL agent sitting across the aisle from her and whispered, "I have important information about Operation Coyote, but I want to talk to a prosecutor as soon as we land in Los Angeles."

The agent got a small notebook out of her bag and wrote on a page, "What kind of information."

She then passed the notebook and pen over to Emilie Portier and watched her write a few sentences, and then Emilie passed the notebook back to the agent. She had written, "There is still another serious plan in play for disrupting Operation Coyote and I know what it is. But I am just Daniel's girlfriend and have nothing to do with his business. I want some sort of deal before I tell you what the plan is and how to stop it."

The INTERPOL agent, Gina Ramos, got up and took the notebook over to where Tim Sullivan was sitting at the back of the plane and showed it to him. He read what Emilie had written and then on another page wrote, "Alright, we will have a federal prosecutor ready to talk to you at the FBI office in Los Angeles as soon as we get there after we land. If the information you give us is important, we can probably make some sort of deal with you." Agent Ramos then took the notebook back to her seat and passed it across the aisle to Emilie. After Emilie read what Tim Sullivan had written, she looked across the aisle at Agent Ramos and nodded.

After Tim Sullivan had observed the interaction between Emilie Portier and Agent Ramos, he got up from his seat and went to the front of the plane, knocked on the door, and went into the cockpit area behind the two pilots.

He then used the pilot's secure telephone in the cockpit to call the special agent in charge at the FBI office in Los Angeles to let her know what was going on. She said that she would have a federal prosecutor there at the FBI office when they arrived from the airport. He also told her to contact the pilot of the FBI Cessna Citation CJ3 and let Larry Greer, John Benson, and Kate Beckett know what was happening.

2:00 p.m. Saturday, March 20, 2021
FBI Cessna Citation Plane Somewhere Over West Texas

The co-pilot of the Cessna Citation had come back into the cabin area and told Larry Greer that there was a telephone call for him from the special agent in charge of the Los Angeles FBI office. Larry had gone up to the cockpit area to take the call and then after about five minutes had come back to where John and Kate were sitting. He said, "I just finished talking to Susan Denison, the special agent in charge of the Los Angeles FBI Field Office. She said that she had received a call from Tim Sullivan on the INTERPOL prisoner transport plane that Emilie Portier, Daniel Lavoy's girlfriend, apparently had information about an imminent plan that was still in play to disrupt Operation Coyote. However, she wanted to talk to a federal prosecutor about a deal before she would tell anyone about the plan and how to stop it. Susan Denison said that she had lined up a prosecutor who could talk to Emilie Portier when their plane landed, and they arrived at the LA FBI office."

John said, "I guess we shouldn't have started celebrating so soon. How long before they can start talking to her?"

"The INTERPOL prisoner transport plane is scheduled to land at the LAX airport at 2:30 p.m. LA time and then it will take about an hour to drive them from the FBI hangar to the FBI office. By the time the prosecutor talks to her, and assuming they can work out some sort of deal, it could be 4:30 or 5:00 p.m. before we find out what the alleged plan is about. By that time, we should be back at the office in Denver."

John said, "I think I will give Denny and Anna a call to see if they have heard about anything suspicious or out of the ordinary going on at any of the bases."

3:00 p.m. Saturday, March 20, 2021
Hampton Inn and Suites Hotel, Casper, Wyoming

Denny and Anna were back at the hotel picking up their luggage and other gear after a short day of coyote hunting and were getting ready to drive to the Casper Airport to meet the King Air which had flown in from Denver to pick them up, when he noticed a call coming in on his cell phone from John. He said, "Hi, John. We were just getting ready to leave for the airport. What's up?"

John told him the story about Emilie Portier and alleged plan to disrupt Operation Coyote and then said, "We probably won't know what is going on for a couple of hours so instead of coming back to Denver, maybe you should go to Fort Collins instead and wait for the transport planes to come back this evening, so we have that location covered. Kate and I will be back in Denver soon so we can keep an eye on things from there."

"That sounds like a good plan, John," Denny said. "We will fly to Fort Collins instead and wait around until the transport planes come in and make sure that the transfer of the coolers from the three planes to the CDC transport van goes okay, and that the van gets to the CDC alright. Maybe you should get Larry Greer to send a couple of FBI agents to the airport in Fort Collins from Denver to give us a hand in case something happens."

John said, "That sounds like a good idea, Denny, I will let Larry know and we will give you another call when we get to the FBI office in Denver."

5:30 p.m. Saturday, March 20, 2021
FBI Field Office, Los Angeles, California

The INTERPOL prisoner transport plane had landed at the Los Angeles International Airport (LAX) at about 3:00 p.m. and had then taxied over to the FBI hangar. There was a permanent FBI satellite office located at LAX and there was a prisoner transport van waiting for them at the hangar. Tim Sullivan and Adam Donahue, plus two more FBI agents from the Los Angeles FBI LAX satellite office escorted the detainees from the plane into the van. The four INTERPOL agents, after a brief stop at the FBI hangar, got back on the INTERPOL Bombardier Challenger 650 prisoner transport plane for their return flight to Panama City.

The traffic on the 405 San Diego Freeway was like a parking lot as usual so it took them almost an hour to get to the FBI main office in the Federal Building on Wilshire Boulevard from the airport. Once they finally arrived at the FBI office, Daniel Lavoy, Eric Boucher, and Gabrielle Caron were taken to separate holding cells. Emilie Portier was taken to an interview room where Special Agent in Charge Susan Denison, and Federal Prosecutor Marcus Solomon, were waiting. Tim Sullivan brought Emilie Portier into the interview room and got her seated in a chair at a table opposite from Susan Denison and Marcus Solomon. He and Adam Donahue then went into the adjoining room so they could observe the proceedings through the one-way glass.

Susan Dennison just sat looking at Emilie Portier for a few minutes and then said, "Ms. Portier, I am Susan Denison, the FBI special agent in charge of the Los Angeles FBI Office, and this is Federal Prosecutor Marcus Solomon. I now must inform you that this conversation is being recorded by that camera located on the wall behind me. I must also inform you that you have the right to have a lawyer here with you. Please state your full name and that you understand what I have just told you, and that you are voluntarily agreeing to talk to us without being represented by a lawyer at this time."

Looking nervous and scared, Emilie Portier said, "My name is Emilie Portier and I understand this conversation is being recorded and that I have the right to have a lawyer present, but I am agreeing to talk to you without a lawyer."

"Before we get started, Ms. Portier, do you mind if I address you as Emilie?" Marcus Solomon asked. After Emilie nodded yes, he continued, "Emilie, what is your relationship with Mr. Daniel Lavoy?"

"I am Daniel's girlfriend. We have been together since 2017 when I moved to the US from Paris to live with him in his house in Los Angeles. We met through my father in Marseilles who owns a small shipping company that did business with Daniel's company sometimes. I was a fashion model in France and living in Paris, but I was visiting my parents in Marseilles over the Christmas holidays in 2015 when I met Daniel at a dinner party. We started dating and I eventually moved to Los Angeles in January 2017 so we could be together."

"Emilie, what connection do you have to Daniel Lavoy's company, World Security Services?" Marcus Solomon asked. "I have to remind you here that it is extremely important that you be completely truthful in your answer to this question because it will determine how we move forward with this discussion."

Sitting up a little straighter and looking somewhat defiant, Emilie said, "I am not now, nor have I ever been an employee of World Security Services. I know in general terms some of the types of things that the company does, but I am not directly involved in any of Daniel's business activities. He prefers that I do not come into his World Security Services office unless it is for some sort of social function. I hear him talking on the phone sometimes at home, but he usually goes into his office in the house when he is talking about business things.

"When I was on the company plane flying down to Panama City from Los Angeles and while we were all on the yacht, I heard Daniel, Eric Boucher, and Gabrielle Caron talking about lots of things but also about something called Operation Coyote. I also heard them talking on the plane about those two women who were abducted by his people and that they had been found and rescued by the FBI and that his people had been arrested. I also heard them talking on the yacht in Panama City about a Plan B for disrupting something called Operation Coyote."

Smiling slightly, Marcus Solomon said, "Thanks, Emilie, I just want to let you know what is in store now for Daniel Lavoy, as the owner of World Security Services, and for Eric Boucher and Gabrielle Caron, as his most trusted and senior employees. They are about to charged with multiple felonies including for starters, the assault and kidnapping of a US Federal Agent and a Canadian member of the RCMP. We have also confiscated all the company documents, files, and computers we found on the yacht and in the condo in Panama City. This is in addition to all the documents and files we had already confiscated in his Los Angeles and Marseilles offices and residences. We are also in the process of locating and freezing all the company's and his personal bank accounts. So, you see, Emilie, your boyfriend is likely to be spending the rest of his life in a federal prison.

"INTERPOL is also extremely interested in his business activities and will likely also be charging him with numerous offenses, quite possibly including international war crimes for selling arms to known terrorist groups. We are not too interested in charging and prosecuting you since you do not seem to have been directly involved in Mr. Lavoy's business dealings. However, since you had considerable knowledge of what he had been involved in, and chose not to tell any law enforcement agencies, we could charge you with numerous criminal offenses if we chose to.

"So, here is the deal. If you tell us everything you know about this Plan B involving Operation Coyote, and if it turns out to be true, and you also agree to testify against Daniel Lavoy, Eric Boucher, and Gabrielle Caron if we need you to, we will give you immunity on all charges. However, in due course, you will be deported back to France when you are no longer required to be present here in the US. I have a short legal document here that you can sign if you agree to these terms."

Emilie read through the one-page document and then said, "Okay, I agree to your terms and I will sign the document. Do you have a pen?"

Marcus Solomon handed her his pen, and she signed her name. He then said, "Okay, tell us what you know about this Plan B and Operation Coyote."

Emilie said, "I heard Daniel and the others talking on the yacht about having two of Daniel's employees pose as pilots for the company who owns the transport planes that fly from the Operation Coyote bases to Fort Collins every day with the specimen coolers. I also heard them talking about putting some sort of explosive device in one of the coolers coming from the bases in Canada. Some guy named Edward Plummer, who is an explosives expert and works for Daniel, was supposed to make the device and then the pilots were going to put it in one of the coolers coming from Canada. I think this Edward Plummer was supposed to detonate the explosive device once it was in the CDC lab in Fort Collins."

Marcus Solomon said, "And when was this all supposed to happen?"

Emilie said, "I think Daniel said Saturday evening, which is today I guess."

Susan Denison and Marcus Solomon both looked back at the one-way glass window in the interview room at the same time, behind which they knew Tim Sullivan and Adam Donahue were watching and listening. They told Emilie to just wait there for a few minutes and they both got up and went out into the hallway where Tim and Adam were waiting for them.

Tim Sullivan said, "I will call Larry Greer in Denver immediately and let him know what is happening. Based on the time in Fort Collins, which is an hour ahead of us here in LA, the plane from Canada should be en route and due to arrive in Fort Collins in about two hours."

After Tim and Adam left to go make their phone calls, Susan Denison and Marcus Solomon went back into the interview room and Marcus Solomon said, "I just have one more question for you right now, Emilie, do you know who Daniel Lavoy's client is for Operation Coyote?"

Emilie said, "I don't know who it is exactly, but I heard Daniel say to Eric and Gabrielle a couple of times after they were talking about Operation Coyote stuff that he had to call the client in Moscow. It did not sound like Daniel even knew his real name, only that he worked for some intelligence agency in Russia."

"Thank you, Emilie, you have been extremely helpful," Marcus Solomon said. "We will have to hold you here for another day or two until we verify the things you have told us; however, if things work out, we can make arrangements to have you released and probably placed into protective custody until all the legal proceedings are underway with Daniel Lavoy and his people."

8:00 p.m. Saturday, March 20, 2021
FBI Field Office, Denver, Colorado

Larry Greer had put Tim Sullivan on speakerphone in his office when Tim had called from Los Angeles so that John and Kate could hear what he was saying as well. Tim told them about the interview with Emilie Portier and the information about the explosive device in one of the coolers currently being transported in the Cessna Denali aircraft which was due to land at the Northern Colorado Regional Airport south of Fort Collins in about two hours.

They thanked Tim Sullivan for the call and then Larry Greer said to John and Kate, "You better call Denny and Anna right away and let them know about the cooler on the Cessna Denali. I will call the Fort Collins Police Service to let them know that we need a bomb disposal unit to be on standby at the airport by 9:30 p.m. and to coordinate with the FBI agents there. We also have to make sure that we keep everyone back from the cooler drop-off site, so we don't spook them when they are landing at the airport."

John called Denny on his cell phone and when Denny answered he said, "Hi, Denny, John here. We just got a call from Tim Sullivan in Los Angeles and he said that Daniel Lavoy's girlfriend just told them about what Plan B is and that there is an explosive device in one of the coolers on the Cessna Denali flying there from Canada. The two pilots flying the Cessna Denali today are employees of Daniel Lavoy and will have to be detained and taken into custody by whatever means necessary after they taxi the plane over to the cooler drop-off location. Larry Greer has just called the Fort Collins Police Service and asked them to have a bomb disposal unit on standby at the airport there by 9:30 p.m.

"Apparently, the plan was to detonate the explosive device in the travel cooler remotely using a cell phone at the CDC lab after it was transferred into the big walk-in freezer with all the rest of the coolers already being stored there. An explosive expert employed by Daniel Lavoy by the name of Edward Plummer apparently assembled the explosive device and is probably waiting somewhere around the CDC lab to detonate it."

With his serious special forces take-charge demeanour kicking in, Denny said, "Besides Anna and me, we have our two FBI security detail agents with us, Meagan Fisk and Trevor Jordan. We also have the two FBI agents from Denver Larry Greer sent here to meet us at the airport. Plus, Syd and Nelle of course. I think that should be enough manpower if we can surprise the two pilots after they land and taxi over to the usual cooler drop-off location at the CDC transfer van. There should only be twelve to fourteen coolers on the plane. Nelle was initially trained as a bomb sniffing dog by the RCMP so maybe we can use her to find which of the coolers the bomb is in. The bomb squad can then take over."

With his voice sounding very tense, John said, "Okay, Denny, that sounds like it should work. You just must make sure that everyone keeps out of sight until the plane lands and taxis over to the cooler drop-off location. We do not want to alarm the pilots when they are flying into the airport or taxiing over to the CDC van after they land. I think the Cessna Denali is always the last of the three transport planes to arrive at the airport every evening, so the other two planes should have already unloaded their coolers and taxied over to the CDC hangar when the Cessna Denali arrives. As we always do, you should assume the pilots will be armed so be careful when you take them down. It would probably be best to take them into custody while they are still in their seats in the cockpit. Maybe Syd and Nelle can help you out with that maneuver."

Sensing that John was extremely worried about finding the bomb before it was detonated, Denny said, "It's okay, John, we got this. We still have about an hour until the first of the three planes is due to arrive here so we will get ourselves organized. Maybe you can call security services at the CDC to let them know what is going on and you can also alert the transport van driver that we will be here to talk to him after he arrives at the usual cooler drop-off location. Also, call the Fort Collins bomb squad people and tell them to park in the main airport terminal parking area until we let them know that they should come to the cooler drop-off location to pick up the cooler with the explosive device, assuming Nelle is able to find it."

After hanging up with John, Denny called over the rest the six-person team and told them about the plan he had discussed with John. They were standing beside the FBI extended Chevy Tahoe SUV which was in a small parking area beside one of the hangars located about 150 yards from the usual transfer van parking spot at the edge of the tarmac. The SUV was on the opposite side of the hangar from the runway so could not be seen by the pilots as they taxied towards the transfer van.

They all had their Kevlar vests on, including Syd and Nelle who were getting exited about the upcoming action. At about 8:45 p.m. a white, unmarked Mercedes-Benz Sprinter cargo van drove to a spot at the intersection of Aviator Avenue and Stearman Street. Denny walked over to the van and waved to the driver and the other man sitting in the passenger seat. The driver rolled down his van window and said, "Are you one of the FBI agents who I was told would be meeting us here?"

"Yes, that's right," Denny said. "My name is Denny, and I am here with five other agents and two police dogs. They are all just waiting down the side street behind one of the hangars. We are only interested in the Cessna Denali when it arrives. I am told it is always the last plane to arrive at the airport every evening, is that right?"

The driver said, "My name is Greg and my helper's name over there is Oscar. Yes, the two Cessna Grand Caravans always arrive first and then the Cessna Denali generally arrives around 10:00 p.m., because it has the furthest to fly all the way from Canada."

Denny said, "I am going to need you to just unload the coolers from both the Grand Caravan planes into the van and stack them on the shelves as you normally would. When the Cessna Denali arrives, there will be two new pilots in the cockpit, so do not act surprised and just say hello to them as you would normally do. Then unload the coolers from the plane but do not put them on the shelves or mix them up with any of the other coolers already in the van and do not stack them on top of each other. Just place them all carefully on the floor of the van. When you have finished putting all the coolers in the van, just shut the van's side door and get back into your seats in the front of the van and lock the doors. Leave the door to the plane open.

"I will be on the other side of the van with my two police dogs and as soon as you get into your van we will go into the plane through the door and apprehend the two pilots. After we have the pilots in custody, you can get out of the van and one of my agents will direct you to where you should go. Do you understand what I need you to do?"

They both said that they did.

Denny then went back to join the other agents behind the small hangar down the service road from the van. At about 9:15 p.m. the first of the two Cessna Grand Caravan planes landed and taxied over to the van. It took them about ten minutes to unload the coolers from the plane and put them on the custom-built shelves in the van. At about 9:40 p.m. the second Cessna Grand Caravan landed, and they went through the same routine. At about 10:15 the Cessna Denali plane landed and taxied over to the van.

Greg and Oscar got out of the van and opened the rear door of the plane and said hello to the pilots sitting up in the cockpit in their seats and asked them how the flight was. They then unloaded the thirteen coolers and, as they had been instructed by Denny, carefully put them on the floor of the van instead of on the shelves. While they were unloading the coolers, Denny was crouched down and walking fast over the short distance up the service road with Syd and Nelle at his heels, careful to keep the van between him and the front of the plane so the pilots couldn't see him.

He came up to the rear far side of the van and waited with Syd and Nelle at his side until Greg and Oscar had loaded all the coolers into the van, closed the door, and got into their seats. As soon as he heard their door locks click shut, he rushed to the still open rear door of the plane and gave Syd and Nelle the signal to capture. Both dogs immediately jumped through the door and into the plane and rushed to the front. They each selected one of the pilots, who were just getting ready to start the plane back up and leaped over the side of the seats and grabbed one of the pilot's arms in their mouths.

As the pilots were yelling and struggling against the grip of the dog's jaws clamped down on their arms, Denny, Anna, Meagan, and TJ came into the plane with their guns drawn. The other two FBI agents went around to the front of the plane and each pointed their guns at one of the two pilots through the front window. Denny came up behind the dogs and said "Release", and Syd and Nelle immediately released their grip on the pilot's arms and backed away. Denny and TJ came up behind the two pilots and pressed their gun barrels against the backs of their heads.

Very sternly, Denny said, "Okay, guys, don't do anything stupid. Just release your seat harnesses and then put your hands together on the top of your head."

The two pilots did what Denny said and then Denny and TJ helped them up out of their seats and handcuffed them. They then escorted them to the back of the plane, through the door, and onto the tarmac. They then walked them about fifty yards away and forced them down onto their knees. Denny told them not to move while Anna, Meagan, and the other two agents pointed their guns at them. The two CDC van drivers, Greg and Oscar also went down to where the rest of the group was standing.

Denny called the Fort Collins bomb squad vehicle and told them to drive over to where they were. He then opened the van's side door and told Nelle to get into the van. He gave her the signal for finding explosives which was "Find Boom" and pointed at the coolers lined up on the floor of the van. Nelle understood immediately, even though she had not done any explosives work for several years. She made her way along the line of coolers, sniffing carefully at each one, and then at the seventh one in the line, she sat down suddenly and looked up at Denny and gave a short bark. Denny told her what a good dog she was and told her she could go over and sit beside Syd next to Anna.

When the bomb squad vehicle arrived, Denny showed the team leader the cooler that Nelle had chosen. The bomb squad vehicle was a steel-reinforced van towing a trailer with a containment vessel shaped like small water tank. He said that they also had a special portable X-ray system that they used to radiograph the suspected bomb before they intervened. He said the purpose was to determine if a chemical charge was present and to check the status of the detonator. A technician wearing a specialized protective suit went into the van with the portable X-ray machine and went down the line of coolers testing each one.

When he got to the seventh one, the cooler Nelle had picked, he looked over at the squad leader and gave him the thumbs-up. He then continued down the rest of the line of coolers with the portable X-ray machine. He got out of the van and came over to the squad leader and Denny and said, "There is only one explosive device and it is in the seventh cooler down the line, the same one the dog picked."

The squad leader smiled and said to Denny, "Well, I guess it is still hard to do better than the nose of a well-trained dog, even with all our fancy equipment. It looks like the explosive device was designed to be quite stable while being transported, so I think we will just carefully take the cooler out of the van and put it our containment vessel. We can then take the cooler to our remote detonation location and detonate it in a safe place."

The technician in the bomb suit then took the cooler out of the van and took it over to the containment vessel and then closed and sealed the door of the vessel. Everyone started breathing a little easier and the bomb squad team all got back in their vehicle and drove away. Denny walked over to the group and told Greg and Oscar that they could now go on their way back to the CDC lab with the rest of the coolers. He then told the two FBI agents from Denver that they could go get their SUV and put Tom Blakely and Derek Andrews, the two pilots, into the back so they could take them back to the Denver FBI office for formal processing and to be placed into custody.

After the two FBI agents had loaded the two pilots into their SUV and left for the one-hour drive back to Denver, Denny turned to Anna, Meagan, and

TJ and said, "Well, that was all pretty exciting. I think the two heroes of the night were definitely Syd and Nelle."

Still looking a little excited, but relieved that it was all over, TJ said, "Those two dogs were amazing. Is this how you guys always work with them?"

Looking at Syd and Nelle as they were sitting beside the group, Anna said, "You wouldn't believe some of things they have done. They have saved our butts too many times to count. They are just as important in our work as any person on our team."

Laughing, Denny said, "They are listening to us so we should be careful that they don't start figuring out how important they are and that they still only get paid in dog treats. I guess I should give John, Kate, and Larry Greer a call and let them know that it is all over here. We might as well have the pilots bring the King Air over here and pick us up so we can all go back to Denver as well."

CHAPTER 21

9:00 a.m. Sunday, March 21, 2021
FBI Hotel, Denver, Colorado

Denny, Anna, Meagan, TJ, and the dogs had arrived back in Denver on the King Air at about 12:30 a.m. Denny, Anna, and the dogs had gone to the FBI hotel for the night, and Meagan and TJ had gone home to their respective residences in Denver. John and the rest of the team had met in his and Kate's suite for breakfast and to review the events of the previous days.

Denny and Anna gave them the play-by-play of the previous evening's events at the Fort Collins airport. Syd and Nelle were very alert since their names seemed to be mentioned quite often. There were several pats on the head and "what good girls" said by John and Kate several times. They even got their own order of bacon from room service.

John and Kate also gave Denny and Anna the more detailed play-by-play of the events in Panama City, expanding on the brief phone discussions that they had while they were there and Denny and Anna were in Casper, Wyoming. Denny and Anna were particularly amused by the story of how Daniel Lavoy had tripped and fallen right on his testicles on the dock beside his yacht.

Denny and Anna both looked at Kate and smiled and Anna said, "Way to go, girl. Too bad I wasn't there so we could have double-teamed him. I guess I will just have to savour the image in my head of him laying on the dock groaning in agony. Too bad you didn't get a video of his accident."

"Well, it happened pretty fast and Kate didn't give me any warning about what she was going to do, otherwise I definitely would have videoed it for later viewing."

Laughing, Kate said, "Sorry, it was just a spur of the moment kind of thing."

10:00 a.m. Sunday, March 21, 2021
FBI Office, Denver, Colorado

After breakfast they all gathered in the small boardroom next to Larry Greer's office in the Denver FBI building. Larry Greer also congratulated Syd and Nelle on their previous night's work. He did not have any bacon, so they just mildly wagged their tails and tried not to look too superior. To them, it was just all in a day's work and they did not really see what all the fuss was about.

After they were all seated, Larry Greer said, "Tom Blakely and Derek Andrews, the two pilots from the Cessna Denali, were booked last night for starters on conspiracy to destroy federal property. There will probably be numerous other charges filed against them once the federal prosecutors get on the case today. As the events were going down at the airport last night, we notified the Fort Collins Police Service and the Colorado State Campus Police and asked them to send a few unmarked police vehicles to look for any suspicious vehicles parked within sight of the main entrance of the CDC Lab. We were able to find an old driver's licence photo of Edward Plummer and we sent it to them as well.

"Two Fort Collins police officers came across a Dodge Ram ProMaster cargo van parked in a spot directly facing the main gate of the CDC lab about two hundred yards away. They called in reinforcements and then knocked on the driver's door window and motioned for the driver to roll the window down. They recognized Edward Plummer from his photo and told him to get out of the vehicle and get on his knees with his hands on the top of his head. He initially protested but then saw two other police cars pull up in front of his vehicle and the officers get out and point their weapons at him.

"After he was handcuffed, the officers checked in the rear cargo area of his van and found a small workbench with shelving and various tools and different kinds of rolls of tape and wiring supplies in several boxes. They also found two cell phones on the passenger seat. They radioed their office for them to send a crime scene forensics team out to the site and to also notify the FBI. We sent our own forensics team to the site and they came up with some interesting evidence.

"It seemed Edward Plummer's Dodge Ram ProMaster cargo van doubled as a mobile bomb-making workshop, superficially disguised as a mobile small appliance repair shop. In addition to the other bomb-making supplies, they found numerous types of detonation devices. They did not find any explosives, but we assume that he probably kept his supply in a safer location.

"One of the cell phones was a burner phone with only one number programmed into the memory. The forensics people assumed that this was the number he was going to call to detonate the bomb in the travel cooler once it was inside the big walk-in freezer in the CDC lab where there are still several hundred coolers being stored. The other cell phone was his personal phone with a facial recognition security system. Since he was available, they were able to open his phone and look at the call log.

"One interesting number they found had called him several times in the previous few days from Panama City. Interestingly, the number matched one of the burner phones INTERPOL had found on Daniel Lavoy's yacht and which is now in the possession of the FBI in Los Angeles. It seems we have now probably connected most of the dots in Daniel Lavoy's plans to disrupt Operation Coyote.

"However, the one big question that still needs to answered is, who exactly was Daniel Lavoy's client? His girlfriend, Emilie Portier, told the federal prosecutor in LA that she overheard him telling the others on the yacht in Panama City that he needed to call his client in Moscow. She said that Daniel Lavoy probably did not even know his real name, only that he worked for one of the intelligence agencies in Russia. I guess it probably did not really matter to Lavoy as long as they paid the extremely high fees for his services. So far, I guess he, Eric Boucher, and Gabrielle Caron are refusing to say anything to the federal prosecutors in LA. So anyways, we have done our jobs so now it is up to the lawyers and bureaucrats to figure out the rest. I'm sure there will be some diplomatic consequences for the Russians, but that is way above my pay grade."

John said, "With today's coyote brain specimens, we will have a total of about 1075 delivered to the CDC lab in Fort Collins. The COVID-21 Task Force will have to decide about shutting Operation Coyote down, or letting it continue if the CDC thinks they need more specimens for the vaccine testing and development. I understand that the task force is meeting in Washington later this afternoon."

"Yes, that is what I have heard as well," Larry Greer said. "I guess we will just have to wait and see what they decide. In the meantime, why don't we all relax for the rest of the day, it is Sunday after all. I will give you a call as soon as I hear anything. I think all the bases have been instructed to just continue operations as usual until they hear otherwise."

"Looking relieved, John said. "Sounds good, we could all use a little downtime after the last few days. We will be at the hotel if you need to talk to us."

5:00 p.m. Sunday, March 21, 2021
FBI Hotel, Denver, Colorado

John and Kate had spent the afternoon relaxing and watching TV in their hotel suite. John had called his three daughters in Edmonton to let them know he would probably be home in the next few days. The conversations were mostly about what the grandkids had been up to and what was happening with their jobs. His daughters knew better than to ask their father about any of the details about his latest assignment.

Sometimes they would read about or hear something on the news about some big international INTERPOL operation takedown that just happened to coincide with the latest work destination of their father. When they would ask him about it, he would usually say that he was just there doing some consulting work and did not know too much about the details of the operation. Sometimes they persuaded Anna to provide a few more details, and quite often they wished they had not asked. It was usually better not to know the details of what their father, Denny, Anna, and Kate did, otherwise it was hard to get to sleep at night when they were all gone somewhere on an assignment.

Kate called her daughter, Dianna, in Portland to catch up as well. Denny and Anna also called their people in Slave Lake and Edmonton, respectively. Denny's lady friend in Slave Lake, Mary Woods, reminded him about his promise to spend more time at home in the future, and maybe even retire from the RCMP. Denny said that he would talk to John, Kate, and Anna about it again. He said that he thought John was considering slowing down and maybe semi-retiring.

Anna's long-term boyfriend was happy to hear from her as well. Since he was a Canadian Security Intelligence Service (CSIS) international criminal analyst ("spy"), he understood the pressures of her job and that she sometimes needed to be away from home.

At about 5:30 p.m., John's cell phone rang, and Larry Greer was on the line. He said, "Hi, John, I just got a call from the FBI deputy director in Washington who had just left the COVID-21 Task Force meeting. He said that the CDC had decided that the vaccine development was going well, and even a little ahead of schedule, so they have decided that the coyote brain specimens already collected would be sufficient. The FBI deputy director instructed me to contact the team leaders at the eight bases and tell them that they can cease operations as of today.

"The senior managers of all the agencies involved will contact their personnel to let them know what they are supposed to do to return to their normal duties. I was told that Vice President Kincaid will be giving you a call at 7:00 p.m. Denver time to thank you for the job you and your team have done.

"I would also like to thank you personally for what you and your team have accomplished with Operation Coyote. It has been a real pleasure working with you. The task force made the right choice when they brought you, Kate, Denny, and Anna, and those two dogs of yours in to run Operation Coyote. Whenever you are ready to go home, please feel free to use the FBI King Air one more time."

"Thanks, Larry, it has been a pleasure working with you and your FBI team here in Denver as well. If you ever want to visit us in Alberta, I'm sure Denny would be happy to take you to some really good fishing spots."

7:00 p.m. Sunday, March 21, 2021
FBI Hotel, Denver, Colorado

As Larry Greer said, John's cell phone rang at 7:00 p.m. and someone said, "Hello, is this Dr. John Benson?"

"Yes, this is John Benson."

"Please stand by for Vice President Amanda Kincaid."

Vice President Kincaid got on the line a few seconds later and said, "Hello, John. I assume Larry Greer gave you the heads-up that I would be giving you a call."

"Yes, Larry told me to expect a call from you. I hope you don't mind but I have you on speakerphone and I have my team here with me, Kate Beckett, Denny Bear, and Anna Dupree, and of course Syd and Nelle are listening as well."

Vice President Kincaid said, "No, of course I don't mind, you have all been responsible for the success of Operation Coyote. On behalf of President Borden and the members of the COVID-21 Task Force, I would just like to express my sincere thanks for the exceptional job you have all done organizing and managing Operation Coyote. We will never know the number of lives that will now be saved because of getting the Operation Coyote stage of the new COVID-21 vaccine development completed successfully and within the timelines required.

"I have been fully briefed by the FBI about all the problems with Daniel Lavoy and his company, World Security Services, and the personal sacrifices you have all made to overcome the considerable dangers his interference caused. Kate and Anna, I would especially like to express my relief and gratitude that you are okay after your ordeal in South Dakota. I cannot imagine how terrifying that must have been for you.

"I have also heard about the exploits of your two dogs, Syd and Nelle. When I first met them at the task force meeting in Denver back on March 1st, I must admit, I was somewhat amused when you said that they liked to attend briefing sessions so that they knew what was going on firsthand, but I now have no doubt that they probably understood everything that was going on. If they are listening please tell them from me that they are incredibly good dogs and maybe give them an extra treat tonight."

"Thank you, Vice President Kincaid," Kate said. "Anna and I are also very thankful that the events in South Dakota turned out okay. As law enforcement agents, we accept that there are dangers associated with our work, however we also know that we have the support of our fellow officers and team members. In our case, we knew that we had the support of John and Denny in particular, as well of the full resources of the FBI, so we knew that it was only a matter of time before they found and rescued us. Thankfully, we were treated reasonably well by our captors, under the circumstances, although it still might take a few therapy sessions to work through it all."

"Thank you for calling, Vice President Kincaid," said John. "We really appreciate it. We are honoured to have been of service to our countries, and hopefully what we have accomplished with Operation Coyote will help in getting the world back on track after the last year of turmoil."

Vice President Kincaid said, "Thanks again to all of you and I hope you have a safe trip back to your homes."

3:00 p.m. Thursday, April 1, 2021
Denver Post Newsroom, Denver, Colorado

Cheryl Kaplan was sitting at her desk in the *Denver Post* newsroom and going over her story for the final time before she had to send it off to the copy editors before the deadline. It was scheduled to be the lead story on the top half of the front page of the paper's Friday edition, generally the most read edition of the week. The rest of the story would follow on pages three and four. The headline was going to be *"Operation Coyote — The Story Behind the COVID-21 Vaccine."*

Somewhat to her surprise, the FBI and John Benson and Kate Beckett had been true to their word, and had called her on Tuesday, March 23rd and told her to come down to the Denver FBI Field Office. For two hours, they had told her the full story about Operation Coyote. They even told her about Daniel Lavoy and the involvement of his company, World Security Services. They had alluded to the identity of his client as being a Russian security agency but told her that she could only suggest that a foreign country was involved, without stating that it was Russia.

All in all, she thought it was going to be one of her best stories.

EPILOGUE

7:00 a.m. Monday, August 23, 2021
Ada Boulevard, Edmonton, Alberta, Canada

The alarm was beeping on the side table beside the bed in the master bedroom of John Benson's house on Ada Boulevard in Edmonton, Alberta. John reached over and pushed the button down to make it stop beeping and then he turned over and looked at Kate Beckett lying next to him. She was stretching and trying to open her eyes. John leaned over and gave her a small kiss on the cheek and said, "Time to get up and go to your new office."

"That sounds very strange. I am not sure that I am ready to start working with all those crazy Canadians over there. Do you think they will accept me as their new boss?"

Smiling, John said, "Relax, I have told everyone that Syd and Nelle will bite anyone who gives you any trouble."

"Thanks, that should endear them all to me right off the bat. Any other pearls of wisdom?"

"Don't worry, you are going to do fine as the new head of the RCMP K Division Wildlife Forensics Lab. And besides, I will still be using the office next to you in my new capacity as the official INTERPOL chief consulting forensic wildlife scientist permanently assigned to the new Edmonton INTERPOL satellite location. And Anna will be there as well as your lab operations manager."

Kate said, "Yes, you are right as usual. I am sure I will do fine and there will be lots of challenges living up to our new status as a satellite INTERPOL

Wildlife Forensics Lab and Investigative Centre. There are quite a few new staff we will need to hire, and we will have to make sure the new space they gave us on the third floor for the expanded lab will be up to INTERPOL standards.

"I am glad that we had the last month off so I could finish moving all my stuff here from Oregon and then have some downtime to get settled in. May and June were very crazy months, travelling to Singapore, Lyon, and Nairobi for the trials of the leaders of the wildlife trafficking gangs captured during Operation Thunderball. At least that is all over now. Have you heard from Denny in the last couple of days?"

As they were talking, Syd and Nelle pushed open the bedroom door and came in and both put their chins on the edge of the bed, with the implied message, "You guys need to get up now and let us out into the back yard so we can do our business."

"Yes, I know it's time to let you out girls." John turned back to Kate and said, "I just talked to him yesterday. He has been busy fishing and supervising the First Nation subcontractors who have been working on our new log cabin in the lot next to his. He said the outside and inside walls and the roof are all done and that the electricians and plumbers are going to be starting this coming week. I might take a drive up there later in the week to check on things and maybe spend a few hours out on the lake fishing with Denny. Syd and Nelle would be happy to see him and they always like going out on the lake in his boat. They can also spend some time playing with Mary's husky, Moses.

"Denny is enjoying his time off and looking forward to his new part-time job as a security consultant and head of security for the new satellite Edmonton INTERPOL Wildlife Forensics Lab and Investigative Centre. He said that Mary Woods, his very patient, long-term lady friend there at Slave Lake is finally talking about getting married since he will hopefully be home more from now on. He said he is still trying to wrap his head around being a married man but thinks it cannot be any worse than getting shot at by poachers. I told him that he better not let Mary hear him saying that or he just might wish that it were only poachers shooting at him.

"I forgot to mention it last night, but I saw on the 11:00 news that the WHO and CDC had a joint press conference in Atlanta yesterday to announce that a new modified COVID-19 vaccine was being made available to all the countries that had experienced occurrences of reinfections of the COVID-19 virus, possibly caused by a mutation of the original virus. However, they said that access to the new vaccine was still being negotiated with Russia because of some ongoing international diplomacy issues which they hoped would be worked out soon."

Kate smiled at John and said, "Gosh, I wonder what that is all about?"

THE END

AUTHOR'S NOTE

I would like to point out to readers that although I have been a professional biologist and environmental consultant for the last thirty-plus years with a B.Sc. in Wildlife Biology and an M.Sc. in Forest Science, I am not a wildlife forensic biologist, epidemiologist, or virologist. Although I did a fair amount of research to educate myself about coronavirus vaccine development, the use of live animal tissue as a method for developing a viable coronavirus vaccine is mostly a theoretical concept, I used to advance the storyline. I am sure actual scientists involved in coronavirus vaccine development would have some issues with my simplified description of the process.

I have borrowed from some of my own background in the development of the John Benson fictional character. I am a professional biologist and live in Edmonton, Alberta, Canada and have three married daughters and seven grandchildren. I had an Australian shepherd/blue heeler cross dog named Sydney (Syd) for seventeen years, and a border collie cross dog named Nelle for fifteen years. They both unfortunately died of the afflictions of old age within about three weeks of each other in early 2018.

In my undergraduate years studying wildlife biology at the University of Alberta, I had a summer job working for the Alberta Department of Agriculture as a "coyote hunter." It was for a scientific study being done by government scientists on the mercury content present in the internal organs of coyotes, an animal at the top of the food chain. I was responsible for collecting the coyote specimens for the study.

I would like to thank my three daughters, Sarah, Andrea, and Lisa, and my two sisters Jane and Nancy, for their encouragement and support during my first attempt at writing a fiction novel. I would also like to thank my good friend Cathie for her encouragement and for her editorial suggestions.

I also thank the staff at Friesen Press in Victoria, British Columbia for their assistance, and in particular the editors and other publication specialists for their help in getting the book ready for publication.

I wrote this novel over several months in early 2020 while I was in self-isolation in my condominium in Edmonton during the COVID-19 pandemic. Although the development of a vaccine for the virus was still many months away at the time, the possibility of a mutated version of the virus emerging to complicate the process was a very real possibility being discussed by scientists. I thought it would be an interesting topic to explore for my novel.

This book is a work of fiction. Names, characters, businesses, organizations, places, events, and incidents either are the product of the author's imagination or are used fictitiously. Any resemblance to actual persons, living or dead, events, or locales is entirely coincidental.

CPSIA information can be obtained
at www.ICGtesting.com
Printed in the USA
BVHW041123231022
649945BV00001B/11